Home from Home

CAROL SMITH

Home from Home

timewarner
b o o k s

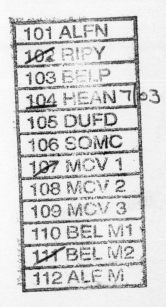

A *Time Warner* Book

First published in Great Britain in 2003
by Time Warner Books

A CIP catalogue record for this book
is available from the British Library.

ISBN 0 316 85979 6

Typeset in Berkeley by
Palimpsest Book Production Limited,
Polmont, Stirlingshire
Printed and bound in Great Britain by
Clays Ltd, St Ives plc

Time Warner Books UK
Brettenham House
Lancaster Place
London WC2E 7EN

www.TimeWarnerBooks.co.uk

Acknowledgements

Grateful thanks, as always, to the efficient Time Warner team – my editors, Tara Lawrence and Joanne Coen, and the brilliant sales and marketing people. Also to Jonathan Lloyd, my agent, who goes where I would never have dared to tread.

A big thank you, too, to Charles Chromow and Bob Prinsky, market observers and US financial experts, for giving me the benefit of their professional wisdom. And most of all to Steve Rubin, for sparing so much of his time to show me how to construct a selling synopsis.

Part One

1

The day the world changed, Anna saw it happen. She had taken the Fifth Avenue bus to 57th Street, on her way across town to a breakfast meeting, when the first plane went over, unnervingly low, and she watched the inevitable impact from a distance. Fifteen minutes later, still dazed with disbelief, she and her publisher witnessed the second strike and the ensuing terrible implosion of the twin towers. In that brief space of time civilisation altered. Over three thousand people were lost, many of them vanished without trace. It was to be weeks before Anna would sleep properly again, months before she finally banished the dreams.

She was late with her book, which wasn't going well. A trauma like this was the last thing that she needed. She would lie awake all night with a pounding heart, reliving, over and over, those harrowing images. In the early hours, as the light began filtering in, she would finally lapse into a fitful doze, only to be woken in what seemed like mere seconds by Sadie, demanding breakfast. Sometimes she just gave up and went back to her desk and tried to get on with her work. From her study window, at the top of the four-storey house, she could see a vista of flickering screens. The city that never sleeps was on overtime.

Paige, with her pragmatic lawyer's mind, told her briskly that she was overreacting. It had been a catastrophe affecting the whole world; now it was time to put it on hold and get back to ordinary living. Too much brooding was simply not healthy, a way of letting the terrorists win.

'Not possible,' cried Anna, in despair. Her father had lived through far worse in his youth but throughout her own life she had always felt protected. It was going to take an almighty adjustment before things returned to normal, assuming they could.

'That's the trouble with you creative folk,' said Paige in her down-to-earth way.

'Meaning I'm some kind of spaced-out nut?'

'No, just that you live in your own encapsulated world.' Implying that Anna really ought to get out more. She was fast becoming a hermit.

But the book was like an albatross dragging her down; her imagination simply was not functioning. Not in any positive way; all she could come up with now verged on the sick.

'Give yourself the weekend off and come with us to the country.' Both Paige and Charles worked harder than most yet equally liked to play. Their house in Quogue was the epitome of good living but Anna couldn't spare the time even for that.

'A couple of days won't hurt,' Paige assured her, but Anna dared not ever relax. The tenuous thread of her seventh novel was threatening to disintegrate. And where would she be should that ever happen, with this expensive new piece of real estate to maintain? The movie money had proved a terrific plus but the financial commitment stretched way into the future. She was far too savvy to depend on another movie deal happening again. Living off one's wits proved an endless treadmill and, for some reason she could not fathom, the books got no easier to write.

'It is just that your standards improve,' said Paige, but Anna refused to believe that.

'Once it is finally finished and delivered,' she threatened, 'you'll not be able to get rid of me at weekends.' Tennis and barbecues and lounging around the pool. Cocktails with the well-heeled Hampton set, every sybarite's dream. She and Paige had been friends since their student days, part of a very tight set. The sister, Anna occasionally reflected, that she'd always rather wished she might have had. Their lives had gone in divergent directions yet still, after almost fifteen years, they remained every bit as close. Paige, with her sharp mind and dynastic beauty, had captured the glorious Charles in their final year. No children (no time) but a brilliant marriage and a lifestyle that could not have been bettered.

'Gotta go,' said Paige, as ever in a rush. 'Catch you again on Monday. Don't overdo it.'

Sunday lunch with her father had become a sacred ritual, about the only time these days that Anna took trouble with food. She would ride the subway down to Tribeca and walk the last three blocks to his street, to the shabby but spacious family home in which she had been raised. These days it was looking well past its best, with cracks in the masonry and a sagging front stoop. The spindly plane trees cried out for attention and the neighbourhood overflowed with full garbage sacks. There were black kids playing in the street outside and they whooped with delight when they saw Anna.

'Yo, Anna. How're ya doin', man?'

'Good,' she yelled, kicking back their ball. Many of them she had known since infancy; a few were her father's pupils.

George Kovac, in his heyday, had been a world-class musician, solo violinist with the Philharmonic, feted, since the age of nineteen, on concert platforms all over the world. His exit from Poland had been sudden and dramatic; he had had to abandon everything, which meant more than just his money and possessions. Now, recently turned eighty and increasingly arthritic, he had relinquished his international career to teach the local children of the community. His pupils were from deprived backgrounds and without proper schooling; occasionally he discovered one with outstanding musical aptitude. George was a genius at coaxing out that talent, charging them only a pittance for tuition. Putting something back, was how he termed it. Better than sitting on his backside, simply growing old.

'Your dad's an inspiration,' was the opinion of Anna's friends, who would frequently make the trek downtown in order to seek his wise counsel. Shambling and craggy, with thick greying hair and eyes fast losing their power, he still remained an imposing figure who cared more for his neighbours' wellbeing than for his own.

Today she was cooking her mother's chicken paprika, ever a favourite with George. The pans in his kitchen were the ones her mother had used. Occasionally Anna would sneak in a replacement, knowing that he preferred things as they were. The house itself was steeped in memories as though time had stood still. Even the noise from the street outside was muffled by solid brickwork and the heavy drapes that hadn't been dry-cleaned in years. The dust and aromas of several decades hung in this room undisturbed, as though Anna's mother's presence were still in the house. She had been a beautiful and inspired flautist who had died suddenly and unexpectedly. Now George spent his days, when not actually teaching, slumped in his decrepit easy chair. Like him, it was sagging and had shaped to his angular frame but he fretted if anyone chose to usurp it. It was all that remained of the old life, she supposed. Anna knew enough to leave it alone.

This Sunday, as always, she served lunch in the dining-room, the only time the room was ever used. The rest of the week her father fended for himself, eating in the kitchen standing up. Anna carefully folded the heavy hand-made lace cloth, relic of a distant age when the world had been at peace, and replaced it with a cheerful cotton one from Macys, more practical and easier to keep clean. She set the table with the tarnished silver that had been her mother's only dowry. How little the two of them had had to set up home, yet the love that had lasted through the years burned as brightly since her death. George shuffled in and looked around with approval, then unlocked a display cabinet and selected two of the long-stemmed hock glasses they used for festive occasions. Ceremoniously he uncorked a bottle of wine, placing it on an antique silver coaster.

When Anna carried in the steaming casserole he sniffed appreciatively and virtually smacked his lips. He regularly went through this courteous little charade though she knew all too well that her culinary skills would never be in her mother's class. Her mother, dead these eleven years, had been an exemplary housekeeper. Anna envied the love he still had for her, hoped that some day she might strike lucky and find something like it herself.

'So tell me about the house,' he said, once they were seated and served. Despite his pretended disapproval of the profligate way she was spending, he was secretly proud of his only child who had grown into such an independent spirit. If you've got it, flaunt it, was Anna's philosophy, though her father devoutly believed in that rainy day. Carefully she detailed all the things she was doing, new furniture, new fittings, even some structural work. Nothing, it seemed, was she keeping from the old life. She was like an eager bride-to-be only doing it all on her own.

'Your mother would not approve,' he said, sadly shaking his head, though she saw from the twinkle in his eye that he was only teasing. She had always known, since her earliest years, exactly what she wanted, and putting money into property these days seemed the most sensible investment. Especially now, with the stock market on its uppers. There were endless reports on the financial pages of thousands of solid investors facing ruin. Yet her father couldn't help worrying on Anna's behalf; George, who had arrived in the States with nothing, had always been obliged to scrimp and save.

'But that was then and this is now.' She lived in quite different times. And, due to the excellent education he had given her, came from an altogether more affluent class. 'The movie deal is just a bonus,' she explained, 'like a flukeish lottery win.'

He laughed and ruffled her hair with pride. 'My daughter, the money maven,' he said fondly. 'Just be sure that you don't overdo it. No point running to me when you go bust; I have very little put away.'

'My regular earnings are something quite apart,' Anna explained, not for the first time. 'I promise you, I still have a savings account.' She had loved the Lexington Avenue apartment, but moving to Madison was the ultimate dream. She had always wanted a house of her own and now, fortuitously, had achieved it.

The apple dumplings were another perennial favourite, then Anna cleared the table and tidied up. She made the coffee and carried it into the parlour where George was already settled with the papers. Occasionally she worried about him living here alone but he had been in this house all his married life and refused now to be uprooted. Although this quarter of lower Manhattan was no longer considered very safe, George remained one of its fixtures. Here, at least, he was known and respected, still a commanding force in the community. She trusted to the goodwill of his neighbours to let her know if ever anything should go wrong. As it was, they spoke several times a week and, on rare occasions, she even succeeded in luring him uptown. Since she had paid so much money for a house, his curiosity had been piqued. Not even at the height of his professional career had he earned such a sum.

They listened to a concert after lunch and idly discussed the week. Anna confessed that the book was dragging, that she found it increasingly hard to concentrate. She told him about the flickering screens, proof that her neighbours were sharing her disquietude. All over the city were new insomniacs, fearful of what might come next.

'A lot of my friends are too scared to go out. Staying home has become the fashionable thing.'

George, who had seen his whole heritage destroyed, took each day as it came. His pleasure was derived from the simple things of life; his daily walk to the grocery store, his music, his chess-games, the children and, of course, Anna. He was inordinately proud of his talented daughter, had read each of her novels more than once. His sole regret was that her mother had not lived to witness the flowering of her wonderful talent.

The old grandfather clock in the hall chimed four. 'Pa,' said Anna, 'I really have to go.' She still had a mountain of domestic chores to deal with before she felt she could get back to her writing.

'Take care, child,' he said, seeing her to the door, then stood and watched her walk away until she turned the corner.

Rather than taking the subway all the way, Anna chose to walk from 42nd Street, instinctively averting her gaze from the gap in the skyline left by the missing towers. It was a blindingly hot November afternoon and, since she spent most of her time at a computer, she badly felt the need to stretch her legs. She had forgotten about the marathon. Even as late as this, almost sundown, some runners still straggled by in ragged clumps, cheered on by an enthusiastic crowd, many waving flags. It was like an endless street party, block by block; people in shirtsleeves came pouring out of their doorways, carrying glasses and yelling with zealous enthusiasm. The Stars and Stripes was everywhere, draped over buildings, on the hoods of cars, fluttering from lampposts and fire hydrants. The *Times* had published a full-page reproduction which was taped to the inside of countless windows. A strange, sad tribute to the thousands who had gone. A moment of unfamiliar patriotism.

By the time she reached home, Anna was exhausted; thirty-two blocks in this unseasonal heat. And yet the unaccustomed exercise had done her a power of good. Her skin was flushed, her eyes were bright and her muscles had a healthy tingle. She stood on the sidewalk, groping for her key, and felt the familiar pride of acquisition. The front of the building was still covered with scaffolding, from when they replaced the guttering and repainted the cream stucco façade, but the door itself was a work of art, solid oak with a black wrought-iron knocker. She had bought the place off a Japanese bank who had used it solely for corporate entertaining. When they suddenly relocated back to Tokyo, Anna had snapped it up at a bargain price. Here, in this much coveted district, 74th Street between Madison and Park, real estate values had long been sky-high, the more so since what was happening in the stock market. Scared investors were moving their assets fast into bricks and mortar and Anna, by pure luck, was already a jump ahead. This house represented all she had ever wanted. It made her feel positively grown-up.

She was at the computer, doing her daily stint, when Larry Atwood, her architect, walked in. Sometimes he got on her nerves with his free use of her key but he always explained that he hated to disturb her. Not that hearing his authoritative voice off-stage wasn't sufficient distraction. She could not resist popping down to see him as he handed out daily instructions to his men. There were four of them, working on separate shifts, and they seemed to have been with her for ever. She had managed to get them to turn down the radio but that didn't deter them from whistling and guffawing. Or stopping for endless coffee breaks, even whole afternoons. They had knocked through the wall between kitchen and breakfast-room, to open up the space that she desired. And the original mouldings on the ceilings had been restored; the house was slowly reclaiming its elegant past. Sadie was in there, with dust on her fur, rubbing her beautiful head against their legs. She was constantly angling for attention, this cat. Anna picked her up and nuzzled her neck.

Larry, for once, was wearing a decent suit instead of his usual jeans and sturdy trainers. Off to a meeting at City Hall, he explained, to do with planning permission for another job. He was an outgoing, laughing man with mackerel eyes; Anna had known him since Yale. And, because of their long-time friendship, he was charging her less than he might. Despite her new-found prosperity, she was grateful.

'Everything on schedule?' she asked. As if.

Larry laughed and nodded. 'Shouldn't be too long now till we finish. I'm sure you can't wait to be shot of the lot of us.'

Anna simply smiled and shrugged and put on a fresh pot of coffee. She knew her role in this all-male commune, would indeed be heartily relieved when they had gone. But she had to admit that their work was first-rate. Step by step, the formerly down-at-heel brownstone was being transformed into a magnificent home. She had lived here now for the past four months and the restoration work had at first seemed unending. She found herself camping upstairs on the upper floors, venturing down only when she knew that they had gone. But out of a cloud of brick dust and confusion, her dreams were taking on substance. Soon she would be able to show it off to her friends. She was dying to know what they'd think of this latest achievement.

'When can I fix the house-warming party?' she asked. 'I don't suppose there's a chance that it might be inhabitable by Christmas?'

'No,' said Larry, calculating rapidly. 'March, at the very earliest, I would guess.'

The breast cancer committee meeting was boring and painfully slow. Anna got home at a quarter after nine, wondering why she still bothered. Public awareness was all very well but these days she had far too much else on her plate. It dated back to her journalism days when she'd adopted the charity as a fighting cause. She had produced some impressive results in her time; now it was little more than an irksome chore. Mainly she disliked the overbearing chairwoman, a wealthy Sutton Place divorcee with delusions of grandeur. All they ever did these days was bicker and drink a particularly nasty sherry, of which it appeared she kept an endless supply.

'I guess you've done your bit,' sympathised Paige when Anna, armed with a restorative vodka, rang her that night for a moan. 'They have nothing better to do, those women, than retail therapy and lunch.'

Anna, guilty at her lack of moral fibre, worried that she should not let them down.

'Without me there, and the buyer from Barneys, I reckon they'd very soon come to a grinding halt.'

'You've made your contribution,' Paige reminded her. 'Without you they would never even have got started. Plus you've got a book to finish. You can't do everything at once.'

'Maybe I'll take a sabbatical,' said Anna, not relishing the thought of having to broach the subject. Mrs Kaufman was a formidable woman who rarely stopped talking long enough to hear what anyone said.

'Shall I write you a sick note?' suggested Paige. 'Asking if you can play hooky for a while?'

Anna smiled. 'It's a tempting thought.' She looked at the pileup of reading she had to get through. Slack off for a moment and it overwhelmed her, like leaves at the beginning of fall. There were times when her life resembled an unmade bed and she didn't know how to start straightening it. She was also on the committee of PEN, the international writers' association, of which the AGM was imminent. It was getting too much, her head was spinning. With a further eight months to work on this wretched book.

'What you really need is a vacation,' said Paige. 'I told you, you should have come with us to the country.'

Having freshened her vodka and scrambled some eggs, Anna stretched out in the living-room to catch up. The top two floors were more or less complete and this was the room she liked best. Comfortable off-white upholstered sofas set off the Botticelli flowered rug that she had picked up in the summer sales at half its original price. The handsome Roman blinds, which she had duplicated throughout, were in a neutral heavy linen which, though they would be a devil to keep clean, gave the whole place a feeling of summer brightness that never failed to raise her spirits, especially when, like now, she had come home late. She loved the house with the passion of new acquisition and often felt reluctant to go out at all. Everything in the world that she valued was here on these four spacious floors. Upstairs were her workroom and panelled library, next to her elegant bedroom and en suite bathroom. Occasionally she fantasised about pulling up the drawbridge and spending the rest of the winter here alone. She had always been satisfied with her own company, a reason for her continuingly single state.

Sadie, purring like a sewing-machine, draped herself over Anna's knees and graciously allowed her to fondle her ears. Mainly what Anna was ploughing through was junk mail and periodicals, plus a pile of newspapers she hadn't had time to catch up with. Habits died hard and she was still subscribing to several monthlies from her previous life – the *New Yorker,* the *New York Review of Books* as well as *Publishers Weekly.* There had been a time when she could fit it all in but right now her energy was sapped. Were she more strong-minded, she would cancel all subscriptions but then might run the risk of missing out. Now was not the time to sort things out; once the book was out of the way, she would try to tidy her life.

Sighing, she flicked through each wordy publication, pausing to browse the occasional feature; occasionally ripping one out. As she watched the pile of rejects grow, her spirits started to lift. At last, at almost midnight, she was through, with only the *Yale Alumni Magazine* left. There was rarely anything of much interest there these days but she could not always be sure. Skip an issue and she might miss some news, the death or advancement of one of her close contemporaries. And that would never do; Anna was very much a creature of habit. She skimmed through rapidly, planning a leisurely bath. The writing had gone well today, she felt herself slightly less pressured. Her irritation with the breast cancer committee gradually eased away. Paige was right, it was probably time to resign.

Shoving the somnolent Sadie aside, she put on a Schubert piano sonata that usually did it for her. Background music; her parents would not approve, but it bathed her overwrought nerves with exquisite balm. Paige was right, she took on far too much. She had cleared her life ruthlessly in order to write full-time and already it was silting up with more unnecessary clutter. Across the street the screens still flickered and the Stars and Stripes adhered grimly to the glass. Her appetite for this city was waning; even the dull roar of traffic invaded her space.

It was only then, on the brink of switching off the lights, that her eye was caught by the ad.

2

Genevieve Hopkins was waiting for a call. One already several days too late. If he didn't ring by tonight at the very latest, she was bound by foolish convention to turn him down. And that would be a blasted nuisance since she'd spent so much already on the outfit. The frock itself had been relatively simple. Candy had steered her into the charity shop where they'd picked up a nifty little Fifties moiré silk in a flattering hyacinth blue. Candy had an unerring eye for style; unaccompanied, Genevieve never would have chanced it. It was the shoes and bag that had run her into debt even though she agreed that she couldn't have done without them. Four-inch heels that made her totter like a drunk but displayed her slender ankles to perfection. But Hector hadn't rung her yet. And now she was having serious doubts that he would.

She wandered disconsolately around her cluttered house, picking up armfuls of washing from the floor. The boys had been home for the weekend and treated the place like a tip. Since their father had defected with that bitch from Sales and Marketing, they had been steadily growing out of control. It had been almost a relief when they both went off to college, though at times she felt that her life had lost its purpose. She ought to be doing more work on her book; instead she was glad of almost any excuse to postpone the beastly chore. Talk about displacement activity; her enthusiasm for her chosen profession had been on the wane for years. Having to produce a new novel every twelve months had become little more than a yoke she could not duck out of. And, although at first the advances had seemed like riches, these days she could never figure out where the money all went.

David had been a steady provider; she was bound to grant him that. Unimaginative and pedantic though he could at times be, they had nevertheless rubbed along very comfortably together. So that when, three years ago, he had suddenly dropped his bombshell, the fallout had knocked her right off course. He was the only proper boyfriend she had ever really had; the thought of facing the future without him had thrown her into blind panic. Two hungry teenagers meant that she couldn't opt out so, instead, she'd been forced to grovel to the bank, who had helped her work out a rough kind of financial plan. One she found almost impossible to stick to; bills kept coming in that she didn't expect. She would call her agent and anxiously explain and the resourceful woman would as often as not bail her out. A commissioned piece for the *Daily Mail*, a short story for *Woman's Own*, even the occasional charity lunch, though Genevieve was a nervous speaker. One way or other she usually managed to cope. It was precarious living from hand to mouth but still she managed to stumble on and, at least, they hadn't yet had to repossess the house.

17

Then Hector Gillespie had entered her life, bringing her sudden renewed hope. She had met him at a private view, been introduced by an acquaintance. He was shorter than she was, with a weighty paunch, but she liked his mellifluous Highland burr as well as his air of authority. He was, by profession, an opera critic with a regular column in a Sunday paper and a row of books to his name. His knowledge and blatant erudition had only added to her insecurity; she was genuinely astounded when he called. Since then they had met sporadically and soon he had coerced her into bed. She didn't find him in the least attractive but needed the affirmation of his desire. If only, she sometimes thought, he would marry her, all this financial roller-coasting could stop.

But Hector was coming up to fifty and had never committed himself yet. Though inclined to pomposity, he was socially presentable and much in demand at events as a single man. He was out on the town almost every night and, she feared, not exclusively with her. There were several women whose names he let slip but she had not yet plucked up the courage to ask who they were. Or whether they were sharing his sexual favours; she rather suspected that they were.

'Ask him,' advised Candy, when she confided her fears over lunch. 'It is always better to know the truth.' She had been a single parent for eight years, was expert at sniffing out phoneys.

'But what if he says yes?' wailed Genevieve, unwilling to face the prospect of life without him.

'Then at least you'll know and can decide what you really want. I'd dump the bugger if I were you, there are plenty more fish in the sea.'

But bright-eyed Candy, with her beguiling smile, was svelte and silvery as well as ten years younger. She muddled by with her forays into fashion and raised that difficult child all on her own. Genevieve couldn't imagine how she managed. Candy was far more courageous than she could ever be.

She broached the subject as they walked home through the rain. 'How have you managed all these years alone?'

'One day at a time,' said Candy briskly. 'And never allowing myself to feel victimised.' Trevor, her ex, had treated her badly and only stayed in touch because of the kid. She rarely mentioned him any more, felt only irritation when he called. But a boy needs a dad so she allowed him regular access though, over the years, his visits had grown steadily sparser. If she let it bother her, it would doubtless get her down, but Candy was made of sterner stuff than her friend.

'They are none of them worth it,' she said with her bright smile. 'Give me my girlfriends any time for loyalty and laughs.'

Genevieve wished she could share her optimism but never felt wholly complete without a man.

And now Hector was doing his same old thing and not phoning. The gala performance of *Arabella* was something she longed to attend. Not so much for the music as the occasion. In the presence of royalty, the stars would be out in force and Genevieve yearned for a bit of restorative glamour. Hence the new outfit. She was heartily sick of how she looked and wearing the same tired old clothes almost every day. She went to the gym on a regular basis, thus still had the figure for the hyacinth blue dress. It was at the gym that she had first encountered Candy. They had fallen into an easy friendship though Genevieve still knew very little about her. Simply that she found her amusing; life-enhancing in her way.

She had never particularly liked this house, not from the day they moved in. It was the first suitable one they had found, early on in their marriage when Genevieve discovered that she was pregnant. Not a natural homemaker, she had simply had to make do and, when a second baby closely followed the first, moving became the lowest of her priorities. Highbury, in those days, before the trendy Blair government, was barely on the fringes of civilisation and even though now it was steadily upgrading, her attitude towards it continued lukewarm. When David defected she had found herself stuck, too poor to make the move to a better neighbourhood. Also, too dispirited; whatever was the point? Alone with her two raucous sons, she felt that she had failed.

Lately, since Hector, she had pulled herself together and even given the outside a fresh coat of paint. But the rooms remained cramped and dark and overcrowded; she had even succeeded in blinkering herself against the garish carpet on the stairs. All the improvements she had once planned to make had faded, along with her dreams. She occasionally saw the disdain on Hector's face on the rare nights he stayed over. Usually she had to go to him, at his bachelor pad in Devonshire Place. With her makeup and toothbrush in an overnight bag, she felt like an ageing call girl. Even worse was returning on the early morning Tube, concealing her rumpled hairdo under a scarf. It wasn't in the least romantic; in fact it made her feel slightly soiled. Candy was right, she really should dump him. But what, if she did, would she do for a social life then? She was a woman of a certain age with children who were virtually grown-up. There was no way now that she could lie about her age, whereas men like Hector, with few commitments, could continue to play the field for as long as they liked.

Genevieve's problem was endemic to her generation; she had

launched herself straight into marriage from being a student and thus had zero experience of playing the field. Without a regular partner, she wasn't quite sure how to cope. Most of the longtime friends she had made only ever socialised in pairs. And an attractive unattached woman, even one of her vintage, was sometimes perceived as a threat by the smugly still married. The advent of Hector had provided a new lease of life; somebody wanted her, she was grateful for his attention. He was older, shorter, fatter; all those things. And yet she felt defined by him, no longer just somebody's cast-off.

'Get out there and have some fun and find yourself somebody else.' Candy was always so positive, the reason Genevieve liked her so much. It seemed that she never got miserable herself but bounced back fighting, with a brand-new scheme, if ever her plans went awry. She was an excellent foil for Genevieve, spunky, original and fun.

'Love is like a seesaw,' Genevieve's American friend, Anna, was fond of saying. 'When you find your end dipping too drastically, it's essential you kick the ground very hard or else the game is lost.'

'Love is all very well,' said Genevieve wistfully, 'but I'm not at all sure I would recognise it now, even if it bit me on the bum.'

It all had to do with self-esteem, but Genevieve was far from being convinced. Anna was confident and brave and fulfilled and exulted in her independent lifestyle. Somehow she had managed, all these years, never to have had to rely upon a man. She was popular and gregarious yet entirely self-sufficient. Genevieve envied her that endless freedom.

'It comes with practice,' Anna assured her. She had had her

own sexual mishaps in her youth. The solitary life was a mindset, she explained. Once you gritted your teeth and took the plunge, it was possible to get used to almost anything. And it gave her the space, so essential to a writer, in which to think and contemplate and read.

'Don't you ever get lonely?' Genevieve asked her.

'No more than anyone else. If you don't have to fit yourself around another person's needs, it is that much easier to accommodate your own. If ever you feel a sudden urge for company, you can always call up a friend, while on nights you are not in the mood for going out, there is nothing to prevent you staying home. No rows, no discussions, no having to find a babysitter. The only person to worry about is yourself. Feet up, mudpack, *The Sopranos* on the TV. You can do what you damn well please and that's what I like.' She neglected to mention the sleepless nights, when her brain was racing overtime and the three a.m. blues set in. Then she would give almost anything for someone at her side, to hold her tight and comfort her and drive the phantoms away. But those moments of total panic were rare and not worth mentioning now. Childhood was something well in the past; she had to fight her battles on her own.

Anna had obviously done a lot of thinking and had things under control whereas Genevieve lived her life almost always on the edge. Jumpy, apprehensive, scared of her own shadow. That was the principal difference between them. And yet, for the past five years, since Santa Fe, the two contrasting women had been good friends. Sharing the same humour, liking the same books; these days they kept in regular touch by email.

They had met in New Mexico, at a literary convention, the sort of thing at which Anna normally sneered. She had been invited as a prize-winning novelist on a panel of 'celebrity' writers, whereas Genevieve was there at her own expense, part of the regular networking her publishers insisted was essential. Anna's own books were intelligent and well-crafted, attracting good reviews and growing sales. The movie deal was a huge boost to her readership, though she was level-headed enough to know that it might not ever get made. Fashions changed, the studios were fickle, but news of the sale had proved a publicity boost; a 'name' director with a stable of successes and an Oscar nomination in the can. With the chance, maybe, of getting to write the screenplay, a field into which she had always wanted to stray. And then, of course, there was the purchase money. Nobody could quibble about that.

Each had recognised a kindred spirit among the varied and colourful oddballs who hang around on the fringes of such occasions. They were largely failures, which was quickly apparent; real writers, as Genevieve was rapidly finding out, simply do not have the time to spare. These were mainly pathetic wannabes, who either financed their own publication or else hawked around a tired old typescript in the vain hope of breaking through.

'The truth is,' said Anna, with her customary frankness, 'there are very few writers of any sort I can stand.' Bores and pedants, most of them, interested mainly in sales figures and self-promotion, which had very little to do with art or even value for money. They laughed. Genevieve, when she loosened up, became instantly much prettier. The slightly gawky British manner softened into radiance when she relaxed. And, at Anna's anarchic instigation, had sunk several rounds of margaritas. At that stage she was not yet divorced, yet already alarmingly lacking in self-esteem. The extent to which she had been mentally undermined was obvious to Anna and painful to observe.

'Men are very much overrated,' Anna pronounced. 'I have yet to encounter one I could not live without.'

Yet Genevieve's novels, when Anna got round to them, were sly and quirky and engagingly fresh, not at all what their rather crass packaging seemed to imply. Genevieve had to be the world's most bashful writer, but that was all part of her slightly wistful appeal. It would be hard, because of their charming insularity, for her books to break into the American market but if even one received critical notice, to Anna's mind the rest should naturally follow. That was the power of word of mouth, her reason for being in Santa Fe. It all boiled down to self-belief and refusing ever to give up.

'Your problem,' Anna was bold enough to say, 'is that they are publishing you all wrong. You are far too good a writer for those sugary girlie jackets.' The so-called 'chick lit' phenomenon was already virtually over. 'You need to be taken seriously up-market and given the real distinction that you deserve. Your wicked humour and sharp observation should be aimed at a far more intelligent readership. Take Nancy Mitford and Barbara Pym. I honestly believe that, properly packaged, your rightful place should be alongside them.'

Naturally, such inspiring words were balm to Genevieve's ears and she tried very hard to believe what Anna was saying. And, indeed, here they were, after all sorts of changes, the firmest of buddies, practically joined at the hip. Anna also had strong opinions about Hector, regardless of the fact she had never met him. She had seen the effect that he had on her friend which, for her, was quite enough. British women could be unbelievably feeble; she could not understand why Genevieve didn't fight back.

'Leave him,' she urged her, unwittingly echoing Candy. 'You are far too good to be messed around in this way.' As long as Genevieve put her life on hold, waiting to see what might transpire with a man who quite clearly did not love her, she stood no chance of ever meeting anyone new. She was like a cab with its meter light switched off, giving out negative signals.

'Be bold,' advised Anna, 'and put yourself about more. You're a great-looking gal with a burgeoning career. It is he who should feel the privilege of knowing you. Who the fuck does the bastard think he is?'

Her words, of course, fell as usual on deaf ears for poor Genevieve simply lacked the basic courage. Like now, for instance, hanging around at home, forlornly awaiting a call that would never come.

3

'Get this!' said Anna to Paige next morning, reading it over the phone.

> Italy, Tuscany. Beautifully renovated
> XIV-century villa, 40 minutes from Siena.
> Six bedrooms, pool. Easy day trips. In
> exchange for house/apartment in midtown
> Manhattan. Four months April–July.

It was signed simply 'Yale grad '78'. Followed by an email address.

'What do you think?' All night she had been turning it over in her mind, considering all the ramifications, wondering if she dared.

'Sounds just what the doctor ordered,' said Paige. 'Why are you even hesitating?' The great thing about being a professional writer was that you could work wherever you chose. No being stuck in an air-conditioned office or fighting the crowds to get home.

'If you guys would come I would jump at it right away. Confess, it sounds like everybody's dream. You, me, Charles, whoever you care to include. We could all of us do with a break in the sun, especially somewhere like Tuscany.'

'I wish,' sighed Paige, on her way out of the door. 'But with all that's going on at the moment? Dream on.' September had thrown the city into chaos. She was finding it hard to keep herself totally sane.

Anna paced the floor, unable to settle. Tuscany in the spring, a dream; right now, there was nothing in the world she could think of that she would rather do. To escape from this oppressive place and finish her overdue book without the nightmares. The only real problem was that she couldn't drive.

'What do you think?' She bounced it off Larry who said he'd come like a shot, if asked.

'I wasn't actually inviting you,' Anna told him sweetly. 'Though in any other circumstances, of course, you'd be at the top of my list. But I'm afraid that, right now, I need you here more. The house has got to take precedence.'

Larry understood that, of course he did. Life would be easier for everyone concerned without Anna hovering, breathing down their necks. Her irritation with their noise and roistering spirits hung like a heavy blanket in the air. From the number of times she popped down to check their progress, he could tell they were ruining her concentration. Without her constant presence there, they could finish the job that much faster. Though it wasn't, of course, his place to suggest it since she was the one picking up the tab.

'If I weren't here,' said Anna, reading his thoughts, 'I reckon your team would be a whole lot happier. But suppose I went ahead with the swap, what would the advertiser think? About having workmen still around. Do you suppose he would mind?' The house, after all, consisted of four spacious storeys. Plenty of room in which to spread out and still not be inconvenienced by the builders.

'If it's not till April, we'll be more or less out of here.' And the swap would be an incentive to hurry them along. With the basement kitchen and dining-room complete, there really wasn't a lot more left to do. Certainly nothing structural, only the finishing touches. Nobody, surely, could be upset by a couple of taciturn painters.

'I'll think about it,' said Anna. It was just too perfect, there had to be a catch. She went to bed wondering whether she dared go ahead.

Anna's email caught Genevieve on the hop. She had stayed up far too late last night, imbibing too much wine. He hadn't called and she wallowed in mortification, conceding herself unworthy of such a man. While the kettle boiled, she studied the *Daily Mail* with its two-page spread of photographs from last night. There they all were, the glittering and the great, posing on the steps of the opera house. Two lots of minor royalty, Princess Michael and the Wessexes, were pictured regally shaking a sea of hands. Genevieve, still in her scruffy pyjamas, sniffed; the little hyacinth number had gone unworn. She searched for a glimpse of Hector but in vain; he obviously wasn't sufficiently grand to be snapped. Either that or too short, she suppressed a smirk, and wondered who he had taken in her place. One of those faceless women, she had no doubt. Younger and smarter, with a knowledge of opera and plenty of scintillating chat. In his world, she knew, she could not compete and wondered why he had bothered with her at all.

She made the tea and slumped at the table to drink it, gazing despairingly at her untidy kitchen. An old-fashioned airer was laden with football gear; her older boy had come home last night and left her his laundry to be done. It was probably just as well that she hadn't gone out. He had arrived from Nottingham without prior warning, expecting to be fed. Then was off again for an all-night party from which he had not yet returned. At least one of them had an active social life; after all, he was almost twenty-one.

'All right for some,' thought Genevieve glumly, running her fingers through her unwashed hair. Just the sight of her growing boys accentuated her feeling of life passing her by. David was off with his fancy piece, leaving her to clear up the mess at home. It wasn't fair but when had it ever been?

The table was cluttered with all kinds of things: ironing, unwashed dishes and her computer. Unlike Anna, with her pristine and orderly study, Genevieve worked wherever the mood took her, surrounded by a chaotic sea of muddle. But at least it meant she was close to the kettle and could make endless cups of tea without getting up. The telephone rang; it was almost eleven. She knew, as she rose to get it, that it wouldn't be him.

A girlfriend, ringing to commiserate; Genevieve smiled in spite of herself and went to the fridge to fetch the bottle of wine. Which, she found, was more restorative than tea, even at this hour in the morning. She settled down for an intimate natter, telling herself that her writing would just have to wait. Anna worked a disciplined eight-hour day and also very often through the weekend. Her novels appeared regularly, eighteen months apart, usually to rapturous reviews. But, then, Anna led a bliss-fully untrammelled life, with only that old dad of hers to dis-tract her. And, from all Genevieve had heard about George Kovac, he was every bit as independent as his daughter, an adored friend and confidant to whom she could tell anything, rather than any sort of ageing encumbrance. She sniffed again. Recalling Anna's seesaw analogy, she felt she deserved some-thing much better.

After forty-five minutes of therapeutic chat, during which she drained off the bottle, the friend had to change for a lunch date across town so Genevieve finally switched on the computer. There was little point in dressing, she had nowhere to go and didn't expect her boy back for several hours. His incursions into town had two main purposes, to catch up on his social life and dump his dirty washing. The other boy was every bit as bad but, at least, further away.

Before she returned to her own turgid prose, Genevieve checked her email. Which was when she discovered Anna's mes-sage and a sudden gleam of hope came into her eyes.

The email outlined the Tuscan plan and wondered if Genevieve was up for it. Was she ever? Anna didn't need to ask. She had never felt more in the mood for running away. But then, immedi-ately, the doubts came crowding in. Who would look after the house while she was gone and what if one of the boys should suddenly need her? They were both almost adult and living their separate lives but, as a parent, she hated to let them down. There was also the question of cost to be considered; Genevieve was almost perpetually skint. Yet the villa, as Anna pointed out, would be free; she surely couldn't afford to turn it down. The main objec-tive would not be riotous living but to get on with their work in peaceful surroundings, away from the distractions of everyday life plus the noise and pollution of summer in the city. She should think of it as a kind of retreat, monastic if not entirely spiritual.

'I'll call you at noon, your time,' added Anna, which meant more or less now. She obviously knew that her indecisive friend would take more than a little persuading. Yet Genevieve, now that the thought had occurred, seemed the absolutely obvious choice. Even, in some ways, better than Paige since she wouldn't have anyone else in tow. Not that Anna didn't dote on Charles; it was just that drawn-out threesomes rarely worked. Two was much better when it came to a period of time and they got on well, had similar tastes as well as pressing deadlines to be met. Also Genevieve spoke rudimentary Italian and, still better, could drive. Anna was bent on wooing her hard, though fully aware it was likely to prove uphill work. Genevieve suffered from that ultra-British condition of resolutely refusing to have fun.

'Provided we stick to a regular work routine,' said Anna, when she made the promised call. 'Think how wonderful it should be. The villa sounds vast, six bedrooms and a pool. Close to Siena, too, which I hear is marvellous.'

'I am not sure I can afford it,' said Genevieve automatically, getting cold feet in her familiar negative way.

'What's to afford? It all comes free, apart from the day-to-day living expenses which we can split between us; it won't be much. Tuscany is notoriously low-cost and airfares are so low right now, you will hardly feel the pinch. Cheaper than staying in London, believe me, and I'm sure that, like me, you could use some R and R.' As well as space from those two loutish lads, though that she didn't add.

'But the house,' protested Genevieve, still not wholly

comprehending. She was always uneasy when it came to matters of finance.

'Simple,' said Anna. 'I will do a straight swap.' The point, after all, of the ad.

'You'd allow a total stranger into your home?' Genevieve was amazed. 'How could you possibly bear that?' She knew how obsessive Anna was; the house was all she had talked about for months.

'I've been in it such a short time,' admitted Anna, 'that it hasn't yet truly started to feel like home.' Besides, there were always workmen about and lovely Larry continually dropping by. She could certainly use some rest and recreation herself, and not just from her workload.

'How can you be sure it would be safe?' persisted Genevieve. 'What guarantees would you have?'

'The key thing is, the guy's a fellow Yalie. You can't get much more respectable than that.'

Genevieve continued with her usual feeble wavering, swinging, as if in fever, from hot to cold. Basically she loved the idea, yet was also, though she didn't say it, worrying about Hector. There might be some perfectly plausible explanation as to why he had had to stand her up and hadn't called. Anna succeeded in buttoning her lip. This was one decision that Genevieve could only make for herself.

'Don't leave it too long,' was all she said. 'Or someone else is bound to snap it up.' If they hadn't already, which was more than likely. Opportunities like this were rare. They'd be fools not to grab it right away.

A whole week went by and Anna had given up, resigning herself to a long anxious summer in the city. Christmas was fast approaching, with its usual razzmatazz, though this one looked already like being muted. She spent Thanksgiving quietly with her father, during which she told him cautiously of the Tuscan plan. What had seemed like such a brilliant idea faded with every day of Genevieve's silence.

'Do it,' said George, as positive as Paige. 'I tell you, if I were younger, I would come too.'

'You'd be more than welcome.' There was plenty of room and at least, that way, she would not have to worry about him.

He laughed but shook his head. 'You are too kind. But my days for jetting around the world are over.' He reached across and gave her more wine. 'But you should do it while you still can. You work far too hard as it is.'

'And you'd be all right?'

'Of course I would. I am not yet senile, you know.'

But it wasn't that easy if Genevieve wouldn't come. There were very few people Anna knew who had the leeway simply to cut and run and head off into the great unknown on a whim. Most of her friends had regular jobs, with Genevieve, perhaps, the sole exception. And she knew too much to bank anything on her after all these years of close friendship. Genevieve's problem, adorable though she was, was a total inability to fight back. One hostile act and she crumpled into subjection. It was hard to imagine how the British Empire had lasted as long as it had. Anna gritted her teeth and went back to her work. She was still hardly sleeping, or even seeing people, but gradually getting on top of things again. The flickering screens had become less intrusive but everywhere she went she heard the same topic. To the extent that she preferred to stay home. Sadie was so self-centred, she didn't care.

And then, to her amazement, the telephone rang and it was Genevieve, weeping fit to bust.

'He's done it again,' she wailed when she could speak. 'Booked for Bayreuth with another woman because he feels *The Ring* would be wasted on me.'

Anna, scandalised, was also amused. This man really did sound the pits.

'I didn't think the two of you were still speaking,' she said. 'You told me last week it was over.'

'He called and we went to a movie,' admitted Genevieve. Which was when this ugly secret had emerged. Even then, it became apparent, he had not intended to tell her but the other woman, Miriam, had called while she was still there.

'Apparently, like him she's an opera freak.' Probably younger and prettier too.

Anna could not imagine how Genevieve could possibly still be bothered; he sounded such an utter waste of space. But her friend was obviously hurting a lot so she managed to soft-pedal on her comments.

'He's always putting you down,' was all she said. 'It's high time you taught the jerk a lesson. Come to Tuscany and let him stew. Trust me, it's no more than he deserves.'

Jubilant that Genevieve had finally made up her mind, Anna wasted no time in answering the ad. She was certain the villa would no longer be available and checked her email every half hour, desperate for a reply. Which, to her surprise and relief, came quickly. A friendly message from one D. A. Sutherland, saying that her house sounded just the job. He needed to be in New York for four months and what she described was exactly what he had hoped for. Safe and central, a perfect match. He didn't even mind about the builders. Provided there was suffi-cient space in which he could comfortably work, he wasn't fazed.

And as for Sadie, he was an animal lover and would enjoy the privilege of having her around.

'He sounds divine!' said Anna to Genevieve, when she called to tell her the swap was going ahead.

'Almost too good to be true,' agreed Genevieve. 'Do we happen to know if he is married?'

Anna grinned; her friend was so predictable. 'I haven't a clue,' she said. 'But I'm afraid that's purely academic anyhow since we're not going to get to meet him. He'll be here in New York while we are there.' She suspected Genevieve was starting to get cold feet and so briskly overruled her. 'See!' she added triumphantly, 'I knew it would all work out. I told you, you can always trust a Yalie.'

Just to make doubly sure, however, since she secretly acknowledged that Genevieve did have a point, Anna checked with Paige. Who efficiently looked him up in the alumni directory for '78 and reported that he was, indeed, there with a rather impressive résumé.

'Hear this,' she said. 'Marine biology, magna cum laude, and also on the rowing team. Brains as well as brawn.' Which reminded her, she had a cousin around that age who had also rowed for Yale.

'Can't do any harm to check him out,' said Paige and dialled the Baltimore number.

Her cousin, Wilbur, was positive in his praise. Now quite a fat cat attorney, he had once been a fun-loving jock.

'*Dan* Sutherland?' he said. 'A terrific guy. One of the all-time greats. A marvellous all-rounder with a first-class brain who might have turned his hand to almost anything. Popular, gregarious, also very well-heeled. He would have made an excellent politician. And he certainly had no problem with the ladies.' He

35

laughed in a slightly suggestive manner but made no attempt to expound. Wilbur was one of those laddish middle-aged men who have never quite left their fraternity days behind. 'Do tell him hi from me if you happen to see him, though I rather think these days he spends most of his time travelling. He became some kind of high-flying photographer doing worthy things for the environment. Why exactly do you need to know?'

Paige explained about the possible house swap and, again, Cousin Wilbur was fulsome in his praise. 'I seem to recall now there was some sort of Italian connection. Tell your friend not to hesitate. Believe me, I'd go like a shot if it were me.'

'Well, that's okay then,' said Anna, relieved, glad of his reassurance. Now that the plan was starting to take shape, she could scarcely wait to get going. Sunshine and solitude and a peaceful, healthy life; it should certainly make up for the rotten past few months. Once Christmas was over, there were only three months to get through and pleasant anticipation would make the time go faster. She would sort through her summer wardrobe and buy some sharp new outfits, just in case. She had insisted to Genevieve that they were going there mainly to work but wanted, just on the off-chance, to look her best. Her father was right, she should grab it with both hands for he knew, more than most, how things could change.

'Do you reckon we ought to have some sort of a contract?' she wondered, then firmly dismissed the thought. It was fuddy-duddy and out of tune with the casual spirit of this friendly exchange.

'Well, on your head be it,' warned Paige, the cautious lawyer. 'Though I can't deny I would kill to be coming too.'

Candy and Genevieve each had important news. Genevieve went

first. Candy was green with envy when she heard about the Tuscan plan. It was a howling February with gale-force winds that rattled the windows and sputtered soot down the chimney. The two hadn't met for several weeks because of the Christmas holidays but now that Hugo was safely back at school, at last Candy had the time for some relaxation. Until half-term; the weeks went speeding by. Sometimes it seemed that the child was on permanent vacation. They sat in the Dôme, nursing their second espressos, unwilling to brave the elements for a while. By mutual consent, they had given up on the gym, at least until the weather was slightly less harsh. Candy, for once, looked exhausted and drained, with mauve shadows under her eyes. Although she would never admit to it, caring for Hugo took it out of her since he never, not for a second, could sit still. Genevieve, who didn't like to pry, marvelled at how Candy coped. At least her own husband had stuck around while the kids were growing up. But Candy had never been married, which must make a big difference. Nor had she ever even lived with Hugo's father. Whatever had happened had not been intended, though Candy would always declare brightly how lucky she was.

'I got my little bundle of joy without having to put up with his dad,' she would say and certainly, for most of the time, she appeared relaxed and content. Hugo's father was some kind of roving reporter who never seemed able to hold down a permanent job. They did not see that much of him, which Candy found a blessing, though there must have been times she could have used some support, especially with that hyperactive child. Genevieve thought wistfully of Hector and how much she was missing him already. At least the trip should act as a diversion and keep her from fretting too much.

Now it was Candy's turn to divulge and she instantly brightened up. 'I showed some of my rough autumn sketches to a
buyer from Harvey Nichols. And, after a really short wait, she
has told me she likes them.' Colour was returning to her pallid
cheeks and, as she talked, her eyes regained their sparkle.
Genevieve hugged her with genuine delight, thrilled at this
unexpected piece of good fortune. This could be just the leg-
up Candy required to put her up there with the other London
designers. She had seen some of the beautiful clothes her friend
had made and the workmanship was exquisite. If anyone
deserved success, it was Candy. As Genevieve knew from her
own experience, the creative life is rarely easy. And having to
live from hand to mouth, without the security of a regular
income, can be exceedingly hard. Even without the additional
burden of a kid with learning difficulties.

'If I can get them to her by the end of the summer, they might
even give me my own line. Can't you just see it, "Macaskill
Modes"? But tell me more about Tuscany,' Candy begged. 'It does
sound the chance of a lifetime.' What wouldn't she give to be
somewhere in the sun, with time and space to work on her
designs. Genevieve told her about the house and how it had all
come about. And when she let slip that her friend in New York
was the novelist Anna Kovac, Candy's eyes positively bulged.

'*The* Anna Kovac? I just adore her books. Couldn't put the
last one down. And now I am pleased to see that it's going to
be filmed.'

Both sank into contemplative silence and Candy toyed with
the sugar. 'I don't suppose,' she said cautiously at last, 'that I
could come along too?'

Genevieve thought rapidly but could see no reason why not.
The house, from all accounts, was vast, and with three of them

there, instead of just two, she would feel that much more secure.

'What would you do with Hugo?' she asked, afraid of what the answer might be. Their summer idyll destroyed by that child . . . but Candy quickly reassured her.

'No problem, his father can take him,' she said. 'It's time the idle bastard pulled his weight.' And most of the time he'd be away at his special school. She would fix things so that it would not be a problem.

'I'll have to check with Anna,' said Genevieve. 'I'll get back to you as soon as I possibly can.' She was not at all sure that Anna would want to be bothered by a third person tagging along, particularly someone she did not even know. Anna took her writing very seriously; the fewer disturbances, the better.

But Anna, somewhat to Genevieve's surprise, seemed perfectly relaxed. The more the merrier was how she saw it, provided they all stuck to strict work routines. It was essential that she finish this book and she needed to do a lot of catching up. And so it was fixed for the start of April, with Candy coming to join them later, after the Easter holidays were over and Hugo back at school. Anna and Genevieve would meet at Pisa airport and rent a car to take them to Montisi where arrangements would have been made by Sutherland for them to collect the keys.

'So we're not going to get to meet him at all?' said Genevieve, sounding wistful.

'No, as I've told you, we should pass him in mid-air. Which is the whole purpose of the exercise.' A shame because he did sound intriguing, especially so since Wilbur's ecstatic response. This trip, however, was not about socialising, but a quiet retreat in which to catch up on their work. Away from the horrors of city life and the memories Anna was trying so hard to suppress.

4

The scent of sunshine was almost palpable when she stepped off the plane in Pisa. Just the short walk across the tarmac evoked a myriad fragrances of early spring, combined with a sharp new sense of hope in the air. It could be she was imagining it but, for the first time in many months, Anna felt a surge of sudden optimism. They had arranged to meet at the Hertz desk and there already was Genevieve, whose flight had come in forty minutes earlier, looking flustered and preoccupied until she saw Anna and waved.

'I've sorted out the car,' she said, after they had embraced. 'It's only a small Fiat but, I promise you, more than adequate for just the three of us.' She hated the thought of driving in Italy but was determined not to let Anna know. It was only a pity that Anna had not learned; surprising, considering how good she was at almost everything else. Still, soon there would be Candy to help share the load and it could not be remotely worse than the horrors of driving in London.

They stowed their luggage in the neat little car, then Genevieve spread out the map. 'We take the autostrada towards Florence. Then down the main artery to Rome, which has a turn-off at Sinalunga. Montisi is somewhere in that area, slightly, I think, to the south.'

Anna looked at her watch. It should take them the best part of an hour, which meant they would be at the villa by just about five. After sitting on a plane for so long, she longed to chill out and unwind. And sample the famous Toscana wines about which she had read such good things. With Genevieve concentrating hard at the wheel and Anna holding the map, they edged into the stream of traffic and, unexpectedly, Genevieve found herself relaxing. Compared with London's arterial roads, this seemed remarkably undaunting. Which, combined with the balmy weather, snapped her straight into holiday mode. They had pulled it off and now here they were, with a full four glorious holiday months ahead. It was good to be with Anna again after more than a year and a half. She looked thinner but every bit as chic, with a new crease of worry between her eyes, unsurprising after all she had been through. But that sort of detail would keep for later. Genevieve focused on her driving.

'Tell me about Candy,' said Anna after a while. She had folded the map and was now relaxing; the road signs were easy to follow from this point.

'There's really not a lot more to add. She is bright, hugely talented and fun. With a wicked sense of humour.' She always had everyone in the gym in stitches with her off-the-cuff remarks and rapid-fire repartee.

'Sounds good to me.' Ten years younger, Anna also knew, but that ought not to present any problem. Provided she allowed them to get on with their work; not too much larking about.

'So how are things with Hector at present? Did you let him know you were going away?'

'No,' said Genevieve, proud for once. She really cared about Anna's opinion, was scared of appearing too much of a wimp. The truth was, he hadn't been in touch. But the way she was feeling now, in these great surroundings, she couldn't care less if she never saw him again. She peeled off her sweater and rolled up her sleeves and let the pine-laden breeze waft through the car.

'Shall we open the roof?' asked Anna, entering into the spirit.

'Why not?' It was a brilliant day. And they had certainly had more than enough winter this year in London. The sleet had rattled the panes and the wind had howled. It was weeks since they'd last even glimpsed the sun.

So they drew into a lay-by and did just that. The road, which at first was industrialised, rapidly mellowed into open countryside with undulant hills of a smoky purple and the signature cypresses of Tuscany.

'*We're on vacation*,' crooned Genevieve, thoroughly happy, drumming on the steering-wheel and running her fingers through her streaming hair.

Montisi, when they found it, looked enchanting. Pure mediaeval, with a narrow, twisting main street on which, they had been told, they would find Raffaele's trattoria. He was the keeper of the keys who kept an eye on the villa. The sun was already beginning to sink and gild the austere stone buildings with its light. The local inhabitants they passed were mostly dressed in dusty black and some of the men were even leading donkeys. There was a pungent mingled aroma of cabbage and manure and the general earthiness of a country village. Chickens scattered left and right from their wheels. The sinking sun was a

great orange orb in the sky. They easily could have gone back
in time. It must have remained unchanged for centuries.

'I love it already,' said Anna, delighted, peering at the instructions she held in her hand. And there it was suddenly, round
the bend by the twisted fig tree, the trattoria with its faded
painted sign. 'Guess this must be it,' she said and they both
undid their seatbelts and got out of the car.

Even as early as this there were people in there drinking,
mainly gnarled old farm workers with faces as ruddy as the soil.
There was a huge brick wood-burning oven in the centre and
a forest of bottles behind the bar, mainly of regional wines. Great
smoked hams and festoons of garlic hung from the weathered
beams. In New York or London it would all be fake but this,
without question, was the genuine thing.

'Just smell that woodsmoke,' breathed Genevieve with relish
while Anna strode over to the bar.

The man who hastened across to greet her was stocky but
well-built and powerfully muscled, with twinkly treacle-brown
eyes. '*Signora,*' he said with a glance of appreciation at her well-
toned body and silk designer shirt. Anna shoved her huge dark
glasses defiantly up into her hair.

'We are looking for Raffaele Manenti,' she said and saw from
his instant smile that they had found him.

'What may I do for you, *signore,*' he asked, offering them seats
at the bar. He uncorked a bottle of a rough local wine and
handed them each a brimming glass. Then placed in front of
them a plate of bruschetta and a bowl of olives. The wine was
delicious, with a subtle hint of sandalwood. The shady interior
of the trattoria contrasted dramatically with the sinking sun.
There was a feeling of somnolent timelessness in the place; the
smell of the woodsmoke, the aroma of fresh herbs, the tang of

the olives which were stuffed with anchovies. Both of them instantly felt at home; they might have been sitting here for years. Even this man with his warm and friendly smile already seemed unnervingly familiar.

'We are here to pick up the keys,' said Anna, reluctantly snapping herself out of her trance. 'To Mr Sutherland's villa.'

The Italian continued to study her politely, blank incomprehension on his face.

'Signor Sutherland?' she repeated more succinctly, searching through the printed-out instructions for the villa's actual name. '*Casavecchia*. It is somewhere here in Montisi; you must know it. Yours was the contact name that we were given.'

'*Si, signora*. I know it well. And also Signor Sutherland. But he has let me know nothing about the keys. Apart from a brief phone call from his secretary in Patagonia. The line was crackly, I could hardly hear a thing. I confess I was not expecting you so soon.' Actually, not at all, his expression implied.

Anna sighed and looked helplessly at Genevieve. Everything till now had gone so smoothly, surely they couldn't screw up at this late stage. After they had built up such hopes and both had travelled so far. She was tired and hungry and the musky, eloquent wine had gone straight to her head. She longed only to be able to crash out and not have to worry any more.

'He specifically told us to come to you for the keys. He knew we were arriving this afternoon.' He was almost certainly already in her own house; that was the arrangement they had made. She had left him amply provided for, with the keys in the architect's care.

Raffaele shook his head and looked pensive while generously topping up their glasses. 'I have not heard from Signor Sutherland direct. Not for many months.'

44

'But wasn't he just here?' asked Anna, puzzled.

'Signor Sutherland is only occasionally here. Most of his time he spends travelling abroad.'

'Oh.' This was a hard one. She was now not sure what to do. It had all appeared so clear-cut in that brief exchange of friendly emails. She wished she had some form of tangible proof that they really were who they said. That was the downside of electronic mail, so much had to be taken on trust. She had an urgent desire to talk to Paige and ask what she would advise. How Paige would laugh, but that wasn't important. This could surely be no more than just a minor crossing of wires.

'Couldn't we just stay here and eat?' suggested Genevieve. The enticing smells from the fragrant wood stove were getting to her in a major way. All she had had on the cheapo flight had been an overpriced sandwich.

'But if someone has been in touch with you, then surely it must be okay.' Anna, though weary and disconcerted, was suddenly right back on track.

Raffaele silently polished a glass and made a great show of considering. It was clear to them both he was not being obtuse, merely hedging until he had made a decision.

'*Un momento,*' he said at last, squeezing Anna's shoulder reassuringly. He disappeared into the kitchen at the rear and they could hear him talking rapidly on the phone. Anna looked at Genevieve and shrugged. At last, or so it would appear, something seemed to be happening. And the wine and the ambience were certainly excellent. She felt extremely reluctant to move on.

After a full five minutes Raffaele reappeared, profusely apologising for having kept them waiting. He spoke in rapid Italian to one of his waiters before ushering them out into the street.

45

In his hand he carried a bunch of large iron keys. It seemed he had decided to believe them.

'I will show you the way,' he said courteously. 'Please follow me.'

He reversed his dusty old battered car out from under the fig tree and led them slowly back down the narrow street, then up a rutted cart track that ran off at a sharp angle. Through fields of tall foliage that looked like bamboo, they bumped along at a snail's pace, to emerge eventually on a kind of plateau with staggering views across a great sweeping valley. Raffaele paused to allow them to catch up, then waved his hand expansively at the view.

'All of this is Tolomei land,' he said. 'The region is known locally as Valdombrone.' His car vanished down another precipitous path and there it was, a carved wooden sign almost hidden by the foliage, informing them that they had reached *Casavecchia*. The path levelled out to a long straight track, sprouting with weeds and summer grasses, at the end of which were a pair of vast gates, chained and solidly padlocked. Raffaele got out and fumbled with the keys, then pulled back one of the gates to allow them through. Genevieve drove past him into a spacious walled courtyard in front of an imposing three-storey villa, painted a pleasing sun-washed terracotta. A double flight of steep granite steps led up to the massive front door and facing the villa from across a well-kept lawn was a smaller building, also terracotta, which, on later investigation, turned out to be a chapel. Fourteenth-century and unrestored, imbued with an aura of sanctity and beeswax. With faded annunciation scenes and even a Latin inscription above the door. This was all so different from anything she knew, and Anna found herself suddenly steeped in emotion.

Instead of expecting them, luggage and all, to struggle up the steep front steps, Raffaele led them to a door round the side that opened straight into the kitchen. The room was vast, with a low-beamed ceiling and burnished quarry tiles upon the floor. It was cool and dark and refreshingly still after all the travelling they had done. It looked untouched through the centuries except that the fixtures and fittings were modern, selected with discreet and admirable taste. There was a great black stove that could cater for hordes and, to Anna's delighted surprise, an American fridge-freezer with an ice machine on the front. Raffaele unbolted the doors to the terrace and they followed him outside. He pointed to a narrow flight of steps.

'Those lead up to the pool.'

In order not to waste more of his time, they left the luggage in the car while he took them on a rapid tour of the house. It was certainly palatial, with six spacious bedrooms, linked in pairs by interconnecting bathrooms, as well as comfortable lounges on each floor. There was even a long, narrow nursery containing a row of small beds. At the bottom of the staircase were a pair of imposing carved doors.

'Signor Sutherland's private quarters,' explained Raffaele. 'I think you will find they are locked.'

'Don't worry,' Anna assured him, getting the message. 'I promise we will be as good as gold.' She had taken the precaution of locking her own bedroom door though had left her study available in case Sutherland should want to use it. Since he was planning to work from home, she thought he might welcome the space. She had left a note telling him to use her office equipment and not to worry about the phone. In New York local calls were all-inclusive. Besides, he was there as her guest. The best thing about a house swap, she could see, was having small necessities on tap.

Raffaele, on the point of leaving, stopped and turned back to Anna. 'Let me get this straight,' he said. 'You spoke to Signor Sutherland in person?'

'No,' said Anna, 'that is not what I said. We never actually spoke. Everything was arranged by email.' She wondered if he had any idea what she meant. 'Here,' she said, digging out her business card. 'Why not check it out with him direct.'

'No need,' said Raffaele, politely refusing the card, 'I understand he is travelling at present. But do, please, make yourselves at home and anything you need, just let me know. I will arrange for Maria, the housekeeper, to come in. She will let you know where everything is.'

'*Grazie,*' said Anna, relieved, formally shaking his hand. At last, with luck, she was going to get to relax.

The second he left, they were back up the stairs, properly checking out the accommodation. There was so much space, far more than they would need; it wasn't at all easy to make a choice. Eventually, after a lot of thought, Anna opted for the suite on the second floor. It overlooked the courtyard and chapel and a rather quaint circular fishpond, surmounted by a leering, leaping satyr. Here, she reckoned, it should be quieter; here she could set up her laptop by the window and perhaps gain inspiration from the view. Genevieve took the high-ceilinged ground-floor room which opened off both dining-room and terrace. Although less secluded, she loved its lofty dimensions and tall French windows, with filmy drapes that swayed and danced in the breeze. Candy was welcome to the whole of the attic floor. First come, first served; besides, she had younger legs.

They lugged in their bags and dumped them in their rooms, then went back out on to the terrace. The lingering last rays of the sun dramatically streaked the sky with purple and orange. Genevieve went in search of wine and quickly returned, triumphant. A rack in the kitchen was crammed with bottles; provided they kept a note of what they drank, they could always replace it when they left.

They climbed the steps to take a look at the pool. It was discreetly concealed behind thick shrubbery with a magnificent, unimpaired view across the hills. As the sky grew darker, the stars popped out, as brilliant and sharply defined as diamonds.

'Happy?' asked Genevieve cautiously. She still could not quite believe they were here; it always took her a day or so to unwind.

'You bet!' said Anna, beside herself. This had all the signs of turning into one of her more inspired gambles.

By the time it was fully dark and the bottle finished they retreated back to the house where the lights were on and enticing smells were wafting from the kitchen.

'*Buona sera, signore!*' said a good-humoured voice and an olive-skinned woman, with a spreading waistline, stuck her head shyly round the door. She was, she explained in her limited English, Maria, here to prepare their evening meal. She indicated that she lived nearby and would send in someone on a regular basis to clean. Cook for them, too, should they ever require it. All they needed to do was let her know.

She lit the candles in the elegant dining-room and, like royalty, the two of them sat down. The meal she set before them was a feast: pickled vegetables, followed by crab ravioli and then a fragrant *ossobuco,* the best either of them had ever had. Maria popped in to say goodnight; the fruit was already on the table and there was cheese and fresh bread in the kitchen. She offered to make coffee but Anna waved her away.

'Go,' she said, 'you have done us more than proud. With food like this on a regular basis, what hope have we of ever keeping our figures?'

Maria laughed and spread her hands wide to demonstrate the way they were likely to swell. She was a handsome woman in, perhaps, her early sixties with the glowing patina that spoke of a healthy life.

'Buona notte,' she said, with many nods and smiles. It was clear she was happy that they were there, to breathe back life into this wonderful house.

Anna scrabbled in the dining-room armoire and emerged with a dusty bottle of grappa. 'I'm game if you are,' she said, nodding towards the terrace, and Genevieve managed to find the appropriate glasses. They had both of them been travelling for hours. Yet the magic of this enchanting place already had them in thrall. To think, had it not been for that serendipitously spotted ad, Anna would still be disconsolate in New York and Genevieve in rainy London, fretting.

'To us!' said Anna, raising her glass beneath a bright canopy of stars.

5

'Shopping,' explained Anna over her second cup, sitting at the table making a list. She was already dressed and immaculately groomed when Genevieve emerged around nine, bleary-eyed and virtually comatose. She was wearing cute Viyella pyjamas and her hair looked like a bird's nest. She was never at her best at this time of day.

'I thought you were planning to work regular hours.' Blindly she groped around, looking for something to eat. All there seemed to be were last night's leftovers hence, presumably, Anna's orderly list.

'I've already done two hours,' said Anna. 'I always aim to start no later than seven.' Which, to Genevieve's blurred reckoning, meant three a.m., New York time. Small wonder then that Anna was so successful; she deserved every accolade she got. It might play havoc with her social life but Genevieve had never known her complain. And whatever went on in her private life that

Anna wasn't telling, it had to be better than anything in her own.

Genevieve hacked herself a hunk of cheese and broke off a handful of grapes. The sun was brilliant and the terrace doors wide open. She poured herself coffee from Anna's cooling pot and drifted outside, barefoot, to savour the air.

'What do you like for breakfast?' called Anna, still engrossed in her list. Odd, considering how long they had been friends, that they really did not know each other's tastes. Although they met more or less every eighteen months, they had never, till this moment, even shared. Anna existed on caffeine and aspirin; Genevieve led a more self-indulgent life.

'Glad at least one of us still has some energy.' This morning she felt distinctly shaky; the grappa hadn't helped.

'I haven't been sleeping properly in weeks. I kind of got out of the habit,' said Anna, whose brain was whirring in massive overdrive after her early morning session. It was going so well, she'd been reluctant to leave it, but first things first and the shopping had got to be done. Anna was never comfortable until things were properly sorted. She lived a regimented life of timetables and lists, whereas Genevieve simply muddled along. Talk about chalk and cheese, they were diametric opposites, yet still managed never to get on each other's nerves.

'Cereal will do me. And fruit,' said Genevieve. Beyond that she could not possibly project. She slumped on a warm stone bench in the sun and found herself drifting off again. That huge feather bed had been such a rare treat and the house so silent she could have slept hours longer. Sometime she would have to start thinking about work but not today. She could not remember when she had last had a break, away from the cavilling demands of all those males.

'Somewhere there should be pool furniture,' said Anna, her mind already racing ahead. 'Once we've stocked up with necessities and found out where everything is, we'll begin to get the hang of things and make ourselves properly at home.'

She had left her own place stuffed to the gunnels with every possible item her tenant might need. Food to see him through the first few days, despite the fact that Manhattan supermarkets virtually never close, and the nearest one was only one block from her house. Champagne, well chilled, plus a case of chardonnay; bread and orange juice and eggs. Every necessity she'd been able to think of. Her grandmother would have made him chicken soup; Anna had done the next best thing. There was even expensive shower gel in the guest bathroom, with an extra toothbrush in case he forgot his own. She so much wanted him to love her house, regardless of the fact they would never meet. She just felt she owed him so much and was grateful. To think, if she hadn't bothered to read the Yale mag, she would never have found this paradise. Talk about lucky. One glance at that mind-stopping view was enough. She must be sure to leave him a note.

'Come on,' she said briskly, rinsing out her mug. 'Get your act together and let's go explore.'

Even by mid-morning it was hot and this was still only April. Anna wore stone-coloured chinos with matching shirt, and the delicious raspberry sneakers that had caught her eye in Bloomingdales. Already the worry lines were easing from her face and her bright dark eyes, inquisitive as a robin's, were, as always, fully alert. Genevieve, more conventional, had chosen a sundress over a plain white T-shirt, with serviceable rubber flip-flops on her feet. She carried a wide wicker basket she had unearthed to help transport all those items on Anna's list. As one who actually liked to shop, Genevieve would rather opt for daily excursions, but the super-efficient Anna, who didn't drive, preferred to stockpile and thus save time, plus energy and gas. And, since they were going to be cohabiting so long, Genevieve didn't attempt to argue. It was, as it happened, a major relief to have someone else to make all the daily decisions.

They drove back down the narrow track. Beyond the boundaries of the villa's extensive grounds, the bamboo opened up into acres of vineyards, picturesquely studded with scarlet poppies. The warm, loamy air came wafting through the car windows; there were crickets doing their number in the undergrowth. The heat was rapidly intensifying; they were wise, thanks to Anna, to have made an early start.

'What did he mean, I wonder, about it being Tolomei land?'

'I really have no idea,' said Anna. 'Though I'm sure we will find out.' She loved every aspect of this mediaeval area; felt she had stepped right back in time.

Genevieve parked outside the trattoria and Raffaele saw them and came quickly hurrying out.

'*Buon giorno!*' he cried, with what seemed like genuine enthusiasm. 'Is everything all right with you ladies? How are you settling in?'

'Brilliantly,' said Anna, 'and thank you so much for Maria. She made us feel completely at home. What a gem!'

Raffaele's smile widened and he bowed in acknowledgement. 'Anything at all we can do for you, just ask.' This morning he appeared to be much more at his ease. Whatever doubts he might once have had seemed to have vanished overnight. Which was good. If they were going to be living in this village for four months, they needed as much goodwill as they could get. It was not an acknowledged tourist spot, another big plus in its favour.

'We are off to do a major shop,' explained Genevieve, dragging out the basket.

'Then you must go first to the market,' said Raffaele, 'which is just around the corner, next to the car park. There you will find the finest vegetables and fish that is freshly caught. And after that, Simonetta's general store which should have anything else you could possibly need. And if *she* lets you down, do please let me know. I am here at all times to make your stay memorable.'

His teeth were exceedingly white against his tanned skin and his dark curly hair, clipped close to his scalp, was showing faint touches of grey. He was burly yet fit, with a touch of the gourmet's paunch but, combined with his fighting physique, that hardly mattered. Genevieve found him a fine-looking man. She reckoned him just about forty.

'I wonder if he is married,' she said, as they walked in the direction he had indicated.

'Why, do you fancy him?' Anna was amused. At least that might help to keep her mind off the interminable subject of Hector.

'Not especially but he does seem awfully nice.' In two brief meetings, she had already observed, he had been so much warmer than the buttoned-up men who were all she ever met in London.

'That's the Italian male for you. Horny and priapic as a goat. Beware of the Latin lover.'

Anna was scrutinising her list as they found the market and went in search of vegetables. 'I suggest we work from a kitty,' she said, as both made their random selections. A string of fat pink garlic, great handfuls of basil and mint, juicy succulent tomatoes fresh off the vine. 'That way it's easier to keep things straight. Better than having to divvy up every bill.'

Genevieve had no problem with that; besides, it was all unbelievably cheap. She balanced a vast watermelon on her hand then stashed it at the bottom of the basket. If they lived like this she was bound to lose weight; the Mediterranean diet was famously healthy. She was also tempted by aubergines but they wouldn't last long and already they had more than enough. If Anna would allow her to pop down here every day, she could keep them in fresh vegetables all summer.

After they had loitered in the market for a while, they both began feeling hot and thirsty and agreed it was time for a break. They found a café with tables outside, in the shade of a huge plane tree, and settled down for a glass of wine even though it was not yet quite eleven.

'This is definitely the life,' said Anna, feeling the pressures of the past few months beginning to ease away. She was pleased with how the book was progressing and planned to put in more hours after lunch. She had brought from New York a fat folder of research notes and would soon embark on the intricate business of weaving the narrative strands together into a seamless whole. This was the part of the process she liked best, when the first draft was completely sketched out. It was a bit like embellishing charcoal with oils, once the underlying pattern had been established.

'You are amazingly disciplined,' said Genevieve, impressed. 'I sometimes go whole weeks without writing a word.'

'People have different ways of working. There are no hard and fast rules.' This was a subject on which Anna was something of an expert. 'I just find a strict routine works best for me.' She grinned. 'Guess it's because I'm so anally fixated.' Now that she was feeling less oppressed, her attitude to the book was slowly improving. It would be her seventh in just ten years. At last she felt she was more or less into her stride. Learning to write was like anything else, progressive. And the more one did, the better it should become. At least, that was the theory; she was still not entirely convinced. Which was why she was glad to be having this long break away.

'Take it slowly, stage by stage,' she advised whenever she lectured. 'Provided you write even a sentence each day, it will steadily grow, like a scarf. The secret of creative writing is mainly the basic slog of getting it down.' There was no such thing as a muse, she told them, it was you alone facing that empty page. Which made writing such a solitary profession. 'Don't get it right, get it written.' It was a craft as much as an art; she said; those that failed to make it often just lacked the energy and courage. Plus, of course, an iota of talent, but that was something, surely, that went without saying.

They rose reluctantly and wandered on, in search of Simonetta's store. They needed oil and balsamic vinegar, unwilling to use up those that were in the house.

'He's already been more than generous,' said Anna. 'Let's not eat the poor man out of house and home.' Although he was scarcely ever there, she wanted to leave things exactly as they had found them. The villa was magnificent and she felt a sudden urge to meet him and thank him for allowing them to be there.

'Talking of married,' she said, echoing Genevieve, 'I also wonder if *he* is.' Despite the fact there had been no mention of a wife, the villa had a distinctly feminine touch. Even the table linen toned with the plates, something a man would hardly do. Unless, of course, Maria had done the shopping, though somehow her homely image didn't quite fit. Maria was of solid yeoman stock, there was no mistaking that, born and bred in Montisi without a doubt, with a finely arched nose in the Roman style, denoting generations of in-breeding.

'Careful,' said Genevieve, grinning at Anna's lapse. 'You are starting to let your hormones show.'

'Nonsense,' said Anna, 'I was merely wondering. All that marvellous, luxurious space just for a single man.' It was the writer in her, she might have added, always delving into people's lives. The stuff of which her novels were made, accurate first-hand reporting from the front. But she couldn't be bothered, it was far too hot. Besides, Genevieve knew as much as she did.

They also needed other basic staples, like washing powder, soap and kitchen matches. They dawdled along the winding main street, peering into every shop they passed. Knitting patterns, toiletries; basic requirements such as surgical trusses. It was quite astonishing what was on display in a small, backwater village such as this.

'I shall know where to come when I need one,' promised Anna as, laughing, they located Simonetta's store.

It was double-fronted, with a wide-open door behind a beaded curtain to keep out the flies. On the counter was a bacon-slicing machine and the smoky fragrance of ripe pancetta melded with that of some marvellous fruity cheese. Like Bisto kids, they stopped dead in their tracks and inhaled. A handful of shoppers were standing just inside, comfortably chatting and obviously not in a hurry. Life in Montisi was hardly frenzied and they welcomed a new bit of theatre like the entrance of these two newcomers. They smiled and nodded and stood aside while the woman behind the counter positively beamed.

'*Buon giorno!*' she said, with a radiant smile, as if she knew already who they were. 'The ladies from *Casavecchia*. What may I do for you? I hope you are enjoying our lovely village.'

Both smiled and said that indeed they were and the local ladies stopped their chatter in order to try to understand. Anna carefully worked through her list while Genevieve packed things into the basket.

'Any time you need anything,' said Simonetta, 'I can almost promise I will have it in stock. If not, it can be ordered from Sinalunga. I can even have it delivered,' she added. 'Eraldo can bring it on his bike.'

With much smiling and nodding and shaking of hands, they finally succeeded in disentangling themselves. Simonetta, it was obvious, was a kingpin of the village and therefore a valuable force to have on their side.

'Let's treat ourselves to lunch,' suggested Anna, once they were safely outside. 'I don't much feel like having to cook today. Besides, we have already done a full day's work.'

Genevieve laughed in absolute agreement. 'Provided you don't let me pig out on pasta. I don't want to go home looking like a blimp.'

Over lunch the conversation drifted predictably to Hector; despite the way he treated her, he was rarely very far from Genevieve's thoughts. Yesterday's fighting spirit seemed to have faded a little and the old wistful note came creeping back into her voice. She admitted that he had not been in touch and that this time she was sure he would not return.

'If he's still seeing other women,' said Anna staunchly, 'then he's certainly no way good enough for you.' Why she held such definite views, she was never exactly sure. She saw things always in black and white and was adept at ending relationships. Let them step out of line even slightly and that, for Anna, was the end. She terminated relationships just like that, allowing them no leeway. Yet, deep in her heart, she occasionally wondered why it should be that she viewed things this way. Everyone, surely, was allowed one mistake; she tried not to be judgemental about her girlfriends. It was possible the secret lay in her parents' close marriage. They had met fairly late, when her father was middle-aged, after indescribable horrors in both their pasts. Looking back, as she often did, Anna realised how lonely life had been as an only child with preoccupied parents with eyes only for each other. And then her mother had died far too young. It was something Anna almost never discussed, a void concealed deep in her soul. Not even to be shared with Genevieve, who tiptoed through life, afraid of her own shadow, too meek to stand up for herself.

And now was saying plaintively: 'I miss him.'

'Why, in particular?' asked Anna.

'He takes me to interesting events. Openings, screenings, cocktail parties. Occasionally first nights.' When no-one more exciting was available; she had few delusions about that.

Anna, irritated, clucked at her. Whatever her secret reservations, she grimly stuck to her guns. If he stepped out of line, then dump the swine. No man was worth so much pain and aggravation.

'Don't be so thoroughly weedy,' she snapped. 'How often do you need to hear it, you are beautiful, talented and *fun*. Any decent man in his right mind should consider it a privilege to be seen out with you.'

'*Signore,*' said a now familiar voice, and there was Raffaele hovering above them. His warm brown eyes simply glowed with geniality. Now *there's* a man, reflected Anna to herself, who looks as though he might have the requisite balls.

'Come on,' she said, as he swept away their plates. 'Let's get back to the villa and find out what's what.'

It was mid-afternoon and the place was pristine, with no sign at all of the ravages of last night. The kitchen was scrubbed and the dish towels rinsed and drying. Someone had done a truly immaculate job.

'I think I could easily get used to this sort of life,' said Genevieve. They lugged in the shopping and stowed it in the cool, capacious larder, then went in search of other essentials, starting with the pool furniture. In a basement room beneath the kitchen they unearthed a horde of delights. A ping-pong table, complete with bats and balls, as well as a washer and dryer. And, folded neatly along one wall, a row of garden chairs in plain bleached linen with huge square sun umbrellas to match.

'Very classy,' said Anna, with approval, as they carted them up to the pool. There were also matching cushions for the wooden recliners. Further evidence of a woman's subtle touch.

'I am sure he can't live here alone,' insisted Genevieve. Everything was in such exquisite taste.

'He is a photographer. Maybe he's gay.' Anna enjoyed putting in the boot.

'Unlikely if he spends his life working in the rainforests.' She imagined him as a sort of Indiana Jones. Genevieve had always been romantic.

'Don't be so sexist. You can't ever tell. Men sometimes give you surprises.'

'He is probably trying on all your clothes. I hope he doesn't stretch them.'

'As long as he doesn't frighten the builders. And keeps his mitts off my fur coat.'

'Raffaele said nothing about a missus. But maybe that's just the Italian way.'

'Lord of the manor and all that, you mean. Keeping her firmly out of sight. More likely she accompanies him to the jungle, carrying the cameras, making up the hammocks, sweeping out the tent while he works. If I had a husband who travelled all the time, I'd be damned if I would let him out of my sight.'

'I thought you didn't want one.' Genevieve was amused. Anna often came up with contradictions. Although they were more or less the same age, their life experiences could not have been more different.

'I don't. But I would, if you see what I mean.' The sun was high and the wine had done its work. They changed into swimming things and went back to the pool.

'What we really need,' said Genevieve, 'is hats.'

'Next time we go to the market,' promised Anna, surprised at how thoroughly indolent she felt. All this exertion was having its effect. Two minutes later and both were fast asleep.

Later that afternoon, Anna stood at the open window, refreshed, serene and still damp from her shower. As she dried her hair, she gazed across the wide expanse of rolling hills towards the distant mass she knew was Siena. Her lunch, her nap and later her swim had added to her feeling of utter contentment. She felt stretched and rested and unfamiliarly calm; all she was missing slightly now was Sadie. She hoped Mr Sutherland was a genuine animal lover, but he'd hardly have claimed that he was if it wasn't true. And Larry would still be in and out, adding the finishing touches. She knew she could trust him to keep his eye out for the cat. Below her, on the manicured lawn, Genevieve crouched by the pond. It was green and sluggish, with its sinister ancient fountain, and looked as if no-one had cleaned it out in years. There were dragonflies and fat lazy bees; it felt as if time had stood still for a couple of centuries. They had been inside the chapel and admired the faded frescoes. Whoever owned this house in the past had certainly lived well.

'I wonder if there is a ghost?' said Genevieve.

'No way,' said Anna, stamping on the thought. 'The vibes, for one thing, are much too good.' She knew about these things.

'Could be a benevolent one. Here to watch over the house.'

'We already have Raffaele and Maria doing that. We don't want to risk overcrowding.'

Tonight they planned a quiet meal on the terrace, lemon pasta with a tomato and mozzarella salad. They had found a couple of hurricane lamps as well as a drawerful of candles. It was fun being just the two of them, able to gossip and catch up on each other's lives. Although they emailed regularly, it was not quite the same as conversation. Genevieve had her hair wrapped in a towel and was wearing a brief cotton robe. In just one day she was starting to get quite a glow. Colour suited her, she so often looked washed out. She deserved a bit more fun in her life, had been decidedly wobbly since David's defection. Anna had met him only twice, briefly, and privately thought him a bit of a stick-in-the-mud. But a woman accustomed to having a husband must find it exceedingly lonely at times when he left. Hector sounded a nightmare whom she hoped never to meet. Genevieve was far too sensitive for that kind of offhand treatment; she needed someone to encourage her and see her for what she was.

Her hair was dry. Anna unplugged the dryer, then sorted through her clothes for something to wear. She hadn't done any work since lunch but was determined not to slack off. Genevieve hadn't even opened her laptop but, then, her attitude towards her work had always been somewhat lax. Though opposites, they made a great team, got on without any problems. Respected each other's feelings and privacy, even laughed at each other's jokes. There were very few people Anna knew with whom she could comfortably travel. Genevieve was the rare exception; she was really very glad that she had come. In a few days Candy Macaskill would arrive; Anna devoutly hoped she was going to fit in.

6

Candy arrived at the end of the week, in a flurry of baskets and bags. She looked like a rather beguiling gypsy in flip-flops and a home-made patchwork skirt, with a battered straw hat crammed down on her flyaway hair. Genevieve had offered to meet her off the plane but Candy, for reasons of her own, preferred the local bus.

'It makes it more of an adventure,' she explained when eventually she came panting up the track. She stood in the middle of the cool, dark kitchen, spilling her bits and pieces all over the floor.

'I've brought you some home-made lemon curd,' she said, delving into one of her many baskets.

Anna, to her private relief, took to Candy instantly. She was slight and elfin with a cloud of dandelion hair and a wide, infectious smile that lit up the room.

'Candy's an unusual name for a Brit,' commented Anna.

'Though I must say, it certainly suits you.'

'I changed it the second I left school,' Candy confided. 'Couldn't bear the one my parents had lumbered me with.'

'What was it?' asked Anna, intrigued.

'Promise you'll never tell anyone?' said Candy. Anna, hugely amused now, nodded.

Candy, having checked theatrically for eavesdroppers, leaned forward and hissed in mock horror: 'Beryl! Can you imagine being stuck with a moniker like that? I'd have either ended up a suburban hairdresser or else working for the Town Hall.' She did have a point.

She loved the villa and raced all over it like a child, clapping her hands with sheer exuberant joy.

'This place is really ace,' she said, bounding back down the stairs. 'Mind if I take the attic so I can spread out?'

Neither minded; both were happily settled and those steep polished stairs were inclined to be slightly unnerving. Candy's motley baggage was stuffed with sketches and fabric samples which transformed the long, low-ceilinged room into an exotic bazaar. Candy loved it. After sharing a damp crowded cottage all these years with a hyperactive child, so much space and those glorious views were far more than she had expected. She brought her sketchpad down to the kitchen and entertained herself, as the others cooked, with lightning cartoons of the two of them at work. After they had eaten and cleared away, she allowed them to leaf through her impressive portfolio.

'It's not remotely finished yet.'

She was undoubtedly very talented; both of them loved her designs. She had skilfully captured the season's prevailing spirit in her own individual, slightly airy-fairy style.

'These should be a big hit with Harvey Nicks,' said Genevieve, whose favourite store it was. 'And put you on the fashion map in no time.'

'Let's hope,' said Candy, in desperate need of a breakthrough. It was hard to make ends meet with no steady job.

She had badly needed this time away though had not been quite sure what to do about her son. Although the school looked after him very well and he only ever came home for occasional week-ends, she felt guilty at simply pushing off for four months in Italy without him. Well, three and a half, if she counted the school holidays, though still a lot of time for her to be gone. There was no-one else she could really turn to; her parents were dead and she had no siblings. They were just two orphans of fate. And yet the idea was too good to let go; she was tired and embattled at the thought of all that extra work. Making ends meet on a freelancer's earnings took up most of her energy and the prospect of working with Harvey Nichols was something she must not let go. Not if it killed her; not at this stage. It was a dream she had had for so long. The last time they had had any sort of a break had been two weeks at Butlins in Skegness two years ago when Hugo was coming up for seven. It was not Candy's usual sort of choice at all but another mother had tipped her off and, actually, both had enjoyed themselves very much. There were organised activities every moment of the day to occupy Hugo's attention and wear him out, while Candy was able to relax at last and simply catch up on her sleep. It was bliss. If she could only afford it, she would do it again, but the Italian jaunt was more attractive. She had had to make up her mind fairly fast so, after a lot of deliberation, she had gone against all her natural instincts and picked up the phone and called Trevor.

To say he had been surprised was an understatement. It was months since she last had initiated a conversation and usually ended up cutting him off mid-sentence. But this was a question of priorities and Candy was in no position to take a stand. If she was going to get that portfolio done, she needed not to be running around after the kid. It was that simple. So she had braced herself to be sweetness incarnate and heard herself asking for his help.

Trevor, to give him credit, had reacted graciously. No, he said, he was not too busy nor planning to go anywhere. In actual fact, he had very little to do since the assignment he had been working on for months was very nearly finished.

'He will be at school most of the time,' explained Candy, 'with just the long vacation to be got through. If you could possibly take him then?' She could hardly believe her good luck. For once the man was acting responsibly, almost like a proper father, and furthermore appeared not to mind her having asked.

'No problem,' said Trevor, just as nice as pie. 'In fact, I will really enjoy it. It is time I got to know him a little better.'

When they'd made their arrangements and Trevor had rung off, Candy had danced a wild tarantella then rushed to tell Genevieve the news.

'He was almost civilised,' she said in jubilation. 'I can't imagine what's got into him.'

'Maybe he's growing up,' suggested Genevieve, though that had never made any difference to David. 'And genuinely wants to bond more with his son.'

'Whatever,' said Candy, 'it means that I can come!' And she had whooped away to rummage through her clothes.

Now that they were well and truly into their routines, Anna rose every morning with the dawn. She had imposed a rule, with which Genevieve complied, that they only break for a very brief lunch, then not meet up again till the cocktail hour. After which they were free to do whatever they liked; let down their hair, have fun.

'What about using the pool?' asked Candy wistfully. 'Is that off limits as well?'

'You can please yourself,' said Anna. 'I am only telling you what I've found works best for me.'

Breakfast for Anna consisted of one cup of coffee, which she brewed in a small tin percolator and then carried upstairs to her desk. She had re-established her narrative flow and the book was purring along. By the time she came down at the end of the day she felt energised and fulfilled. Genevieve, who preferred a leisurely breakfast, got up a little later. But, inspired by Anna, she was on the job by nine and managed to stick at it, more or less, until they convened on the terrace for lunch at one. After that, she usually sloped off to the pool to take a lengthy siesta in the sun.

Candy, however, never stirred until noon and often appeared for lunch in her negligee.

'I was up till after three,' she would tell them, yawning. 'I always function best in the early hours.'

She talked to Anna about her books, was a genuine and avid fan. She had read them all with a flattering degree of attention which warmed Anna's heart towards her even more. However ditzy she might seem on the surface, there was a real and original intelligence working beneath.

'It's good for the morale to know someone is actually reading them,' said Anna. 'There are times it can seem like writing into a void.'

*   *   *

Candy, to the surprise of the others, turned out to be an inspired and instinctive cook. She would wander around the extensive grounds and return with fistfuls of this and that which she'd then transform, with an apparent lack of effort, into something tasty and unusual.

'It comes from growing up poor,' she explained. 'I am used to having to scrape by.'

Sorrel soup and home-made pesto; she discovered a munificence of herbs growing wild and garnered them carefully so as not to impede their growth. She even occasionally made her own pasta, beating in unexpected flavours that never failed to delight. There were tomatoes staked carefully close to the kitchen door where they caught the early morning sun and, behind the compost heap, neatly planted rows of beets and lettuces. Someone here at some time in the past had been a thrifty gardener and made the most of the resources they had at hand. There were also luscious black figs in abundance which Candy sliced with prosciutto from the market and sprinkled with basil and mint.

'In another life, you might well have been a chef.'

'I have neither the patience nor dedication.'

'I wonder who does the garden?' pondered Anna. They had seen no sign of any sort of outside help. 'And why the vegetables if the villa is hardly ever used?' None of it quite added up.

She asked Maria next time they saw her, waving her hand in appreciation over the neatly staked rows. Maria beamed and nodded with pleasure, then modestly indicated herself.

'I,' she said in her halting English, 'try to keep them watered and weeded and also thin them out. Occasionally Raffaele comes up to dig. We like to keep things nice in case the owner should suddenly return.'

'Does no-one else ever use the house?' It did seem a terrible waste. Maria shrugged and gestured in the air, talking fast in her difficult local patois which even Genevieve found hard to understand. As it happened, Genevieve had popped into the village so Anna could only guess.

'Is the villa often rented out?' she asked. Maria shook her head.

'I think,' said Candy, 'she said something about family. Though who that family is, she doesn't say.'

'They are probably mostly all related in Montisi. In-breeding in these country villages is a fairly usual way of life.'

'But Sutherland isn't an Italian name. I wonder how he fits in.'

'Maybe he has an Italian wife,' said Anna, which made the best sense. Since he had been at Yale, he was obviously not a local, but it could be that he had married into the community.

'Ask her,' said Candy, but Maria just gabbled on and soon they waved and smiled and wandered away. Anna told Candy the little they knew and she entirely agreed about the elegance of the house. As a designer herself, she had a very perceptive eye, had picked up many small details the others had missed. The positioning of the mirrors, for instance, and the super-abundance of softly shaded lamps. The house, though austere, had been furnished for comfort and the kitchen was almost professionally equipped, with rows of bottled preserves upon the shelf.

'I am pretty certain this is not the work of a man. If we took a peek inside his private suite, all would undoubtedly be revealed.'

'We can't,' said Anna, 'we promised Raffaele. Besides, the doors are locked.'

'Coward,' said Candy. 'It's the obvious way. There must be some method of gaining access without having to force the lock.'

'Not that it's any of our business,' said Anna. Sutherland, after all, was in her own house; she hated to think of him snooping through her things. It went against the spirit of the arrangement. She had left everything but her own bedroom unlocked, even her filing cabinet. Trust was the keynote of swapping homes; she was starting to feel quite an expert. She had left a long memo on the kitchen table, detailing everything he might need to know. Telephone numbers for the vet and the maid, the whereabouts of the nearest liquor store, the dry-cleaner, the post office, the subway. She had also provided a metro map in case he used public transport. And Larry's number, should anything go wrong. Though, of course, he could always call her here, which seemed to make better sense.

'We could always ask Raffaele, he is bound to know.' Candy was like a puppy with a bone. Anna detected the gleam in her eye and knew she had mischief in mind.

'What, and look like silly schoolgirls? I don't think so. After all, what difference can it make?' She was ultra-sensitive about personal privacy, especially since her profile had become so much higher. The idea of anyone asking questions about her own life filled her with instant dismay. The thing that stood in Sutherland's favour was that Paige's cousin had known him at Yale. That, to her mind, was the best recommendation, a guarantee of good behaviour.

Candy laughed. She didn't remotely care but got a buzz out of sending Anna up. 'You realise,' she said solemnly, 'that in all probability his wife is now living in your house? Using your dishes, soaking in your bath, inviting the neighbours in for drinks. Stealing the affections of your cat, countermanding the architect's instructions. Don't worry,' she added, 'there's no problem with that. She seems to have excellent taste.'

72

'Stop!' said Anna. 'You're making me nervous.' The thought had halted her in her tracks. Surely he would have mentioned a wife, wouldn't he, since he was planning to be there for so long? All he had said was that he needed space to work and did not object to the workmen being around. She saw from her grin that Candy was only joking, but that didn't stop her feeling slightly uneasy. She loved the house with such a passion, she hated the thought of another woman there. Illogical, maybe; there were three of them here and yet it was not quite the same. She thought of checking with Larry, then dismissed it. There was no point in worrying about something she could not control. A deal was a deal, she had accepted his terms and, in all honesty, felt that in fact she had come out of it better. Her place was still a building site while the villa was sheer perfection.

The market became a favourite venue and pretty soon they were very well known in the village. Montisi was so far off the beaten track that tourist invasions were rare. The inhabitants were courteous and reserved, with a moving dignity that guaranteed respect. Many of the older women still dressed, head to foot, in black. To begin with, even Genevieve had problems understanding them, found the local dialect hard to crack. But Candy was immediately in on the fast track; smiles and nods worked every bit as well. So that soon they found themselves accepted and knew many of the stallholders by name.

'Hats,' prompted Genevieve, the first time they took Candy there.

'Hats,' agreed Anna, so they made that their first port of call. All sorts of other things lurked within that market. Between the food and vegetable stalls were dotted piles of tablecloths and a garish array of clothes.

73

'Who buys them?' asked Anna, as Candy fingered through them. Multi-coloured rayon housedresses, styles that might well have come from another age. All they needed were bandannas and mops to do a Fifties' Doris Day act in chorus.

'Real women,' said Genevieve, 'who actually live here and can't afford much for a lesser priority like clothes.'

'This would really suit you,' said Candy, pulling one off the rack. 'Try it on.' It was cotton in a wraparound style, designed to fit all sizes, and did, indeed, go really well with the new healthy glow in Genevieve's cheeks. Cornflowers on a lilac background; over the plain white T-shirt she wore it was demure, with a soupçon of sauce.

'How much?' asked Genevieve and Anna rapidly calculated.

'Nine dollars. Can you believe that?' she said as Genevieve forked through her purse.

The hats were a riot and they ended up buying two; Candy already had her battered old straw. Anna opted for a jaunty trilby in raspberry cotton that echoed her shoes while Genevieve chose something more flexible in raffia which, gussied up, Candy assured her, might even do duty for a wedding. 'Stick a few cornflowers under the band and you're there.'

Companionably, they wandered on, comfortable in this new threesome.

Next on the must list was Simonetta's shop. Candy needed insect repellent and the others more of that wonderful cheese. Also, the pasta was running low and they could use some tins of *ceci* just in case. Besides, Simonetta, they had rapidly established, was the fulcrum of gossip in this village. No expedition into Montisi was complete without dropping in on her.

'You will love her,' said Anna. 'She has a wicked sense of

humour and her English is really very good.' Which made a change; in this part of Tuscany few of the natives spoke much English, though the girls were rapidly picking up on the nuances. By the end of the summer they should be fluent, assuming they lasted that long.

It was close to one and siesta time; for once the shop was deserted. Simonetta popped out with her radiant smile and insisted on giving each of them a glass of sweet wine and a biscuit so dry it was almost impossible to swallow.

'It means she likes you,' said Genevieve quietly. 'A local Montisi custom.' She bought the cheese and an armful of beet leaves to make that delectable local soup. In a very short time they were turning into peasants and moving more and more into local fare. Genevieve was secretly pleased. Despite her declarations that she really no longer cared, the weight was miraculously dropping off without effort.

'No junk food,' Anna reminded her.

'Also all those stairs,' added Candy. Plus the long, hot walk back when they didn't take the car and went down to the village for fresh bread. Anna's Spartan regime was certainly working. All three of them were feeling and looking good.

'Isn't this pure bliss?' said Genevieve, as they lazed in the early evening out by the pool. Candy was doing her nightly thirty laps, determined to keep up the good work of the gym; not, so it would seem, that she really needed to. In her brief bikini, she looked like a waifish child with her wild Botticelli tangle of seaweed hair. She certainly had a load of energy; just watching her swim made Genevieve feel limp. Anna was silently writing in her notebook; these days it seemed that she rarely let up.

As the sun slowly sank, the fireflies appeared, like jewelled

Tinkerbells hovering over the grass. From all around them came the fragrance of the *genista*, the bright yellow broom so abundant in these parts.

'Plantagenet,' said Genevieve, out of context. 'That's where it got its name.'

Anna, still scribbling, was not really listening. She had suddenly hit a roll, she said, and needed to get it all down.

'I find,' she said at last, snapping the notebook shut, 'that it helps to leave a paragraph halfway through. Gives your brain something constructive to do, even when you think that it isn't switched on.' Here, she found, she was sleeping like the dead. At last the terrible images were fading.

'You know, I don't miss New York one bit.' Except, of course, for beloved Sadie. 'I wonder how Sutherland is settling in.' Or should that be the Sutherlands? They were still no wiser. There was one thing, though, on which all three were agreed. They could not have felt more at home in his beautiful villa.

'I hope he's as happy there as we are here,' she mused. Pretty soon the work would be done and Larry and his labourers would move on. Part of Anna felt disappointed not to be there to see it finished, though this paradise that she was living in now was effective compensation. The house would be like a birthday present, something to look forward to at the end of four glorious months.

Candy came dripping out of the pool and perched on the edge of a recliner, towelling her hair.

'Drinkypoos time,' said Genevieve, getting up. 'What do you girls fancy doing tonight about supper?'

Since Candy had joined them, they tended to go out more. She was so turned on by the sheer fact of being abroad that it seemed unfair to expect her to stay home and cook. She had never been to Italy before, was overwhelmed by the foreignness of it all. The trattoria had become their favourite hangout, though there were also a couple of other small places nearby. They always got a huge welcome from Raffaele, who in some ways resembled a large and bouncy dog and kept a regular table just for them. He certainly had an attractive personality as well as being an accomplished charmer with his taut, suntanned skin and flirty eyes that occasionally swam with emotion. Italian yeoman stock, earthy and sound. Feet on the ground and eyelashes to die for.

'I wonder if he's married?' said Candy, unaware that she was treading familiar ground. There had never been so much as a glimpse of a wife, unusual in such a tight community. The others told her she had a one-track mind, always on the lookout for a man. He was far too old for her, anyway; she should take her place in the pecking order and wait for it to be her turn. Anna and Genevieve swapped glances; it was fun having Candy here.

'She is probably stuck in the kitchen, poor soul, slaving over a hot stove.' Genevieve, these days, had few illusions about the opposite sex.

'Looking at least ten years older than he does. In one of those voluminous black dresses.'

'With sweat stains under the arms . . .'

'. . . from that stall in the market.'

'Wearing slippers with holes in to ease her aching bunions . . .'

'. . . and with chronic lumbago from the mountains of washing-up.'

'With a bunch of anxious *bambini* at home. Scabies and rickets, you name it.'

Raffaele nodded benignly, enjoying their riotous high spirits, though luckily not quite fluent enough to follow their actual drift. It was a balmy, wonderful Tuscan night and the aroma of woodsmoke was fast going to their heads. They had ordered baked chicken with rosemary potatoes, were growing daily more relaxed about their figures. Especially where their drinking was concerned. Raffaele, without any consultation, brought a litre bottle of the rough local red that had now become their usual. He was amused and happy to watch them having fun. They certainly added some colour to his establishment and helped enliven the rest of his clientele who were mainly farmers and local tradespeople, often with their whole families.

Anna had lately been having exotic dreams. 'Do you think it might be the poppies?' she asked the others. 'Growing among the vines,' she persevered when both of them started to cackle. 'No, really. I'm being serious. Remember where opium comes from.'

She did have a point and the dreams were not only colourful but stayed in her head when she woke, which was unusual, though nightmares, of course, often linger on in the shoals of the subconscious.

'What you're suggesting,' said Candy, giggling, 'is that you're perpetually stoned.'

'If you like, though only mildly.' It was a pleasant enough feeling, she could not fault it; her brain felt remarkably relaxed. Maybe it was simply that she had ceased to worry and her cares were easing away. Her father, when she last telephoned him, had sounded remarkably spry.

'Don't waste your money,' he told her sternly. 'I am perfectly able to cope.'

Genevieve, too, was feeling less anxious since her most recent calls to both her boys.

'*Ma*,' they had said, in perfect echo of each other. 'Why don't you just quit fussing?'

That night, when they returned to the villa, they went skinny-dipping in the pool. The moon was full and the water bright silver; they lay on their backs and watched a shooting star. The real lives they had left behind seemed suddenly remote. Anna had finally stopped worrying about Sadie and they hadn't heard a mention of Hector in days.

'Can't we just stay here for ever?' begged Candy. 'I feel as though I have died and gone to heaven.'

7

Time passed and the temperature rose. May came in with a glorious flourish, tinting the lambent scenery with shifting light. The rolling hills turned pink or mauve, depending on the time of day, and distant Siena lay shimmering in the heat like the mythical kingdom of Oz. In the villa the windows and doors stood wide open to encourage the static air to circulate.

'We really must go there one of these days,' said Anna, standing on the terrace in shorts, a glass of chilled wine in her hand. Genevieve, beside her, nodded; Candy had yet to appear. The attic, and now most of the other rooms too, were strewn with a jumble of fabrics and fine ink sketches as the fashion portfolio spread its wings and flew rapidly out of control. Candy, now that she had settled in, was firing on all cylinders; she was certainly very gifted, no denying that. And knowing that Hugo would be safely with his father meant she no longer had that nagging worry. She slept long hours which paid dividends;

awake, she was the most delightful company. Anna was happy too with her own steady progress and even Genevieve's book was gathering steam.

They walked around wearing very few clothes, careless of possible intruders. The villa was so isolated that anyone approaching would be seen from sufficient distance that they would have plenty of time to cover up. Not that they ever had visitors at all, other than Rosa, a smiling village girl who came in regularly twice a week to dust and do light housework. She was sweet and willing but apparently spoke no English, which Candy found frustrating. She would have made an ideal spy who could tell them all the things they were dying to know. Genevieve tried talking to her in Italian but either she did not understand or pretended that was so. It was hard to tell.

'Damn,' said Candy, 'we will just have to work on Maria.' Though with her, too, they usually drew a blank.

Occasionally Rosa cooked, which was always a treat. Although they all took turns in the kitchen, it was nice, at times, to be able to sit down to an authentic Tuscan meal, served on the table on the terrace, shaded by a couple of the huge umbrellas.

Candy, when not comatose in bed, spent many hours stretched out topless by the pool. 'What?' she said, the first time Anna approached her, almost as though she were doing something wrong.

'You should be wary of taking so much sun,' warned Anna, the practical city girl. The last thing she wanted to do was nag, but this was potentially slow suicide. But Candy, for so many years deprived of life's little luxuries, blatantly chose to ignore her advice. After years of working so hard just to make ends meet, these minor health scares failed to bother her. Even her frenzied sketching had come temporarily to a halt; all she wanted to do right now was bake her brains and just wallow in the sun.

Paige, despite her horrendous workload, stayed in regular touch with Anna by email, one of the marvels of modern technology, far better than telephones or letters to Anna's mind. Paige had a witty and distinctive turn of phrase that always made Anna crack up. Wry and irreverent, her sharp observations were always bang on target. The city, she reported, was stupendously hot, with temperatures high in the nineties. If it weren't for the weekly bolthole of Quogue, she didn't know how they would ever survive.

'I am beginning to think we made a colossal mistake, not taking you up on your offer and coming too.' But Charles was embroiled in the financial gloom that hung like a pall over the city and Paige, too, had more work than she could comfortably cope with. Normally, by this time of year, things were becoming pretty dead, but the mood in New York was manic and intolerable, with people scared of what might be coming next and seeking ways to ward off further catastrophe.

'I envy you your freedom,' Paige wrote, 'as well as your God-given talent. Being able to do your own thing wherever you choose. Lazing around in your Tuscan paradise while the rest of us poor mortals slowly succumb to the traffic fumes. I hope you get cellulite from eating too much pasta; it isn't fair that you should get off scot-free.'

Dear Paige, still stalwart after all these years. Anna could see her clearly as she had been, that first semester at Yale when they'd roomed together. Paige, with her golden patrician beauty, had dazzled the men in their year but her mind was level and her judgement sound; she had never allowed herself to get carried away. Till the advent of Charles, she had played the field and always kept things light-hearted. And their relationship was still as firm as it had been then; top of the things Anna missed about New York was the regular banter of her closest friend.

'Saw Larry and Phoebe last night,' Paige reported. 'We took your dad to the Philharmonic and they were in the next row. Both looking blooming; because of what's happening business is going really well. People are scrambling to sell off their investments and put the cash into bricks and mortar instead. Larry is experiencing a sudden bonanza. Instinct tells me that his next significant career move might well be into politics. He would certainly make an extremely capable mayor.'

That was a surprise but Paige was usually right. Her naturally delving legal brain picked up clues that others might overlook and Larry, too, had been a close pal since Yale, part of their tight inner circle. Anna was pleased and grateful that they were spending time with her father; it helped to assuage any lingering guilt about leaving him so long on his own. But Paige, along with her other friends, had always adored the old man. He was wise and caring and generous with his time, always prepared to listen and give good advice.

'I wish my own dad could have been like yours,' was one of Paige's regular laments. Hers had been a tight-assed corporate lawyer who, although endowing his children with trust funds and first-rate education, had fallen sadly short on most of the rest. And ended up changing wives at a late age before drinking himself to death.

'Why ever would you need him? You've got Charles,' was Anna's stock reply. She envied the Colliers their solid union, perhaps the best marriage she knew at close hand. She had never, herself, wanted to be tied down yet exulted in Paige's contentment. If she should ever have the good fortune to find a soulmate of her own, she hoped she might one day be similarly happy. But that was something she rarely discussed, not even with her intimates. Anna, at heart, had long been a loner, a cat that walked by itself.

'Any news of my house?' she emailed back. It was all very nice that Larry should be thriving but she hoped not at her own expense. Since he was doing it all at cut price, she wasn't in any position to argue but she worried that Mr Sutherland might be inconvenienced.

'He didn't say,' replied Paige. 'And I confess I forgot to ask. If I find a reason to be in your neck of the woods, I will go and take a peek at it myself.'

'Don't bother,' replied Anna. 'You've enough on your plate as it is.' But she longed to know how things were shaping up. And so she called Larry direct.

'Everything's fine,' he told her breezily. 'We are coming in bang on schedule. With luck, we'll be out of there in a couple of weeks. I must say,' he added, 'that you made a brilliant investment. Have you been keeping an eye on Dow Jones?'

'Not really,' said Anna, who had seen only occasional headlines. 'What precisely is going on?'

'Corruption, corruption, corruption,' said Larry. 'Many of the biggest players are starting to come unstuck. People are panicking and selling off their stock but most have already left it far too late. The party is over but they're only just catching on. Millions have lost their retirement plans.' There was the faintest hint of satisfaction in his voice. He, too, had been shrewd enough to put all his savings into property.

'How's my tenant? And is he coping?' Anna hoped he loved her house as much as she loved his.

'I haven't actually seen him yet. He seems never to be around.'

'Is Sadie okay?' she asked, instantly alarmed, afraid her pampered pet was being neglected.

'Sadie's fine,' said Larry soothingly. 'Always looks sleek and content. And the house itself is in apple-pie order. You'd hardly know that anyone was living there.'

'Is his wife there?' She felt she had to know.

'I wasn't aware he had one. The only person who occasionally drops by acts more like a PA. In and out at the speed of light, sorting through mail and returning calls, too busy even to chat.' Also too snooty, he privately thought. He hadn't warmed to her at all.

For a reason she could not identify, Anna felt oddly relieved. She hadn't liked the thought at all of another woman in her space. But knowing that Larry was keeping an eye on things, meant she could finally relax. She lapsed back into her pastoral idyll, shoving all thoughts of New York to the back of her mind.

She awoke with a start in the early hours at the sound of horrendous screeching. Because of the heat, she had left the windows open and thought at first it was coming from her room. Her pulse raced unnaturally fast and she rose in terror. The moon was almost full again and the garden was bathed in brilliant light. Peering cautiously over the sill, Anna could see nothing unusual on the lawn. What sounded like a pack of hyenas voraciously slaughtering chickens or, at the very least, a vixen on heat, was causing no discernible havoc below. Unperturbed, the garden slumbered on. But the noise continued with shattering resonance until, after a while, Anna went back to bed. Her heart was pumping overtime and she found that she could not settle. She would have been tempted to creep down to Genevieve's room if it weren't for those dark, daunting stairs. She tossed and turned, pulling the sheet up high, and eventually managed to drop off again into a fitful doze.

When, as usual, she arose in the early dawn the disturbance had ceased completely. While her coffee was brewing, she stepped outside to watch the sun rise slowly over the hills. The grass was still glistening with morning dew and only the crowing of a distant cockerel disturbed the absolute tranquillity. In New York, all night, she could hear the rumble of traffic, punctuated by sirens and occasionally screams. This was a totally different environment; Anna basked in its peace.

'Frogs,' said Genevieve knowledgeably at lunch, familiar with them from her country childhood. 'In the mating season they certainly do make a racket. Until you know what they are, it can be scary.' She hadn't been able to hear them herself since her room faced in the opposite direction and the walls of the villa were fourteen inches thick, one good reason it had survived intact all these years.

'Frogs?' said Anna, unconvinced. 'Well, show me where they are, then.'

Genevieve knew already. She led Anna triumphantly to the ornamental pond, surmounted by the wicked, leering satyr. Both stared into its murky depths, but beneath the water lilies, nothing stirred.

'They must be sleeping it off,' said Genevieve, disturbing the surface of the water with a twig.

'I wish they'd keep their damn rutting to themselves,' said Anna, though now they had identified the sound, it would not seem nearly so bad. Nature red in tooth and claw or green in libidinous flipper. She grinned. In Manhattan it would have meant murder or worse. She could not begrudge them a little amphibious fun.

That night they ate poshly in the dining-room, with candles on every surface. The ancient mirrors, with their tarnished glass, lent a grandeur that was compellingly authentic. If you half-closed your eyes you might almost believe yourself back in the fourteenth century. On occasional evenings they even lit the fire, just to add a homey touch, but the weather at present was so stiflingly hot they welcomed the cool of the huge high-ceilinged room. It was warmer outside on the terrace than in here, even now that it was dark.

Candy had really excelled herself and thrown together an impressive fish stew. She had spent the whole morning poking around in the market while the others were virtuously at work.

'You have got to eat it all up,' she commanded, 'because in this heat it won't keep.' Mussels and squid and a handsome red mullet; she had even discovered some saffron high on a shelf.

'Well, someone certainly appreciates the finer things in life.' She had noticed numerous little gourmet details like that. The quality of the wine was excellent too. No matter how rarely there were visitors here, their host was clearly a perfectionist.

'I wish we could meet him,' she added. It was becoming an obsession. The more they saw, the more they longed to know.

'Leave him a note,' suggested Genevieve. 'Perhaps you can set something up.'

'Candy, you'll be the death of me,' groaned Anna, handing over her bowl to be refilled. At home she rarely bothered to cook and long ago had given up entertaining. Writing was such an absorbing commitment, she seldom felt comfortable away from her screen. Basic things like eggs and cheese could keep her going for weeks.

'You work too hard,' was Candy's comment, passing her the bread. 'You really should try relaxing more, especially while we are here.'

Genevieve pulled a second cork. 'Let's take it up to the pool,' she said. 'But, please, chaps, tonight no grappa.'

Candy gathered up the scented candles and placed them strategically around the edge of the pool. The flickering flames competed with the fireflies and they even found a glow-worm on the steps. It was like entering an enchanted glade, a fairy-land of delicate dancing light. With a whoop of delight, Candy ripped off her clothes and dived headfirst into the pool.

'The water's divine, come and join me,' she screamed. 'The last one in does the dishes.'

Genevieve found it hard to open one eye. It was hot and swollen and throbbing like a metronome. She also had a fierce compulsion to scratch – anywhere, everywhere, all at the same time. Something pretty nasty seemed to have stung her in the night. As she cautiously moved, she realised she was covered in abrasions. Horrified, she jerked fully awake, swinging out her legs from under the sheet. Despite the diaphanous mosquito netting, which she'd had the prudence to draw around the bed, the little blighters had still contrived to sneak in. In all, she counted thirty-nine hits, with others that hadn't yet peaked. With her fair complexion, she had always been susceptible; this morning she resembled the Elephant Man. She found Anna in the kitchen, similarly suffering, though her olive skin meant that she had fared less badly. Bright pinpoints of calamine dotted her face like pale measles. And certainly had done little for her mood.

'It was those damned candles around the pool. They must have attracted every bug within range.'

Even Candy was up early too, slathering herself with lotion. 'That's it,' she declared, 'no more skinny-dipping for me. Definitely never again by candlelight.'

The heat continued though the itching gradually ceased. They made an emergency trip to Simonetta to stock up with cures and preventatives, and henceforth ensured, before lighting candles, that the mosquito screens were in place. Anna and Candy were unused to country living and Genevieve considerably out of practice. But it did not, in any way, cramp their style nor reduce their general enjoyment. If anything, these minor hitches made them appreciate what they had got all the more. Anna slept like a log these days; even the mating frogs failed to keep her awake. Her brain had cleared, her creative juices were flowing. Her skin was pellucid, despite the disfiguring bites. New York featured less and less in her thoughts as, incidentally, did her house. Or even her father, whom she tried not to call. She did occasionally drop him a postcard but knew how he hated any fuss. She had inherited from him her independent nature and knew when to leave him alone. Too much attention and he started to feel old and she knew that both Paige and Charles were doing staunch duty. She would try to find a way to repay them but that would have to wait until she got back. In the meantime, she must respect his privacy by appreciating this place while she was still here.

Trudging back from the village one morning, laden down with groceries and wine, having recklessly chosen the overgrown shortcut, knee-deep in grass and wild flowers, Anna and Genevieve stopped suddenly in their tracks. It was just past noon and the sun was at its highest. They had opted for exercise instead of the car and now both were hot and exhausted. Also Genevieve was developing a blister and couldn't wait to get home and kick off her shoes.

'What's that?' asked Anna, shading her eyes. A heat haze shimmered in front of the gates; what she saw was more like a mirage. Genevieve was peering too. 'Looks like a bunch of bikes,' she said. 'Surely that cannot be.'

To the right of the gates, the ground swelled steeply upwards, surmounted by a tuft of scrubby trees beyond which rolled the endless verdant scenery with not another habitation in sight. Their villa was the last along the track. What had caught their eye was indeed a cluster of motorbikes, unattended but parked in a tight circle, as if part of some sinister alliance. They counted eleven, which was slightly unnerving; so much for their rural retreat. An involuntary chill ran down Anna's spine and her steps grew instantly more cautious. A lifetime in Manhattan had sharpened her instincts.

'Looks like an invasion from the local Hell's Angels,' she muttered, devoutly hoping that she would be proved wrong. Together they stealthily crossed the lawn towards the villa's main front door which, as always, stood wide open, allowing the breezes to blow through. There was no sound of voices nor movement from within. Everything drowsed in the slumbrous midday heat. No sign of Candy either, though the remains of her breakfast were scattered all over the table and the teapot, when Anna felt it, was still lukewarm. They stowed the shopping, then Anna strolled up to the pool to find out what was going on. And there was Candy, stretched out in the sun, wearing only the briefest of bikini bottoms, hat pulled low, oblivious of the world.

Anna, disapproving, shook her awake. 'You ought to be more

careful,' she said. 'You never know who might be lurking around.' She told her about the motorbikes and Candy vaguely remembered having heard them. She'd been half asleep and had taken no notice, assuming that they were simply passing by. Anna advised her to cover herself up while she went to find out what was going on. There were times when Candy resembled a careless child, altogether too laid-back for her own good. Candy pulled on her T-shirt but continued to lie prostrate. She couldn't care less, thought Anna grimly, advancing towards the impenetrable shrubbery, there to protect the pool from prying eyes.

Suddenly she heard a burst of muffled laughter and a frenzied stirring in the bushes and something large erupted right at her feet. For a startled second, she took it to be a large animal but, as it uncurled and struggled upright, she saw it was wearing jeans and a leather jacket. Presumably a local youth, out on the rampage with a cluster of silly-ass friends. Somehow they had managed to crawl through the shrubbery, where they had been hiding and feasting their eyes. Now, with much scuffling and merriment, they all broke cover and raced away back to the safety of their bikes. She shook her head sadly as the engines started to rev and they took off in a cloud of dust. Something, insidiously, appeared to be going wrong. Cracks were beginning to show in their paradise.

8

They did eventually make it to Siena, one weekday morning late in May, when Anna had reached the end of a chapter and the others were suddenly craving a change of scene. For even paradise can occasionally cloy; too much perfection isn't natural. On Anna's insistence, they left at the crack of dawn and were in the Campo in time for a leisurely breakfast before the tourist invasion was properly underway. Candy, still bleary-eyed, was trying hard to shake herself awake but Genevieve did all the driving without so much as a murmur. Candy could take her turn on the journey home, allowing Genevieve to indulge herself at lunchtime. That was the way things usually fell into place; after so many weeks of endless close contact, a workable living arrangement had kicked in. Considering two of them had never met before, the trio was co-existing remarkably well. By now most groups would be spitting and growing mutinous but these three actually liked each other; even more, always the acid test, could still be civil at breakfast.

Already, as early as this, it was hot but they had become acclimatised. They wore short cotton skirts with T-shirts and sandals and, of course, the obligatory hats. Anna was tanned as dark as a native Italian while both the others had achieved a burnished glow. And Genevieve had distinctly lost weight; she was proud of her flatter midriff. How she had achieved it she couldn't imagine, after all the wine and pasta she had consumed.

'Just goes to show that the gym is a waste of time.' She ordered a cappuccino to follow her melon and recklessly stirred in extra sugar. She was far less stressed because she was so much happier and had stopped just grazing on junk food when she felt the need. Also she no longer had to cater for growing boys. They lived simply and healthily on fish and fresh vegetables, the staples of the Mediterranean diet. And, in her heart, she had even stopped hankering after Hector; felt only the occasional passing pang. Spending time with lively, independent women had turned out unexpectedly life-enhancing. She no longer worried about how she looked and went without makeup during the day, though Candy was doing great things for her morale by overhauling her wardrobe. It reminded her of boarding school, which she had always rather enjoyed. In many ways the success of this trip was due to the fact that she was finally discovering she could cope on her own without a man. A slice of wisdom she had picked up from the others; if nothing else, she would gratefully carry that home. And stand it on the mantelpiece, in place of the more usual straw donkey, a memento of a seismic change in her life.

'If we are going to do the Duomo,' said Anna, studying her guidebook, 'we ought to get in there before the crowds. Which means now.'

Obediently they filed after her as she deftly led them by the most direct route. Anna, it seemed, had a natural radar and rarely ever had to consult a map.

Siena was a truly enchanting city which had remained the same, virtually unaltered, since the Middle Ages. Its steeply climbing mediaeval streets were backlit at night like a stage-set, with seventeen separate neighbourhoods, the *contradas,* proudly picked out with their own distinctive colours. The highlight of the tourist season was the legendary horse race, the Palio, which dated back unchanged to the eleventh century. Then the Campo swarmed with spectators and the whole of Siena came out in force, waving banners to cheer on their chosen teams. Family was set against family; the *contrada* always came first in their loyalties. Like the Montagues and Capulets, they would fight to the death for the cause. That, however, was not for a few more weeks. The race took place only twice a year, in early July and August.

'We could always come back,' said Anna with a grimace, 'if you think you can stomach the barbarity.' To her mind the sport rivalled bullfighting in its grossness, involving unnecessary suffering to animals and bringing out the bloodlust of the crowd.

Genevieve shuddered. 'I am not sure that I could.' Somewhere she had read that the horses sometimes died. But the thought of all that pageantry inflamed her curiosity, even though the race itself lasted an unbelievably brief ninety seconds.

'Well, let's at least think about it,' said Candy diplomatically, 'and see how we feel a little nearer to the time.' Siena was less than an hour from Montisi; they had done it today at record speed. And it would be a shame to miss out on its biggest event, especially since they were here for a whole four months. The chances were she might never return, so she wanted to cram in as much as she possibly could. Even if Harvey Nichols should come through, and Candy was by no means sure of it, she had never in her life been flush with money and living as a one-parent family took up everything she earned.

For the next few hours they wandered and admired, soaking up the atmosphere and pausing for regular pit stops. The heat was fierce but they were in no hurry, with plenty of time just to wander and explore and savour the colourful street life at their leisure. Anna's favourite spectator sport was sitting outside at a café table, watching the world go by. It was, she felt, far more educational and rewarding than focusing only on inanimate things and helped to fire her writer's imagination, part of the main purpose of trips like this.

'This place is great,' said Genevieve with longing. A hazy daydream was starting to take shape of one day, conceivably, moving here to live. The climate, the food, the easygoing people, especially the hunky, good-looking men. As Anna was constantly reminding her, writers can live wherever they choose, provided they have a lifeline to civilisation. These days, with laptops and the internet, the world was potentially their oyster. And the flight time from London to Florence or Pisa was now just under two hours. She thought about Highbury, with its polluted, traffic-clogged streets, as well as the terrible weather they had been enduring. The wraith of Hector flitted fleetingly through her mind but she banished it sternly before it could take hold. Thus far, she was coping remarkably well without him. She might just drop him a postcard to rub that in.

'I think I have more or less had it,' announced Anna by mid-afternoon. 'Does anyone mind if we think about heading back?'

Her calves were aching from all the uphill walking and they had gutted the city, at least for today. There came a point in sightseeing when you needed to stop before it all merged into one uniform blur. She had friends in New York who would rubberneck till they dropped, while retaining no lasting impression of what they had seen. Along with the millions of Japanese tourists who seemed only ever to venture forth in flocks and saw life entirely through their viewfinders. Snaps and guidebooks served their purpose, but it was also essential to savour firsthand the essence of a place and its inhabitants. The beauty of staying so close to Siena was that they could easily return at any time.

As they slowly strolled back to where they had parked the car, down a narrow side street they chanced upon a truly magical shoe shop. The window was lined with rows of pretty sandals, all in the finest Italian leather, at stupendously reasonable prices. They stood like kids in front of a sweet shop, noses practically pressed against the glass.

'Italian footwear is the best in the world,' said Anna, the shopping connoisseur. Hopefully she tried rattling the door but the shop was now closed until half past four.

'It's siesta time,' Genevieve reminded her. As big-city dwellers, all three of them, they had several times been caught out this way.

'Ah well,' said Anna, philosophically. 'What better excuse could we possibly need for coming back very soon?'

'Do you mind if we take in San Gimignano on the way back?' It would mean quite a lengthy detour but Genevieve, avidly studying the map, could see an alternative route that should easily work. And since they were not in any special hurry, sitting comfortably in the air-conditioned car would be a welcome alternative to all that strenuous sightseeing. By the time they got there, they would have their second wind and be ready for another bout of exertion. Neither of the others had any objection, so off they set, this time with Candy at the wheel and Genevieve reading out directions.

San Gimignano, just east of Volterra, was one of the most famous Tuscan hill towns. Significant for its dramatic skyline, it was a place that Genevieve was particularly keen to see. According to the book she was reading, recommended by Raffaele, it had reached its zenith in the Middle Ages before the Black Death had decimated its population and power had reverted to Florence. Since knowing Raffaele and listening to his stories, she had become engrossed in the history of the region. He had a way of describing things that made her want to know more. And unlike Hector, who dismissed her as an airhead, the Italian went to considerable pains explaining his heritage to her. Not just in a sketchy way but with all the passion of a natural born teacher. This would be an excellent way of showing her appreciation. A little encouragement could surely do no harm; she was growing increasingly attracted by this warm and eloquent man.

Anna, unaware of all this, gratefully grabbed the chance for a snooze in the car. She had lately been working such long, intense hours that by this time of the day she was pretty much knackered. Softly, as the other two talked, she drifted off and began quietly to snore.

'She's back on the serious narcotics again,' giggled Candy, recalling their opium joke.

'Let her sleep,' said Genevieve. 'She does work awfully hard. And obviously needed this break.' No-one who hadn't been there on the spot could start to comprehend what she must have been through. And, unlike either of the other two, Anna rarely discussed her emotions, preferring to keep her nightmares bottled up.

'It's useless trying to cosset her,' said Candy, who understood from personal experience just how complex these things could be. All those hours spent with doctors and psychiatrists; small wonder that Trevor had eventually wandered off.

'Not too loud,' said the ever loyal Genevieve. Anna had been immensely good to her by talking her through her various problems. Now, if Anna would only allow her to, perhaps she could pay a small part of it back. It was good to see her finally relaxing.

She had, however, overlooked one crucial thing – the effect the spectacle of the towers of San Gimignano was likely to have on her. Anna woke abruptly as Candy pulled into the main drag, looking for a convenient parking space. The sun was starting its glorious descent and the shadows were lengthening dramatically so that the initial impact of what she saw before her hit her like a sudden blow to the heart. She stumbled unsteadily out of the car and simply stood and stared.

'What is it?' asked Genevieve, alarmed and concerned, rapidly grabbing her arm. The colour had totally drained from Anna's cheeks; she looked like a person in shock.

'The towers! I never knew,' she said, appalled by this eerie echo of New York. The tall, imposing mediaeval skyscrapers were legendary in Tuscany, the main reason for the fame of the small walled town. Two, in particular, standing close together, were indeed uncannily like what Manhattan had lost.

'Once,' explained Genevieve, thinking fast and anxious to make amends for what she had done, 'there were as many as seventy of them standing. You could, according to Raffaele's book, cross town by rooftop as easily as by road. They were built initially as fortifications but also as monuments to their owners' egos. The higher, the better, just like modern city life. Some mediaeval Donald Trump must have been getting his rocks off. Think of it, all that boiling oil just to repel your neighbours. No dropping in for a cup of sugar in those days.'

'I presume they only used extra virgin,' put in Candy to lighten the tone. 'If you're going to be boiled alive, let it be with taste.' She, too, was startled by Anna's extreme reaction, had not, up till now, entirely realised how terrible it must have been to witness the destruction at firsthand. The television coverage had been gruelling enough but how much more horrendous to have been there.

Genevieve gave Anna a spontaneous hug, deeply sorry now that they had come.

'Interestingly enough,' and she read aloud from the guidebook, 'this was also once a centre of banking and corruption.'

As well as the site of some serious Renaissance art so that, by the time they had taken it all in, Anna had regained her equanimity. It was strange, she thought, as they walked back to the car, how history could play such devilish tricks. Those forward-thinking builders from the past had contrived to demonstrate that time was an endless whole with nothing really altering at all.

'I'm famished,' announced Anna when they finally headed home. They'd had nothing but snacks to eat all day and now it was very nearly seven. The sun was low and the heat reducing; a welcome breeze was stirring the sluggish air.

'Let's stop off at the trattoria,' said Genevieve, once again taking her turn at the wheel. 'We could all use a break and it's simpler than going home first.'

'Will he be open yet?' asked Candy, but Raffaele's establishment very seldom closed.

'My treat,' said Anna, as they bounced into the forecourt. She felt in urgent need of some space in order to download the day's experiences. In both Siena and San Gimignano, history appeared to have stood still. It would take a while for her brain to adjust and her breathing to resume its natural pace.

The place looked deserted, though the door was, as always, open, and a dusty Land Rover stood outside, a gun tossed casually in the back. A friendly golden retriever came to greet them, head down, tail waving vigorously like a flag. Genevieve gently caressed its ears as the women looked around for some other sign of life. Inside the trattoria it was dark but blessedly cooler. Raffaele was stationed at the otherwise empty bar, drinking with a stranger he didn't introduce.

'*Signore!*' he said, with apparent delight, and led them through to a shady table outside. He brought them bread and a flagon of wine, then rapidly laid a cloth and awaited their orders. No need to take them through the house specials; they practically knew them all by heart.

'Please take your time,' he said, seeing their indecision. 'I will be waiting inside.' He retreated to the coolness of the bar and his unidentified drinking companion.

'So,' said Raffaele later, once they had given him their orders and he was busy with cutlery and plates. 'How are you ladies getting along? Is everything all right at *Casavecchia*?'

'Fabulous!' said Anna, able at last to relax. 'We are having a really great time. The villa is splendid and so well kept up. It seems such a shame that it isn't more often occupied.'

'We are on our way back from Siena,' said Genevieve. 'A truly enchanting town.' She was going to ask him for more of his stories but unusually, for once, he seemed preoccupied.

'Ought we return for the Palio, do you think? Everyone talks so much about it.'

'I would say so, without any doubt. But will you still be with us by that time?' He seemed puzzled, as though that was not what he had been told, though who he could have been talking to was a mystery.

'For the first one certainly, in July,' said Anna. 'We have the villa until the end of that month.'

'So you have been in touch with Signor Sutherland?' He buffed a knife with a spotless cloth before carefully setting it in place.

'Nope,' said Anna, 'there has not been any need.' Now that she knew that her cat was all right, the last of her niggling worries had faded away. She relaxed in her chair, kicking off both her shoes, imbibing the glorious scents of the summer evening. It would take a lot to beat this place. How glad she was to be here and not in New York. But Raffaele, somewhat to her irritation, seemed very much still on their case. How many times did she have to explain? She wished he would learn to mind his own damn business.

'Tell me,' said Genevieve, adroitly changing the subject, alert to just how short Anna's fuse could be, 'that night we arrived and you showed us the way to the villa, what was the name of the family you mentioned that owns so much land around here?'

'Tolomei,' said Raffaele, suddenly brisk. 'They are among the biggest landowners in Tuscany. You may have seen their palazzo in Siena.' He busied himself shaking out their linen napkins and seemed not to want to pursue the subject at all. Anna's eye briefly caught Genevieve's. She idly wondered what he was not revealing.

The stranger had emerged from the gloom of the bar and now stood quietly listening, drinking his beer. Anna gave him a cursory glance, then took a closer look. He was tall and rangy, dressed in faded denim, his eyes obscured by reflective lenses. Raffaele continued ignoring him completely, made no attempt to introduce him or draw him into their group. A local farmer, would be Anna's guess, remembering the Land Rover and the gun. The clothes might be old yet were obviously expensive. You didn't find tailoring like that in a village such as this.

'*Scusi,*' said Raffaele, 'forgive me for asking again, but how exactly do you come to be staying there?' He slung the cloth carelessly across his shoulder and planted both meaty hands on the table. His liquid eyes were serious for once, all trace of his usual flirtatiousness totally gone.

For Chrissakes, what was it with this buffoon? Inside her head, Anna was once again screaming. *Read my lips!* she wanted to tell him; maybe he wasn't very bright. Why couldn't he let the subject drop? She had told him over and over as much as she knew. Her arrangement with Sutherland had been totally straightforward; if he hadn't bothered to fill Raffaele in, that was not her problem. For all she knew, or even cared, he was merely the keeper of the keys. Like Maria, nothing more than a retainer, paid to do a specific job.

'I swapped,' she repeated, struggling to keep calm, heartily wishing he would go away and leave them to eat in peace. 'Direct with Signor Sutherland by email. In exchange,' she added, 'for my own place in New York. He wanted somewhere to stay for four months. I needed to get away.'

'And you're saying that's where he is now?' Raffaele remained unconvinced.

'As far as I know. That was the purpose of the ad. Why is it suddenly so complicated? What's your problem?'

Raffaele, muttering, went back inside for the food. As he passed, he said something fleetingly to the stranger who drained his glass and followed him into the bar.

Anna, exasperated, raised her eyebrows; it was fast turning into a farce. Only she wasn't finding it amusing, not in the slightest way. First the frogs and then the mosquitoes, followed by the Hell's Angels gang. She had come all this way in search of a retreat and refused to allow irritations to rattle her now.

'Look,' she said firmly when Raffaele reappeared, arms weighted down with their order. 'Why not check it out with him direct? Here's my telephone number in New York.' She handed him the business card he had already rejected.

'No need, *signora,*' he said, mollified. 'I assure you that is quite all right. Forgive me for asking so many questions.' His eyes remained troubled but were now evasive. He wished them all *buon appetito* and finally left them alone.

The food was superb and Anna cooled down. She must not allow things to get to her in this way. She regretted having snapped at him, he was only doing his job, but she did find his constant inquisitiveness very trying.

The stranger was waiting with his dog when they walked back to their car, leaning against the Land Rover. Anna glanced at him curiously and he gave a peremptory nod, then stood and stretched and wandered over to talk. He was taller than she had realised at first, with the long easy stride of an athlete, and his skin had that healthy year-round tan which spoke of a life lived largely out of doors. When at last he spoke to her she got a huge surprise; his English was fluent and he had an American accent.

'So what's all this about a house swap?' he asked, as though it were any of his business.

Anna bristled, instantly back on her guard. She'd had more than enough aggravation for one day. There was something about his nonchalant stance that got right up her nose, combined with the fact that he couldn't be bothered to smile. That was the thing about Italian men; despite the charm they so easily turned on, beneath it all they considered women inferior.

'So what's it to do with you?' she snarled, facing him, arms akimbo.

The eyes behind the mirrored lenses continued completely inscrutable. Anna had a sudden urge to knee him sharply in the groin. 'Don't patronise me,' she wanted to shriek. 'Get off my fucking case!'

Instead, she inhaled and buttoned her lip, taking deep breaths to cover her agitation. This hadn't been a good day at all; first San Gimignano, with its horrifying echoes, now this insufferable man.

'I overheard you mentioning that Sutherland was in New York.' He seemed impervious to her worsening temper.

'I guess so,' said Anna, as Genevieve unlocked the car. 'Along with his wife, so I believe. Staying in my house in midtown Manhattan.' Even without the sun it was hot; she wanted only to get home now and into the pool. 'If you're so interested, ask him yourself.' And she thrust the card that Raffaele had rejected into his receptive hand.

'Thanks. I'll do that.' He slid it into his pocket. At last he did smile and his teeth were flawless; despite her fury she noticed that. He clicked to his dog then turned on his heel and abruptly strode away.

'Wowee!' said Candy with appreciation, once they were safely out of earshot. 'You know something? That guy's pretty tasty. I certainly wouldn't kick him out of bed.'

'Down, girl!' said Genevieve, sneaking another look as he calmly started his engine and drove away. A fine-looking man, that could not be denied, although sadly way out of her league. Given the choice, she still preferred Raffaele, with his gourmet's belly and earthy Italian charm. Except when he was in a mood, like tonight, when she had secretly found him slightly threatening. There was more to the man than immediately appeared. She wondered what his link was with the stranger.

Anna alone sat silent though inwardly spitting with rage. 'Bastard!' was all she eventually said though she wasn't entirely sure why.

9

'See if you can find me some basil, there's a love,' said Candy, 'and perhaps, while you're out there, some sprigs of oregano and mint.' Genevieve was hovering in the kitchen, having just completed her morning's work. Anna was still invisible upstairs but the sun was well and truly over the yardarm, no argument about that. It was definitely time for a drink. Genevieve glugged the remains of last night's bottle into Candy's eagerly proffered glass. The white was slightly less palatable than the red but drinking red at lunchtime gave them all headaches. Genevieve, wearing her schoolgirlish aquamarine robe, looked burnished and delectable from the sun. Since hanging around all these weeks with the profligate Candy, she had relaxed many of her primmer domestic habits. Candy, up earlier than usual for a change, wore minuscule shorts and a scarlet halter top which she would whip straight off the minute she got back to the pool. The local Hell's Angels, or whatever it was they were, had been back several times since that initial invasion. Anna disapproved of Candy's flagrant exhibitionism, seriously worrying that she might end up with more than she could handle on her own. But there was no stopping Candy, a dedicated sun-worshipper; for as long as it shone, she would soak up as much as she could.

Today, though, it was her turn to make lunch and she was preparing one of her lavish, imaginative spreads. Crostini were baking under the rather slow grill and she was slicing mozzarella and tomatoes, hence her need of the basil. Genevieve trotted obediently into the garden where a riot of untamed herbs grew along the borders. She came back triumphantly clutching a generous bunch and they both inhaled reverently its uniquely pervasive aroma. Basil was surely the quintessence of summer, certainly here in Italy.

'Heaven,' said Genevieve, opening a new bottle then piling up the dishes to carry outside. She had spread a colourful cloth on the garden table and carefully chosen ceramic plates that would tone. Because everything here was in such perfect taste, it lent an air of festivity to even the simplest of meals. Again she found herself wondering what its owners must be like to have created such a mellow and beautiful home. Occasionally she fantasised about some day being part of such a team. Two kindred spirits, working contentedly in tandem to create the manifestation of their dreams. She cringed even to think of that garishly patterned stair carpet and how she had put up with it all these years. No wonder Hector didn't take her seriously; as a homemaker she was a disaster.

'Better summon Anna,' said Candy. 'It is very nearly ready.' She handed over the platter of crostini, topped with ricotta and anchovies and her own home-made onion relish.

'Mmm,' said Genevieve, sneaking a taste then rapturously

licking her fingers. 'You really are a terrific cook, Beryl. It's a shame you waste so much natural talent working as a seamstress.'

Candy, grinning, flipped her with the dishcloth; the sparring between them had become a regular thing. 'If I'd stayed in Watford and hadn't moved on, who can say what great things I might have achieved. Beryl's Beauty Parlour on the High Street, perhaps, instead of Macaskill Modes.' Several difficult babies instead of just the one. Talk about wrong side of the tracks; Watford, though less than an hour from central London, might have been somewhere on the moon.

It was amazing to Genevieve what Candy could achieve with just a needle and thread and a box of pins. She would half-close her eyes and study what Genevieve was wearing, then boldly attack with a sharp pair of scissors and alter it there, on the spot. Someone a little more chicken, maybe, would not have the courage to risk such desecration, but experience during the past few weeks had proved how inspired Candy was. She was working creative miracles with Genevieve's rather tired clothes, purely out of her own good heart and enjoyment of her craft. Plus, of course, her perpetually sunny nature. It would certainly take a lot to rattle Candy.

Anna came down, stretching and rubbing her neck. Too many hours hunched over a computer could do all kinds of permanent damage. But right now the book was on such a roll, she was reluctant even to break for lunch for fear of losing her narrative flow. Genevieve handed her a glass of wine.

'You can't just sit there writing all the time. Allow your brain time to recharge.' Although she, too, was doing her daily stint, Anna's determination continued to shame her.

'Where do you get your ideas from?' asked Candy, tearing basil and delicately drizzling oil.

'The same place you get your fashion designs.' Anna tapped

her forehead. 'And yes, you are right, it pays to take a break.' She stretched both arms above her head and arched her spine to relax it.

'I'm dying to read it,' said Candy, leading the way.

'You'll have to wait till September,' said Anna, much pleased. Having a genuine fan around was doing her ego a power of good. Writing was such a solitary occupation, she needed occasional affirmation, especially from a declared non-reader like Candy, whose usual fare was trashy paperbacks.

They sat grouped at the end of the long ash table, surrounded by Candy's feast.

'There's enough here to feed the whole neighbourhood,' said Anna, pouring iced water from an earthenware jug.

'Eat before it gets cold,' advised Candy, handing around the crostini. It was a pleasure for her to cook grown-up food for a change. Hugo only ever fancied burgers and baked beans and other junk food. She wondered fleetingly how Trevor was coping, whether he liked the burden of full-time parenting. She grinned to herself as she tossed the arugula salad and reckoned he would be in for quite a shock. Trevor was not known for his empathy or warmth. He had a brief attention span and would quickly walk away.

'I was thinking about my kid,' she said, 'and how he is finding being alone with his dad.' She chuckled. 'They both have a deal of growing up to do. Each is accustomed to always expecting his own way.' Head-on confrontation; she was enjoying the thought. With luck, they should gain from the experience and it might make things easier at home.

'How come you never married him?' asked Genevieve. She had long been intrigued by Candy's hippy existence and wondered how she had ended up on her own. Not through lack of admirers, of that she was sure; Candy positively radiated charm.

Candy shrugged. 'It was one of those things that simply never happened. Both of us always got our timing wrong.' She wrinkled her nose and thought back through the years to the time, long ago, when she'd fleetingly cared about Trevor. He was a freelance journalist, moving around with his work, while she was at art school, waitressing at night in order to make ends meet. By the time they'd arranged to move in together and she told him about the baby, his ardour was cooling and his interests had shifted elsewhere.

'How do I know it's mine?' he'd dared to say, flicking channels to find the football. They both worked such long hours that they rarely met. It had been her idea to share a place; he had never shown very much commitment.

'Who else's?' she screamed, threatening him with the chip pan, for a moment prepared to do him serious harm. Now she momentarily closed her eyes, forcing the memory back into her subconscious. By the time Hugo was born, Trevor had been long gone. She had not heard from him again for several years. That was the last time she had shown serious emotion except where her baby was concerned. Ever since, all her love had been channelled towards the kid; no-one was ever going to hurt her so much again.

'Did you ever regret it?'

'Not for a second.' About that Candy was adamant. Yes, there had been a few hard times when she had worried about paying her bills, but somehow, through courage and sleight of hand, she had usually managed to stay afloat. And, despite the problems of Hugo's slight affliction, she had loved every single moment of bringing him up.

'Didn't you ever want children, Anna?' said Candy. It was something she never talked about.

Anna shook her head. 'Guess I've just been fortunate,' she said. 'And never been troubled by my biological clock.' So many women of about her age went into a last-minute panic, suddenly feeling their chances slip away, prepared to make terrible compromises in order to reproduce. Anna had never experienced that, perhaps because of her happy family background. She had grown up knowing herself totally loved, even though somewhat isolated.

'Also, at your age,' she said to Candy, 'I had more important things to do with my time.'

'More important than sex? Surely not.'

Anna laughed. 'Of course not, idiot. But I wanted a proper career.' She had worked as a journalist, like Candy's ex, but unlike him had really done very well. Freelance commissions from major magazines until, one day when she felt herself ready, she had bravely settled down to write her first book. It was a solitary life but one she had never regretted. Creating whole scenarios brought its own reward. She certainly hadn't felt the lack of tiny pattering feet.

'But, then, there are always your books,' said Candy kindly. 'You have done your bit for posterity. Your name is bound to live on.'

Anna flicked an olive at her. 'Thanks a bunch,' she said.

'Who knows, one day your prince may still turn up,' said Genevieve romantically. 'I wonder how you will feel about things then.'

Anna shrugged. She still had dreams, the main one of which had been that elegant house. 'I'll be sure to let you know when it happens,' she said. 'Though it would have to be a really special guy to come between me and my vocation.'

'And you always have your cat,' added Candy with a smirk. 'All that is really missing is a rocking chair.'

'And a shawl. I suppose I could knit one,' said Anna, entering into the spirit. She loved these two women, was grateful they had come. Could not imagine settling back to total isolation.

'I wouldn't want to be without my boys,' said Genevieve, without much conviction. Everyone laughed. The conversation was beginning to get serious; time to lighten up. Candy disappeared back into the kitchen and returned with a massive water melon which she proceeded to hack into wedges. The fruit and vegetables here were stupendous; it would be hard to readjust to bland supermarket fare.

They lolled around and drank more wine, replete yet still reluctant to clear up. Anna kept nibbling at the leftover *crostini* and Candy urged her to finish the lot as she didn't want to have to chuck them out.

'You always make too much,' complained Anna. 'It is turning me into a glutton.' But she grabbed another slice of the thickly encrusted toast and ate it with keen relish.

The sound of a distant engine caught their attention and all three fell silent, listening to its approach.

'Sounds like somebody coming here.' But who in the world could it be? It was slightly too early for the harvesting of olives and most of the local farmers kept well away.

'Not those bloody motorbikes again.' But this was, quite clearly, only a single engine. There was a crunching of gravel in the villa's forecourt and they all got up and went to take a look. An ancient taxi had pulled up outside and out of it was climbing a short, portly figure, wearing a ridiculous panama hat and carrying a huge striped golf umbrella. He was talking in rapid Italian to the driver who was struggling with an alarming amount of luggage.

'Aha,' he said archly as he turned and saw them watching. 'I thought I'd drop by to see how you girls are behaving.' He paid the driver with a handful of loose change and the man drove off in obvious disgust.

Hector Gillespie, for it was he, having pecked Genevieve awkwardly on the cheek, lunged at Anna with out-thrust hand, in the manner of a paunchy garden gnome.

'I surmise that you must be the famous one,' he said, with a cultivated Scottish burr. 'Certainly, if you can afford to rent this place.' He chuckled as though he were wit incarnate, a man exceedingly pleased with himself. Anna and Candy simply stood there speechless. Both, they found out later, loathed him on sight. He was even worse than either had expected, a caricature of all they had imagined. Genevieve, flushed with guilt, babbled incoherently. It was clear she had not been entirely honest; how else could he have known where she was staying? She must have forgiven him for Bayreuth but not had the courage to tell them. This, thought Anna, they did *not* deserve, especially since they were supposedly here to work.

Formal introductions were made and Hector carried in his bags, followed by Genevieve, clutching his hat and umbrella. She shot the others a stricken glance that met with a total brick wall. It was her mess entirely, she would have to sort it out, with the least amount of disruption to their harmony.

Hector, impervious to the prevailing froideur, continued to prattle on. 'Now don't you go worrying your pretty little heads about making me feel at home. I am perfectly willing to doss down with Gen, until you can sort out something a little more permanent.' Sharp, alarmed glances passed between all three but Hector was having a very thorough look round. He wandered into the dining-room and studied its dimensions with approval.

'Well,' he pronounced, greatly satisfied, 'there is certainly more than ample space.'

'Get rid of him!' hissed Anna behind his back. 'What the hell does he think he is doing here?' How *dare* he. She had noted, inconsequentially, that his nostril hairs were ginger, matching the jaunty little beard that looked as though it were glued on. Doubtless, beneath the baggy flannels and unflattering sage green sweatshirt, his body was covered with a similarly unappetising pelt. Also, she noticed, he walked with a slight limp.

'I can't,' wailed Genevieve, knowing him all too well; this man, so expert at caustic putdowns, possessed the fine-tuning of an ox. It wasn't as if he ever listened, and she *had* been guilty of sending that ill-judged postcard. But now that she saw him again, up close, the slight wistful feeling that occasionally assailed her had vanished without trace. Compared to Raffaele, with his warmth and charm, the pallid Hector could not even start to compete.

That night Genevieve insisted on doing the cooking. Hector was too tired, she explained, to feel like going out. He was on his way back from Bologna, where he had been covering a music festival, and thought he would surprise her by turning up unannounced. Also, she admitted, he was faddy about his food.

'I'm afraid he won't eat garlic,' she warned them, thereby instantly ruling out most of their favourite dishes.

'How can that be?' asked Candy, astonished, 'when he bangs on about being such an international foodie?'

Genevieve was suitably embarrassed. 'Something to do with his Scottish upbringing,' she said. 'His Morningside mother convinced him early on that garlic was vulgar as well as not quite nice; only for peasants and foreigners. The ones who breathe in your face on the Tube during rush hour.'

'Silly mothers raise silly children.' It endorsed everything that Anna had ever thought.

Genevieve settled conservatively for macaroni cheese and a plain green salad. Despite her irritation, which she found hard to suppress, Anna magnanimously opened some rather good wine, while Candy set the dining table with tall red candles in elegant holders to go with the linen napkins that matched exactly. By the time she had finished, the room looked enchanting. With one accord, the ladies retired and decked themselves up to the nines.

Not so Hector, who emerged in the same crumpled clothes, oblivious of the niceties of life. He located Sutherland's excellent sound system and worked through his collection of opera CDs, clucking derisively at his taste in recordings. Then disappeared into Genevieve's room and returned with a handful of his own.

'The man is clearly a philistine,' he sneered. 'Presumably tone deaf.' And proceeded to blast them with selections of his own which prevented any attempt at conversation.

'How could she do this to us?' groaned Anna. After all the years of such close friendship, she could not believe they had been reduced to this. Candy, equally appalled, merely shook her head. She considered saying, to cause a bit of mischief, that her personal favourite was *HMS Pinafore*, then decided the ploy was bound to misfire. The man, besides being a boor, was also a fool. And simply not worth the effort.

Hector took the head of the table, as though it were his rightful place, and lavishly poured the wine that Anna had opened. Genevieve, from habit, served him first, and he started to dig in right away, not bothering to notice that the others were still waiting. After he'd lengthily pontificated on the aria that was playing, from a little-known opera by Massenet that none of them had even heard of, he finally switched his attention to them, though not with any apparent degree of interest.

'How is the book?' he asked Anna dismissively, as though she had only ever written the one, then proceeded to ramble on over her reply which was, as it happened, monosyllabic.

'I know how it is with you ladies,' he said archly, squeezing Genevieve's knee. 'You and your wee potboilers, you take it all so seriously.' He beamed benevolently round at them, while Candy spluttered into her wine, and held out his plate to Genevieve for seconds. Anna noted, with savage satisfaction, that he had a glob of cheese sauce stuck in his beard, while Candy was trying heroically not to laugh. Eventually, as was bound to happen, Hector's eye lit upon her. He liked her daring décolleté and gilded aureole of puffball hair. Also, as Anna had already observed, she was ten years younger than they were.

'And what do *you* do, young lady?' he asked, wiping his face with his napkin.

Candy stared innocently back at him with wide, ingenuous blue eyes. 'I'm afraid I'm a humble dressmaker,' she said. 'I cannot compete with these two.'

'Never you mind,' said Hector benevolently, helping himself to more salad. 'There is far too much emphasis placed these days on the education of women. It is quite sufficient to be decorative, my dear.' And he leaned across and gallantly patted her arm. 'And handy with your needle, too. It should make you an excellent wife.'

Candy, for one long moment, sat transfixed, then pushed back her chair and made a dash for the kitchen. Anna joined her, on the pretext of fetching more wine, and they both stood hugging each other, shaking with mirth. If he weren't so dreadful, it would be even funnier, but how would they ever survive his presence here?

10

Hector expected a full cooked breakfast which it fell to poor Genevieve to prepare. Fruit and flakes weren't enough for him, he needed lots of protein to sustain him.

'No wonder he's so flabby,' remarked Candy. 'He really should be severely cutting down.'

'Maybe he'll have a coronary,' said Anna. Which would be an effective way of getting shot of him.

Genevieve had to abandon her daily routine of starting work at nine. Along with breakfast, he demanded the morning paper, so one of them had to fetch it each day from the village. Hector, needless to say, didn't drive, though Anna was in no position to fault him for that. It seemed he was determined to be as disruptive as he could. He would wander around in a disgusting old bathrobe, allowing glimpses of his corpulent belly, playing his awful opera CDs and noisily rustling the newspaper. Candy escaped him by staying in bed, while Anna got up even earlier in order to make herself scarce. Genevieve would stand miser-ably at the stove, listening to a litany of complaints. The Tuscan sausages were not up to scratch, he liked his eggs to be sunny side up and not flipped over in the pan. She was sent on a hunt for coarse-cut orange marmalade and then for English-style bread. He had also brought with him some Earl Grey tea which he noisily slurped as he lingered on over the crossword.

'Ask him when he's leaving,' prompted Anna.

'I can't,' said Candy. 'Besides, he'd never take the hint.'

It was no use relying on Genevieve who seemed to be firmly back under Hector's thumb. The more he complained, the more she visibly wilted. Gone was the new joie de vivre she had lately been displaying. He disapproved of what Candy had done to her clothes, considered the hems too short and the neck-lines too low. And was totally impervious to the fact she had lost so much weight or that her skin was now glowing with health.

When he'd finally finished eating, leaving Genevieve to clear up, Hector would disappear upstairs, newspaper in hand, and lock himself in the bathroom for half an hour. He would then swap bathrobe for baggy shorts and waddle up to the pool for a soak in the sun. A man that shape should never dress that way but Hector was oblivious of taste. His paunch slopped grotesquely over his belt; his legs were white and, as Anna had guessed, covered in thick sandy hair.

'Gross or what?' whispered Candy, stifling her giggles, though she did take exception to his invasion of her territory, especially since he had a rasping snore whenever he nodded off. If any-thing good had come from his intrusion, it was that she no longer sunbathed topless; in fact, spent less and less time around the pool but moved her recliner defiantly on to the lawn.

'Utterly vile,' was Anna's chilly pronouncement. He no longer had even the power to make her laugh.

Weary of lying alone by the pool, and suffering from a virulent case of sunburn, Hector, waiting to be fed, slipped on his disgusting bathrobe and shuffled off to explore. He had been all over the villa already, peered into everyone's rooms, tut-tutting at Candy's extravagant waste of space and the tip-like chaos of the attic. Luckily he was up there on his own or they might have detected the covetous glint in his eye. This space, remote from the rest of the house, would be just the place for him to settle and get on with some work of his own. He still had the Bologna festival to write up and was also drafting a book on Berlioz. He liked it here, it was comfortable and handy. He might stay on until the women left. But being in with Genevieve, though having its obvious attractions, seemed not to be working out too well. She had been out from under his control too long; he would have to rein her in. He blamed the influence of the other two, especially Anna, whom he found unacceptably abrasive. He had never much cared for American women, who were bossy and over-assertive. He would think up some way of displacing Candy. She could do her little doodles somewhere else.

He slip-slopped down the highly polished stairs and out of the main front door which faced the chapel. Genevieve, since it was almost lunchtime, was out there, harvesting herbs. Hector shuffled across the lawn and she, guilty at the way she was avoiding him, laid her cuttings in a shady corner and followed him inside. The frescoes, which she had looked at before, were, on closer scrutiny, pretty magnificent. Though they were faded and, in places, patchy it was amazing how, after all these centuries, so much still survived intact. Hector put on his reading glasses in order to study them closer. She knew from experience how pedantic he could be. With luck, he might remain in here for hours.

'Must get back to the kitchen,' she said blithely, attempting to push her way past him. 'I will call when lunch is on the table. It shouldn't be very long.'

'Look at this,' said Hector, ignoring her, pointing at a faded coat of arms. It was blue and silver, in the shape of a shield, sporting three crescent moons. He peered even closer, standing up on his toes, attempting to decipher the ancient Latin. '*Mutare vel timere sperno.* It would appear,' he said grandly, 'that whoever once lived here was connected with nobility.' Some sort of dwelling had been continuously on this land right back to the Middle Ages; Hector was impressed. He possessed a strong streak of rampant snobbery that extended even beyond his musical tastes.

Over lunch he raised the subject again and all of them mentally groaned. It seemed they could never sit down to eat without a thundering lecture from this bore. If only he'd just shut up and enjoy the view and be grateful for the food they put before him. But, despite his gastronomic claims, he never seemed even to notice what he was eating but rattled on, often with his mouth full, until he had driven them away.

'Let him take his turn in the kitchen,' Candy had often suggested. But Anna, not liking the thought, resisted; so far it was the only room he hadn't yet invaded. The longer they could repel him, the better. That was her point of view. Besides, she would bet five bucks on Hector not even knowing how to boil an egg. She had encountered men like him before and saw right through his façade.

'How's your Latin?' he asked them now, eager to score further points with his erudition.

'We don't do Latin in the States,' said Anna.

'And I left school at fifteen,' added Candy.

Everyone looked hopefully at Genevieve, who just shrugged. 'We'll check it out with Raffaele,' she said, glad to be able to bring him into the conversation. 'He's lived here all his life and is bound to know. He owns the trattoria in Montisi,' she explained, 'and is also, in a way, our landlord. We can ask him next time we go there.'

Hector, in his usual boorish way, ignored her and, without pausing, continued to hold forth. Roughly translated, the motto read: *I scorn to change or to fear.* Whoever's it was sounded suitably autocratic. He very much liked the idea of such grandeur, would seek out someone with appropriate education, perhaps the lord of the manor himself. Which was not at all a bad idea; he brightened. It was simply a question of tracking the fellow down.

After a few more days of lolling around, Hector began to revive. Having recovered from the excesses of Bologna, his passion for Italy, combined with his natural greed, made him start to feel restless confined to the villa. By that time normal channels of conversation had almost completely dried up; if any of the three of them ever ventured to voice an opinion, Hector always expected the final word. Anna and Candy were heartily relieved when he announced a sudden need for an excursion. Though, it transpired, for one evening only; he was bent on showing Genevieve a good time. At first he suggested that she drive him to Siena but that, as Candy pointed out, meant she wouldn't be able to drink. Hector scowled. He hated having his wishes thwarted yet was also reluctant to appear a spoilsport in front of the other two women. He had a high opinion of his own eligible status and had Candy down as a possible stand-in next time a gap occurred in his social calendar.

'Why not go to the local trattoria?' suggested Candy wickedly. Genevieve looked appalled but couldn't deny him. At least that way they would get to talk to Raffaele and Hector could ask him first-hand about the fresco.

Hector looked deeply condescending. 'I very much doubt that there's anything in this backwater to match my usual culinary requirements. You must remember, I'm a widely travelled man.'

Genevieve, unguardedly, leapt to Raffaele's defence. 'I think you'll find that you're wrong,' she said, realising just too late what she had done. Hector, who always knew better about everything, cocked one quizzical ginger eyebrow at her.

'And is it recognised by Michelin?' he asked – to him, the ultimate test. Genevieve had to admit that she'd no idea.

'But the food is brilliant,' she said, her colour rising. Hector's silent glance spoke volumes; he simply left the room.

'Don't let him get away with it,' Candy exploded the moment they heard his footsteps up the stairs. 'Most of the time he treats you like a servant. Who the fuck does he think he is? And why on earth do you let him get away with it?'

'I'm sorry about him,' said Genevieve helplessly. 'I didn't for one moment think he would come.' It had been a whim, a private revenge; she wasn't accustomed to having such tactics work.

'Well, now he is here,' said Candy firmly, 'do what you can to make the best of it. See that he spends some money on you for a change.' Not just money, time as well. Instead of treating her like an unpaid skivvy; it was disgraceful how much he took for granted. So far he'd shown no intention at all of even con-

tributing to his keep. And when it came to things like clearing
the dishes, Hector was never to be found.

'You're quite sure you won't come with us?' asked Genevieve
hopefully as Hector settled himself in the car without bothering
to open her door. Tonight he had made a bit of an effort and
was wearing a tan jacket with a clean white shirt and a pink
and green striped bow tie.

'Garrick Club, you know,' he had explained while he was
dressing but Genevieve couldn't care less. And nor, she was certain, would the others either. Such petty snobbery was terribly
out of date.

Anna and Candy, standing meekly in the driveway, mutely
shook their heads. They could barely contain their muffled
delight that Hector, after all these days, was actually leaving the
premises. They had all sorts of secret indulgences lined up,
starting with a leisurely swim and followed by Candy putting
highlights in Anna's hair. After which they planned to watch
Terms of Endearment, Candy's favourite ever movie, which she'd
serendipitously discovered upstairs in Sutherland's eclectic video
collection. And Anna had elected to cook tonight, in celebra-
tion of their brief reprieve. Neither could wait to see him go
and get on with the business of the evening.

'I don't remember ever disliking anyone quite so much,' Anna
said as they cheerfully waved them off.

'Poor Genevieve,' said Candy, suddenly doubtful. 'Maybe we
should have gone with them after all. He treats her so badly all
the time, constantly putting her down.'

'By this time in her life,' said Anna, 'she should be able to
stand on her own two feet.' Forget what Hector might think of
the trattoria, she wondered what Raffaele was likely to make of

him. Despite his occasional moments of detachment and the cautious suspicion she had sometimes seen in his eyes, Anna, the professional observer, watched with absolute fascination Raffaele's growing interest in Genevieve. Her own life might be sterile at the moment but Anna had known passion in the past. She'd put money on it; she recognised the signs. If only Genevieve weren't so bashful.

'I confess I'd love to be a fly on the wall,' she said. 'To witness the clash of the Titans.'

'Godzilla versus King Kong, are you suggesting?'

'I was thinking more Godzilla versus Mighty Mouse.'

Genevieve was looking particularly fetching tonight. Raffaele was hurrying forward to greet her when he took in the hovering presence of Hector and practically stopped in his tracks. What was this? A new development he had not expected. All his Italian virility took charge even though he remembered that he still didn't totally trust her. The orders he was getting from elsewhere particularly warned him to be wary of these women. Something very definitely was wrong. Until it was sorted he had to tread very carefully.

'*Signora*,' he said, regaining his composure and courteously including Hector in his bow.

Hector, eschewing Genevieve's regular table, was looking around for something more remote. 'Far too noisy,' he loudly announced, ignoring Raffaele totally as he stalked away to the furthest, darkest corner. Genevieve, embarrassed, gave Raffaele an apologetic shrug but had no other choice than to meekly follow her escort. The restaurant was three quarters full, with the satisfied hum of contented diners quietly enjoying their food. Several of them, already known to her, greeted her with affection and

Genevieve acknowledged each one with a wave and a smile. Hector's expression grew ominously darker. How dare this woman possess a life of her own.

Raffaele, after a suitable pause, presented himself at their table, pad in hand, to run through the evening's specials. This was the part that Genevieve usually liked best, savouring his mellifluous Italian that made the food sound even more enticing than it was.

'Tonight, *signor e signora,*' he began, allowing the words to roll sinuously over his tongue, 'we have seafood bruschetta made with mussels and clams, ricotta and thyme tortelloni with fava bean sauce, and grilled pork ribs, Florentine style.' He beamed at them both expectantly, pencil poised. 'And then, of course,' and his tone grew more seductive, 'we have today's *sopra tutto,* spaghettini with lobster sauce.' He kissed his fingertips expressively and rolled his eyes heavenwards.

Genevieve sparkled, her absolute favourite, but Hector appeared to be only half-listening, his eyes still glued to the printed menu, deaf to the eloquent recital.

'I will certainly have that,' said Genevieve, salivating at the thought. 'With an onion and tomato salad, please. On the side.'

Raffaele, signifying his approval, rapidly scribbled it down. Then turned expectantly to this man he had not met before who seemed to be taking the menu extremely seriously.

'Is the pasta nice and fresh?' asked Hector, ignoring the fact that Raffaele owned the restaurant and treating him condescendingly, like a waiter.

Raffaele stared, for a moment nonplussed. 'For this dish the pasta is factory-made,' he explained, deferential though less so. 'As is the custom in this part of the world.' Normally he might have swivelled his eyes; out of deference to Genevieve, he resisted.

'Bollocks,' said Hector rudely, 'it is simply cutting corners. Everyone knows that pasta should be freshly made.'

'Actually, Hector,' ventured Genevieve timidly, wondering as she said it how she dared, 'in Italy, for certain dishes, dried pasta is the norm.' The fashionable fresh stuff, once so popular in trendy delis, had now virtually vanished from the shelves. The famous Italian chefs stuck to their guns; factory-made was what they recommended for many of their most popular classical dishes. Especially seafood, where the grainier texture liaised more successfully with the sauce.

But Hector was having none of it. He hated not to be right. 'And what about the carp?' he asked with suitably heavy sarcasm. 'Is *that* fresh?'

'*Si, signor,*' said Raffaele, deadpan. Genevieve secretly squirmed. At that precise moment she'd have given anything at all to be able to spirit herself home.

Hector demanded to see the wine list, ignoring her protestations that the house wine was really good. She had, after all, sampled it often enough, though wasn't inclined to admit that to him. He was always implying that she drank too much, though his own intake could hardly be called abstemious. He hummed and hawed and flicked through the many pages, then once again summoned Raffaele to the table.

'Don't you have anything French?' he enquired. Raffaele looked totally disbelieving while Genevieve wanted to bury her face in her hands.

'*Signor,* the wines of Toscana are among the finest in the world.' A glint of dislike was now evident in Raffaele's eye, though Hector was far too self-involved to observe it. He continued to ponder aloud and change his mind then, just as Genevieve was beginning to despair, eventually settled on a bottle of chianti classico. Genevieve was quick enough to glimpse the disdain on Raffaele's face.

The evening was a nightmare from start to finish. Even after the food had been served, Hector continued critical and allowed his opinions to resonate round the room. The tortelloni were too salty, the fish was too bland, while the granita was over-chilled and hurt his teeth. Genevieve kept sneaking glances at her watch, wondering what the others were doing now. She saw them stretched out on the vast upstairs couch, glasses in hand, engrossed in that marvellous film. But anything had to be better than this. Hector, as he guzzled his food, was pontificating about Italy, flecks of fish adhering to his beard. She hated him with a sudden intensity for his rudeness towards Raffaele. Talk about letting the side down; she could have cried. Eventually, to her immense relief, Hector called loudly for the bill and Genevieve made a dive for the washroom in order not to witness him settling up. She had meant to ask Raffaele about the frescoes but that would have to keep for another day. If, that was, she ever dared come here again. Right now she wasn't sure.

They drove home in silence. The roads were deserted and in just a few minutes they were back at the villa's gates. Lights were on all over the house; Genevieve's spirits leaped: the others were still up.

'We're home,' she called, as they entered through the kitchen where everything was clean and tidied up, with a tantalising lingering whiff of garlic in the air. She climbed the stairs rapidly, hoping to shake off Hector, and found them, as she'd expected, on the couch. The television, however, wasn't on; they were just sitting, quietly talking. At Genevieve's entrance, both looked up and she saw, with a sudden jolt of shock, that Candy had been crying.

'What's up?' she asked, in genuine alarm, crouching on the floor in front of her and taking hold of her hands. Candy's nose was red and raw and the whites of her eyes bright pink. Beside her there was a scrunched-up letter, apparently the cause of her distress. Genevieve, receiving no answer, looked at Anna who, with an almost imperceptible head shake, warned her to tread very carefully. But Genevieve cared too much to hold back; over these past few weeks of close proximity, her feelings for her friend had immeasurably deepened. Candy had always been a fun companion; feisty, optimistic and brave. But now she was something much closer than that, as dear to her as a sister. Genevieve couldn't bear to see her cry. It was frighteningly out of character.

'I'll tell you tomorrow,' mouthed Anna so Genevieve, taking the hint, left the room.

'What seems to be the problem with the poor wee lassie?' asked Hector, hovering behind her in his crass, overbearing way, set to stick his nose in and undoubtedly cause Candy more distress.

'Nothing that need concern you. She's just upset.' Genevieve had become uneasily aware of his growing interest in Candy. Here he went again, up to his same old tricks. When would she ever learn? She pushed past him quite roughly, in a flash of sudden anger, almost making him lose his balance and fall.

'And now I'm off to bed,' she announced. 'Goodnight.'

11

The letter had arrived by a roundabout route, brought by a postman on an ancient rusty bike all the way from Sinalunga. Candy, laughing gustily as Anna simmered the sauce, had carelessly ripped it open, registering only that it came from Hugo's father. Doubtless one of his smug reports, to let her know how well they were getting along. Slowly the laughter drained away, along with all the colour from her face. Anna, distracted by her sudden silence, glanced up curiously from the stove.

'Candy, what is it?' she asked in alarm, instinctively turning down the flame.

Candy said nothing, was reading the letter again, then silently handed it to Anna. When she spoke, she was choking with so much emotion that she almost couldn't get the words out. 'The bastard's getting married,' she said. 'To someone he's only just met.'

Anna, scanning the letter, was perplexed. She had distinctly had the impression from Candy that the whole thing was way in the past. 'Is that such a bad thing?' she enquired. 'I thought you no longer cared.'

'You are missing the point. Read on,' said Candy wildly, raking fraught fingers through her puffball hair. 'This woman, whoever she is, is seven years older. And yes, you've got it, keen to start a family right away.' She began to cry, in great gulping sobs, and Anna put an arm around her shoulders. 'They want to adopt Hugo formally and give him what Trevor terms "a stable home". The nerve of the man after all these years. When he hasn't even kept up his child support payments.'

'Hold it right there,' said Anna. 'Calm down. It surely can't be that bad.' No-one could take a child away from its mother, not one as meticulously caring as Candy. She went on reading. The sinister part, the bit that had got to Candy, was that the bride-to-be was a solicitor, specialising in family law. Candy had been solely responsible all these years for raising the child on her own but the cold fact was that a father also had rights. And this woman would know all the legal loopholes. No wonder the bastard had been so compliant when she'd swallowed her pride and asked him to look after Hugo. He had never shown very much interest before; he must have had this up his sleeve all the time.

'I've got to go home.'

Anna poured them each a glass of wine and they sat down at the table. 'There's no point in doing anything hasty,' she said, 'until you know the full facts of the situation.' A married couple might feasibly score points over a single parent but she still refused to believe that they could win. Not when the child was as young as Hugo and had special needs. Perhaps they could reach some sort of a compromise, starting with a calm discussion between the three of them. Paige would know, was at the very least the sort of person that Candy should talk to, assuming that British and American law were more or less the same – she would know this too. Later perhaps she would call New York. Email was fine for gossip and chat but this looked too serious for that. With a sudden pang, Anna realised how much she missed her, her wise and capable best friend.

'I'd best start packing. I hope I can get on a flight.'

'Slow down,' said Anna practically. 'You don't even know where they are.' Which was true; the letter had taken longer than usual to reach her. Trevor and Hugo were off on a fishing trip, somewhere unidentified in the heart of Wales. 'Why go home and be miserable on your own when nothing can happen, in any case, till they return?'

It made much more sense for Candy to remain here, with two supportive companions to prop her up. Also Anna knew in her heart that, selfish or not, she relied on Candy to prevent her from doing Hector serious harm.

'What we all need,' said Anna next morning, when Genevieve had at last succeeded in getting Candy to see sense and stay, 'is a little retail therapy. We deserve it.'

They were sitting out in the garden, drinking coffee. Hector was still incarcerated upstairs. Anna, for once, had taken time off from her writing in order to help cheer up Candy but Genevieve, who had been through it all herself, was able to add hard facts to Anna's cool logic. When her husband had left her for another woman it had all been cut and dried. Apart from the shock – she had not seen it coming – things had been sorted out with remarkable ease. He paid the school fees; she kept the house. They hadn't ever needed to talk to lawyers. But that was another illustration of Genevieve's overly submissive nature; she quickly saw all kinds of good reasons for blaming it on herself. If she had only been a better wife, if she hadn't let herself go; even perhaps if her novels had been more successful. And if she didn't spend her days at the kitchen table, writing books that were rarely ever reviewed, then David might not have lost interest so soon and looked for someone he could be more proud of.

Candy began to laugh. She loved it when Genevieve started to put herself down, she did it even more effectively than Hector. 'Yeah, yeah,' she said, the old twinkle back in her eye. 'And if you hadn't needed to put food on the table and insisted he go out to work, he would never have met her in the first place. Right?'

'Let's go to Siena,' said Anna suddenly, remembering the shoes. Hector had been banging on all week about wanting to see the sights. Although it would be an almighty pain to have to take him with them, they were going to have to endure it some time and could frighten him off from tagging along by saying they were going there purely to shop. 'We can drop him off at the Duomo,' she said, 'and let him do his own thing.'

They were all agreed. No time like the present; each felt the need of a change of scene. When Hector finally emerged, on his way to the pool, they informed him of the Siena plan but said he could stay at home if he preferred. Naturally he wasn't going to do that.

'You might have told me before I got dressed,' he grumbled, but went back inside to put on street clothes and shoes.

'Do you remember where it was?' asked Genevieve, as she parked.

Anna had a rough idea; her homing instinct was as acute as

ever and it was definitely somewhere in this neighbourhood. They said their goodbyes to Hector and watched him walk away, guidebook and newspaper under one arm, reading glasses strung round his neck on a cord. He had left the golf umbrella behind but still wore the foolish hat. Anna and Candy had given up pretending; what a ridiculous figure he was. They both had a hearty laugh at his expense and Genevieve, somewhat guiltily, joined in too. It was still living purgatory having him in her room; she was thinking of suggesting that he move upstairs to the nursery because of his ceaseless snoring.

'How on earth have you managed to stick him all this time?' asked Candy, genuinely baffled. 'The man's a buffoon, not remotely in your league. I can't see how you could possibly ever have fancied him.'

Genevieve gave her a watery smile. 'I suppose I was just grateful for his attention.' Not that he'd given her much of that, at least from what she had told them.

'If we're lucky, we'll manage to lose him at lunchtime too,' said Anna. They had simply said they would doubtless see him around. Siena was a very small town, most of it grouped round the Campo. Otherwise he knew where the car was parked and that they planned to leave no later than four. There was plenty to keep him occupied with all those galleries and churches. It was a glorious day and Candy was feeling much brighter. Ideal conditions, in fact, for a bit of a binge.

They located the shop without difficulty and this time found it open. They stood and drooled, as they had before, then wasted no more time and went inside. Anna could suddenly feel her money burning a hole in her pocket; in the window she saw at least three pairs of sandals she felt she could not live without.

It was months now since she had last been power-shopping; the events of September had totally killed the urge. But now she found the old craving creeping back and could not wait to get spending. It would still be summer in New York when she got home and, by that time, she would be up against her deadline. She might as well stockpile now while she had the time. Besides, these sandals were quite unbelievably cheap.

'Can you believe it?' she said, wriggling her toes, admiring the gilded thongs with their intricate roses. 'Less than fifty dollars a pair. I think maybe I will take them in all colours.'

Genevieve laughed, enjoying her extravagance. Sometimes she felt that her friend had too little fun. And on Anna's tanned feet, with their immaculate toenails, the sandals certainly did look delicious. 'Go on,' she urged. 'What have you got to lose? It is, after all, only money.' And Anna, at this point, was particularly flush though no-one could deny that she had earned it.

They had them also in silver and pink, again both in Anna's size. She tried them on and paraded around and the smiling saleswoman, comfortably overweight, applauded and encouraged her.

'*Bellissima, signora!*'

'What do you think? Should I take all three pairs?' The others chorused their approval. 'At least they should see me through to Labour Day.'

She handed over her Visa card and the woman took it away. They had lived so frugally since arriving in this country, it would scarcely make a dent in her credit balance. She wondered what other treasures she might find, now that she had revived her retail habit. She had bought a pair of the most exquisitely cut pants last time she was in Rome. It was possible that in Siena, too, she might find a similar bargain. Certainly it was worth a look; at least they had plenty of time.

'Leather's the thing,' said Genevieve knowledgeably. 'Just as it is in Florence. Also, fancy stationery.'

'And yummy *panforte*,' said Candy with relish; they had passed a shop window packed full of it. 'Rich and sinful, like Christmas cake. Divine!' She would take some home for Hugo, she decided, which immediately brought on a mini attack of the blues. Poor little mite – but the others had helped her to rally. No-one was ever going to take him away; she would make certain of that.

'*Signora.*' After a lengthy pause, the woman had returned. She still had Anna's card in her hand and a flicker of discomfort on her face. There was, she explained in her halting English, a small problem. Visa were refusing to accept the card, saying that it was over its credit limit.

'Not possible,' said Anna impatiently. This card she kept solely for foreign travel and she knew for a fact it was fully paid up. 'It has to be some mix-up at this end.' Italy was hardly known for its efficiency. 'Please try again.'

The woman obligingly went back to the phone but with the same result. When Anna spoke direct to Visa, they politely refused to honour her purchase because she had insufficient funds.

'But it's a gold card,' she protested, 'and I pay it off every month.' She'd been raised to be meticulous about such things.

'Perhaps,' said the woman, now deeply embarrassed, 'the signora has another card she could use?'

Anna, whose mood had radically changed, shook her head. Genevieve offered to lend her the money; they could easily settle up once they got home. But Anna's enthusiasm for shopping had evaporated. Something needed fixing that could not wait.

'Come on,' she said urgently, 'let's get out of here. I must return to the villa right away and find out what the hell is going on.'

'Don't you have your cellphone?' asked Candy.

'Yes,' said Anna, 'but I don't think it will work for an overseas call. Besides, I don't have the Visa number. Let's go.'

They located Hector, still dawdling in the Duomo, and hustled him, protesting, to the car. Having finally succeeded in making it to Siena, he hugely resented being made to leave so soon, before he was even halfway round the Cathedral. It was packed, he told them, with so many important works of art, that he could happily have spent several days there, just browsing. Richard Wagner, apparently, had been so bowled over by the splendours of the Duomo that he had even thought about setting *Parsifal* there. Hector had, after all, just been in Bayreuth and was always keen to share the fruits of his knowledge.

'Look, for instance,' he said dramatically, 'at that monument over there.'

'No time,' snapped Anna, panting to be off, certainly not in the mood for one of his lectures. He could always stay on in Siena, she told him curtly, and find his own way home.

'But I've made a startling discovery,' he said, strutting with self-importance. 'At least allow me to show it to you while we're here.' Fuss, fuss, fuss; where would it ever end? He knew all too well what women were like; she had probably simply forgotten to mail the cheque. The downside of this Italian jaunt was having to shepherd all three of them. 'That monument is to the Tolomei family and, guess what, it is their coat of arms that also adorns the frescoes in our chapel. Blue and silver with three crescent moons. Even the Latin motto is the same. It would appear we are living on Tolomei land,' he said, as if talking about royalty.

'We knew that already,' snapped Anna, heartily sick of his intellectual posturing. Sick, too, of his deep inherent snobbery which kept on popping up.

'According to my guidebook,' he went on, 'the family claims direct descent from the Egyptian pharaohs, the Ptolemys. Almost certainly apocryphal, I would think, but nonetheless a charming theory. Ptolemy the First, so the history books tell us, ran Egypt like a business, strictly for profit. Whereas the Italian Tolomeis have been bankers for generations. Interesting how it all fits.'

'Cleopatra,' said Candy suddenly, surprising them all. 'My kid just did her at school,' she explained. 'The dozy mare married her brother.'

'As they all were inclined to do in those days.' Hector was not yet prepared to relinquish the limelight. 'Later she moved on to Julius Caesar, immortalised by the Bard.'

'Can't we please get going,' said Anna. 'If you'd just stop yapping and showing off.' The longer they stood here, the worse things might become. She needed to talk to Visa without further delay.

'Now, now, children,' said Genevieve placidly as they all piled into the car. But Hector was already into one of his mammoth sulks while Anna stared grimly out of the window, trying hard not to panic.

The Visa office in New York could not have been more helpful. When Anna called and explained the situation they checked her personal details first, then took a look at her account.

'No, ma'am, there's no mistake,' said the woman eventually. 'Your credit limit is twelve thousand dollars and you've over-spent by seven hundred.'

'But I haven't been using the card,' protested Anna. 'Where were these payments supposedly made?'

All of them in New York or its vicinity; the woman went through the list. Groceries and jewellery, expensive computer equipment. A two-thousand-dollar payment to Louis Vuitton. Someone had systematically cleaned her out. She was appalled.

'But I haven't even been in the States. Not for a couple of months.'

'And you still have the actual card in your possession?'

'Yes,' said Anna. 'Right here. In my hand.'

After another lengthy pause, during which Anna was put on hold, the woman returned sounding guarded and slightly less apologetic and said there was nothing further she could do.

'What the hell do you mean?' asked Anna, enraged. 'Someone has clearly stolen my credit card details. Aren't you going to put a stop to it? This is a disgrace.'

'I'm afraid it's beyond our jurisdiction. According to our records, all these purchases were made in good faith. You are saying you still have possession of the card; is it possible that another family member also has access to it?'

Anna, always quick-tempered, now lost her cool entirely. 'No!' she shouted. 'I demand that you cancel it. I will cut the damn thing up.' And not renew it, was what she meant, as if the woman would care.

The line went silent for another few minutes, then Anna was asked for her confidential password. Luckily that was something she knew; the same as the one for her computer. But the woman told her it was incorrect. She no longer had the requisite authority to cancel her own credit card.

Next Anna tried ringing her own home number but found the

machine was not on. The phone just rang and rang but nobody answered. She tried it again at intervals all afternoon, then gave up and called Larry instead.

'Hi, babe!' he said, surprised to hear from her again. 'How are things going over there? What's the weather like where you are? Over here it's as hot as Hades.'

Anna, never one for idle chitchat, came rapidly to the point. She explained what had happened with her credit card and that she urgently needed to contact Sutherland. 'What's going on with him?' she demanded. 'He never seems to be there.'

Larry admitted that he still hadn't met him. Maybe he was travelling a lot. 'You are surely not suggesting,' he said, 'that this has anything at all to do with him?'

'I have to consider everything,' said Anna. 'And nobody else, other than you and your team, has legal access to my house.' Which included her personal papers; she shuddered. And every-thing else she possessed.

Larry begged her not to get upset. These days this kind of financial scam was becoming run-of-the-mill. It didn't require any special expertise to get hold of someone's credit details and fake a duplicate card. A waiter, a salesperson, an order placed over the phone; theatre tickets, flowers, mail order, magazine subscriptions. The opportunities for fraud were manifold and getting worse all the time. The internet gave out regular warn-ings not to divulge such information. Also, since Anna styled herself with just her initials, A. L., it opened the card up to use by either sex. Slowly her pulse returned to normal. Larry was right, she must not be paranoid. These months in paradise had dulled the edge of her usual city smarts. Why would a man of such obvious prosperity feel the need to indulge in petty theft? Besides, he was highly educated, magna cum laude from Yale.

Too intelligent to believe that he wouldn't get caught when he was the only real suspect.

'How's Sadie?' she asked, slowly calming down, hoping her darling was not being neglected. If he was only rarely there, then who was feeding the cat?

'Sadie's fine,' Larry reassured her. 'Sleek and healthy and obviously much-indulged. He clearly *is* there enough of the time. It is just that we never get to see him. And there's always that female sidekick I mentioned before. Girlfriend or employee, I am still not quite sure. But she seems to be doing a perfectly competent job.'

'Or wife,' prompted Anna.

'Or wife, perhaps, though somehow I really don't think so. Next time I see her, I'll be sure to ask, if only to put your mind at rest.'

All this made total sense to Anna; Sutherland was, after all, a photographer who had wanted this house swap for a definite period because of something urgent he had to do. Of course he would have a PA with him, if only to hold the fort while he was out on the job.

And the good news was that, true to his earlier promise, Larry would be gone by the end of the week.

12

L ife at *Casavecchia* was more or less back to normal. Larry's
reassurance did make sense. Anna now accepted entirely
that she had merely been the unlucky victim of a purely random
crime. Hector kept urging her to go to the police but she couldn't
see, at this stage, what they could do, not while she was still
in Italy. She would have to wait till she got back home and
could have a face-to-face with the Visa people. And she could
not return until the four months were up because of the terms
of the house swap. At least she now had the security of knowing
that an automatic lid had been put on her losses. Since the card
was well and truly over its limit, no-one could use it until it
had been paid off. She also had the comfortable awareness that
her bank account was in better than usual shape, soon to be
even more enhanced by a further injection of movie money. It
took more than a thief to bring her down, now that she was
over the initial shock. Despite the vast expenditure on the house,

which seemed to go on for ever, she had never before in her life been this solvent. Her tension eased, she got on with her book which continued to glide along.

Candy, through Anna's intervention, was also in much improved spirits. The wonderful Paige, who invariably came up trumps, had produced a relevant legal expert who had succeeded in putting her mind at rest. No court in the world, he assured her over the phone, would give custody to an absentee father who had never been anything more than just part-time. So Candy had abandoned her plan of curtailing her trip and was once more hard at work on her designs. The ones already completed were magical and inspired; the portfolio for Harvey Nichols would soon be ready.

'Just think,' said Genevieve, poring over the sketches, 'soon you'll be up there on the catwalk with the stars, rubbing shoulders with Naomi Campbell, too grand for the likes of us.'

'What are you going to spend it all on?' asked Anna.

'Food,' said Candy, 'and shoes for the kid.' She was far too canny to start counting chickens, certainly not at this early stage. The fashion business was notoriously cutthroat. She had heard too many bad stories.

Genevieve was less under Hector's thumb and rebelling. Since she had banished him from her room because of his reverberative snoring, she was able to reclaim some independence and not be quite so much at his beck and call. These days she insisted he at least fix his own breakfast, although she continued to be responsible for bringing in the food. As well as doing the clearing up; he left the kitchen in a right old mess, but they still had the wonderful Rosa to come in and clean.

'I also have a book to finish,' Genevieve reminded him. 'With a deadline every bit as pressing as Anna's.' She managed not to listen to his predictably scathing riposte; so much time spent here with just the others had toughened her up considerably.

So Hector sulked and riffled through Sutherland's music collection, sneering at his limited operatic knowledge. Anna succeeded in closing her ears but insisted he turn down the racket while she was working. She hadn't come here to be blasted by sound; a writer needed silence in which to think. The man persisted in rubbishing their host, while all the time behaving boorishly, with no consideration for anyone else. With luck, he might soon become bored and move on, though so far showed little sign of doing so. He still sprawled inelegantly out by the pool and his pasty complexion had turned an unsightly brick-red.

'I cannot imagine what you ever saw in him,' became Anna's regular refrain. 'The man is pompous and boring and obtuse.' Controlling, too, though she wasn't going to say that. Anna could be stern but was rarely unkind and Genevieve had already put up with enough.

Genevieve had, though, to concede that Anna was right. 'I guess I must have been desperate,' she admitted, remembering the time when her confidence hit rock bottom and she believed no man would ever admire her again. Her husband had dumped her for someone much younger, leaving her alone with just the kids. Hector's timing, just that once, could not have been improved on. She'd been cheered and flattered when he first came on the scene, whereas now the sound of that braying, dismissive voice had seriously started to grate. If she heard one more mention of Maria Callas, whom he always referred to reverently as '*La Divina*', she thought she might at last be tempted to tell him where to shove it.

*   *   *

Still, Hector was now installed in the nursery where, at least, he had a choice of beds. Despite his angling for Candy's attic, he had been firmly relocated to the floor below, in the long, narrow room that was usually the province of kids. That was clear from the four little beds, with their nursery lamps and matching candy-striped covers. And the huge walk-in closet at the end of the room in which they could stash all their toys. There were jigsaws and boardgames in piles on the shelves as well as *Winnie-the-Pooh* and *The Wind in the the Willows*. It seemed that the Sutherlands had spared on no detail. It was good to imagine this friendly house alive with the chatter of little voices.

'Presumably the Sutherlands have children of their own.' There was nothing to suggest that this wasn't so. Except that Raffaele and that chilly, blank-eyed stranger had made no mention at all of any appendages.

Hector, with a deep lack of grace, had carried his lumpy bags upstairs and spread things all over the room. Whatever bad thoughts he had about Candy, his habits were slovenly in the extreme. He left a pile of unwashed shirts and socks for Genevieve to deal with. Rosa, she knew, would have willingly done it but she saw no reason to lumber it on her. Men like Hector viewed women as facilitators, especially ones less fortunate than themselves or who simply did not happen to share a language. Except that Hector's Italian was fluent so that was really no excuse. It was like being back with her two idle sons. Genevieve now heartily regretted ever having sent that ill-judged postcard.

Now, at least, she could sleep at night and so could Genevieve and Anna. The motorcyclists had not returned, the frogs had gone quiet, their season presumably over. Peace ruled once more in *Casavecchia*. Even the mosquitoes left them alone.

*   *   *

'Look what I've found,' said Hector, bursting in on Anna. 'In a trunk at the back of the nursery cupboard.' Anna rested her wrists on the edge of the keyboard and silently prayed for forbearance. No doubt another of his snobby discoveries. Time must be hanging heavily on his hands. She glanced up at him with a questioning expression, then focused with interest on what he was clutching: a girl's straw boater with a blue and yellow ribbon, lovingly wrapped in tissue paper.

'Good heavens.' She held out her hands for it and turned it round and round. It had obviously been worn quite a lot but probably not for a while. It was hard to imagine why anyone would have kept it. Not in a country place like this where it could have no possible use. Doubtless an echo from somebody's past, preserved for sentimental reasons. It might have been lying there for years. 'What else did you find?' she asked.

'Come up and see,' said Hector, leading the way.

He had hit the nursery like a mini tornado, his things were piled on all four beds. The cupboard door now stood wide open, as did the trunk he had found. Anna peered into its tidy depths, already disturbed by Hector. Neat pleated skirts and blue flannel blouses, sensible knee-length games shorts. Plus, in the corner, a battle-scarred lacrosse stick. Boarding school gear from a time machine, completely out of place in rural Tuscany.

'I found it under a pile of old curtains. I was moving things around,' he said, 'to make room for my own stuff.' It was just like him to go snooping where he shouldn't but Anna was nonetheless intrigued. The more they discovered about the Sutherland ménage, the more fascinating it became. Maybe there was a daughter too who went to school in England.

'Do they still wear that kind of uniform?' asked Genevieve when the others came up to witness Hector's find. 'I am sure it's all terribly out of date. Isn't it jeans and T-shirts these days with jogging outfits for games?'

'I wouldn't know,' said Candy, who had left her secondary modern at fifteen. 'But the workmanship is so exquisite it must have cost someone a bomb.'

'I wonder why they kept it, whoever they were. You would think it would do better in a charity shop.'

Candy was now digging discreetly under the layers and came up bearing a filmy white silk dress, with beautiful hand-worked embroidery on the sleeves.

'Confirmation dress,' said Genevieve. 'I would love to know how long it's been hidden here.'

'Well, at least the moths haven't found their way inside. They are obviously better mannered than the mosquitoes.'

'Do they even have moths in Italy?'

'I can't see why not. Provided they can survive in all this heat.'

'Put it all back,' said Anna uncomfortably, feeling that they were trespassing where they shouldn't. 'And cover it carefully with the curtains again. We don't want Sutherland, when he does return, thinking we have been prying into his secrets.' She shot an accusing glance at Hector, who remained impervious. She hated the thought of any stranger fingering through her own private things, was glad she had thought of locking her bedroom door.

'I must get back to work,' she said. 'I'll catch up with you at lunch.'

'Any further thoughts?' Anna asked, as Candy hacked slices of bread.

'Only that there's a whole history here. Which, when you

consider the age of the house, isn't remotely surprising.' It made Candy feel oddly comfortable to know that the house had once led a normal life. Apart from the immaculate accoutrements, it did seem strangely lacking in personal things. No family photographs, no pictures, no books apart from the ones in the nursery. Not even old signs of a pet. Nothing at all to give any sort of clue as to what its owner's tastes might be, other than of the very best.

'I suppose if he's almost never here, there's no point in leaving stuff lying around.'

'Which seems such a waste of a beautiful house. He could rent it out through the tourist season and make an absolute killing.'

'Not if he's connected to the Tolomeis.' Hector was still puffed up about that. 'They are one of the most powerful families in these parts. I would love to know how close the connection is.'

'I meant to ask Raffaele,' said Genevieve, cringing to remember that terrible evening. They had kept away from the trattoria ever since; she could not bear the thought of a similar confrontation. If only Hector would get the message and leave, but he seemed to have dug himself in. He was writing his column and phoning it through without a care in the world.

'Next time we go to Siena,' he said, ' I am going to look for that palazzo.' And undoubtedly ask himself in there for tea; Hector had that sort of brazen cheek.

'Maybe they'll beg him to stay,' muttered Candy. 'How could anyone possibly resist his natural charm?'

Seated peacefully one morning at her laptop, Anna was idly hunting for a word. One of the things she liked most about the writing game was that it stretched and finely tuned the mind. Her latest indulgence was the dictionary on disk; she spent endless contented hours just browsing through it. It might slow her progress but she felt it improved her style. The reviews of each new book bore witness to that.

Something odd started happening on the screen. A block of text she had been polishing for hours suddenly, without obvious reason, disappeared. One moment she was working on it; the next, the screen went blank. Anna cursed and fumbled around, trying to figure out what she had done wrong. When typing fast, as she knew from experience, it was possible to strike the wrong key and throw everything else out of kilter. But this new laptop was state-of-the-art and therefore, supposedly, foolproof. She was careful always to save text as she went along and also to do a full backup after each session. Yet the missing paragraphs had completely vanished; were not even in the recycle bin. Maybe the batteries were running low, though the usual warning had not appeared on the screen. And, since she was mostly plugged into the mains, that shouldn't, in any case, happen.

She rapidly closed all her files and logged off, then checked that the power was on. But when she re-booted, that chunk of text was still missing, which was doubly frustrating since she'd been making such progress and knew that her morning's output had been especially good. Once lost, it was hard to re-create without damaging her narrative flow. After all these years regularly using a computer, by now she ought to know what she was doing. And then, in front of her disbelieving eyes, it started to happen again. Another two pages simply melted away as though the machine possessed a will of its own, a malevolent one at that. Some outside force was manipulating her cursor. Stunned, she watched it move across the screen.

'Genevieve!' yelled Anna, now thoroughly rattled. 'Get up here fast and tell me what's going on.'

*   *   *

Genevieve hadn't a clue and neither had Hector, which did not, of course, stop him pontificating at length.

'As a lifelong Luddite,' he said with smug satisfaction, 'I don't trust any form of gadgetry but still dictate my column over the phone.'

Anna could do without his interference; she wished he would leave them alone and go jump in the pool. What was happening here was seriously unnerving. Were it not for the fact that they were stuck in the heart of nowhere, she would call the helpline and seek professional support. The last thing she needed was for the hard disk to crash, not at this vital late stage of the book. She had to admit that Hector did have a point, not that she would ever let him know. At least with an old-fashioned pen and paper you knew you were relatively safe. Too many writers she'd heard of had lost whole chapters; one, whose computer had been nicked from his house, an entire book. If that should ever happen to her, she doubted she would be able to go on. Just the thought of having to do so much rewriting made her feel positively faint.

'I can't even print it out,' she groaned. She always travelled light, without a printer. She could usually borrow one, if ever the need arose, though presumably not in a rural backwater like this. She did at least have the backup tapes, for which she was profoundly grateful. And a rough early draft on the main computer, which she hoped was not affected by what had just happened.

'What exactly do you mean?' asked Genevieve, hovering bemusedly behind her. Despite the fact that she used a laptop herself, her grasp of computer know-how was pretty sketchy. Anna, whose knowledge of cars was nil, was nonetheless forever updating her technology. She found it fascinating, and the better it was, the more she enjoyed her daily grind.

'My two computers are networked,' she explained. 'This one

and the main one in New York. Which means that, before I go anywhere, I plug them together and they synchronise. Everything there is instantly updated, including my address book and diary. It is hugely handy and saves a lot of effort. And when I get home, I repeat the process.' Computer science could occasionally be a headache but, when it all worked, definitely simplified things.

It might be worth a quick call to New York to check with her technical advisor. The least he could do was reassure her, since his was the brain that had created the system. She clicked on her on-screen address book for his number but was unable to access it. Instead, a blocking message appeared, informing her that the address book was currently in use. 'Another user' had it open and was working with the file. Anna would just have to wait.

'I don't believe it!' she said, profoundly shocked. The night-mare was rapidly worsening. Something was happening that she did not understand and starting to scare her profoundly. She double-clicked on her other files, all with the same result. Her financial spreadsheet, her biographical details; most frightening of all, her online bank balance. They all flashed up the same stark message. Access to them was denied.

'What exactly does that mean?' asked Genevieve, way out of her depth.

'It means,' said Anna grimly, through clenched teeth, 'that somebody, using my main computer, is snooping through my files.'

Somebody in New York was what she meant. Somebody in her house.

She tried repeatedly to get through but the line continued busy. She guessed the handset was probably off the hook. Meanwhile her files remained inaccessible. Whoever was reading them was certainly taking his time. Sporadically, she also tried Larry but never with any success. In New York it was still only mid-afternoon; someone by now should pick up. Although Larry was usually working on site, he ran his tight business from home, aided by his efficient wife, Phoebe, who did all the paperwork.

'Call the cops, why don't you?' again urged Hector, but what exactly did he think she was going to say? That someone to whom she had given her keys was using her home computer? A total stranger whom she had invited in and told to help himself to whatever he liked? There might still be some sort of rational explanation, though Anna was at a loss to imagine what. In frustration, she scrolled through a list of her files to remind herself what was there. A chill ran through her as she read her meticulous notes. She had annotated all her credit card details, including their separate PIN numbers, and also thrown in, as an added bonus, her Social Security number.

'Don't you have a secret password?' Even Genevieve knew that you should.

'Indeed I do,' said Anna sharply. Which only added to the mystery. Nobody but her knew what it was. Sutherland could use the computer for general purposes but supposedly not access her personal data. After a couple more agonised hours, slowly, one by one, the files became free. She ran through them rapidly, skimming their contents. Most of the details of her personal life were laid out succinctly on the screen. She had always been proud of her innate tidiness; could not have made things easier had she tried. The last one to clear was her online bank account which now she opened with fingers that positively shook. The final tranche of the movie money had been due at the beginning of the week, paid in direct by

Warner Brothers according to contractual terms. She had meant to check it but somehow never had. Now she registered, with total disbelief, that her current credit balance stood at zero.

Her anguished cry brought the others running. They found her white-faced and in shock.

'I can't believe it. He has taken all my money. The bastard's cleaned me out.'

If Anna thought things could not get worse, she was wrong. After countless futile attempts to reach Larry, the phone was eventually answered by a faltering voice she barely recognised.

'Phoebe?' said Anna doubtfully. Perhaps she had got the wrong number. There was no reply, just laboured breathing, then words were spoken quietly in the background and a stranger's voice came on the line.

'Who is this please?' The voice was male though not one that Anna recognised.

'Is this the Atwood residence?'

'Who is it wants to know?'

'It's Anna Kovac. Calling from Italy. Will somebody, please, tell me what's going on?'

There followed a muffled conversation, then Phoebe took over again, her voice so distorted it was hard to make out what she said. She sounded like an old or demented person. Or one in the grip of profound and disabling shock.

'Phoebe? What's happened?' asked Anna, in sudden terror.

There was a long fraught silence until Phoebe could find the words. 'It's Larry,' she said at last. 'He's dead,' sounding as though she still could not quite believe it.

'Dead?' repeated Anna, not entirely comprehending. The line

to New York was crackling and not at all clear. She could not believe she had heard correctly, it had to be a mistake.

'Dead,' repeated Phoebe, beginning to cry. 'He had an accident.'

'What sort of accident?' It made no sense. He had sounded so bouncy and full of life the last time they had spoken, only days ago.

'He fell,' said Phoebe, still quietly sobbing. 'They were taking the scaffolding down.'

The scaffolding. Oh God, her house. 'And what exactly occurred?' He couldn't be dead, not exuberant Larry, always so full of life. Anna had known him since her student days.

'Nobody knows for certain. He must have slipped. Somebody called the police.'

'Somebody in the house, you mean?'

'I don't know.' Phoebe was clearly devastated and confused; Anna really didn't like to press her. She whispered platitudes, then rang off, too stunned to take in all the implications.

'That settles it,' she announced to the others. 'Now I have to go home.' To attend the funeral, to be with Phoebe. To try to make sense of what was going on. Most of all, to track down the elusive Mr Sutherland and finally confront him face to face. For a moment she thought about calling her father; childhood habits die hard. Then remembered in time that he was now old and frail. She didn't want to risk alarming him unduly.

The drive to Pisa was balmy and delicious, with the glorious high summer foliage resplendent whichever way they looked. On a happier occasion, they would have driven that much more slowly in order to savour the scenery to the full. Sun-baked stone farmhouses with terracotta roofs; olive groves cut into steep climbing terraces and a strange golden light illuminating the trees against an undulant backdrop of misty purple. Anna was far too upset to take it in. The Tuscan scenery she had found so inspiring had suddenly entirely lost its allure. She was full of grief and all she could think about was this nagging worry that had to be resolved.

Genevieve had loaned her some cash for the trip which, with her traveller's cheques, just covered the airfare. She hadn't bothered with buying a return ticket in case she decided to stay on. Again, the writer's life was flexible. She had half-thought she might move on to Florence or Rome. In New York, she had the security of knowing she still had a separate savings account with just enough put away to see her through until she had sorted things out. Rationally, she knew that it had to be a blunder. Somebody at the bank had screwed up royally. The movie company could just be in arrears; perhaps there was a fault on Anna's phoneline. But until she knew the truth, she couldn't relax.

'Stay in touch and let us know what happens,' said Candy and Genevieve when they hugged her goodbye. Despite the drama, they were also intrigued. 'Promise you'll let us know the minute there's news.'

Candy had agreed to stay on at the villa, at least till they knew when Anna was coming back. There were six weeks of the house exchange still to go and Hugo and Trevor had not yet returned from their trip.

'We always have Hector to take care of us,' said Candy, in a clumsy attempt at levity.

But Larry was dead and Anna's money all gone. Things surely couldn't get any worse than that.

Part Two

13

Anna arrived in New York in the late afternoon and took a yellow cab straight to East 74th Street. The evening rush hour was already in full swing and the traffic predictably snarled up. She writhed with impatience on the bumpy back seat, willing the driver to go faster. This one was taciturn and some sort of foreign. His silence was welcome since she had no desire to talk. The city was sweltering and smelled strongly of tar and scorched rubber; the contrast with the fresh Tuscan air practically made her choke. Even within the cab, her throat felt gritty. Eventually, after what seemed like hours, he made a right into Madison Avenue and pulled up in front of her house. She was travelling light, with only a single bag, and the laptop suspended from her shoulder. Distractedly, she paid the driver, then turned to take a good look at her pride and joy.

With the scaffolding down, the building appeared pristine, better even than Anna had dared to hope. Larry's team had

157

worked miracles. The stucco exterior had been cleaned and repainted a brilliant, luminous cream and all the long sash windows were freshly washed. The windowsills had been re-pointed and the ancient scroll mouldings restored. And the handsome oak door, which Larry had recycled from a building site in Brooklyn, provided a suitably elegant finishing touch. Despite her current preoccupations, Anna's heart swelled with satisfaction. For a work of art such as this had she slaved all these years. She ascended the short flight of steps from the sidewalk and hesitantly rang the bell. Her heart was beating unnaturally fast; she dreaded any sort of altercation. Nothing happened, so she tried again, three short buzzes in a row. At this time in the afternoon, the odds were against anyone being at home, but she would not consider trying to enter without first giving proper warning. She might be the owner but he was the approved tenant; they had an informal agreement to that effect. Again nothing happened, so Anna tried the knocker, listening to it resonate through the house. A sound that sonorous should alert even the hard of hearing, but Anna instinctively knew there was nobody there.

She put down the laptop and scrabbled for her key, then took a deep breath and inserted it into the lock. She wasn't quite sure of the correct protocol but had travelled all these miles and was too het up to care about splitting hairs over details like that. Something decidedly fishy was going on; her sole concern right now was to find out what. And if her tenant happened not to be at home, then that was hardly her fault. She owned the house and had the right. Now was not the time for niceties. Too late it occurred to her that she probably should have called Paige. Having her lawyer along would have made it more official.

She tried to twist the key again, then realised it was resisting. She pulled it out and inspected it closely, assuming she had selected the wrong one. But this was unquestionably the key to the main front door; the other two on the ring were just for the dead bolts. Someone appeared to have changed the locks; she was pretty certain that it wouldn't have been Larry.

She shifted her attention to the right of the door and tried peering through the first-floor parlour window. Her handsome linen Roman blinds were uniformly three quarters closed, designed to conceal the interior from passers-by as well as from the searing effects of the sun. She pressed her face close to the sparkling glass and adjusted her vision to the dimness inside. Then froze with shock at what she did not see. It seemed that all the furniture had gone. Her pictures and ornaments had disappeared too, even her clock from the mantelpiece. Emotion as powerful as an electric current coursed through Anna's veins. Something unbelievable had been happening in her absence. Her instinct to return had been spot on.

She retreated rapidly back down the steps and tried the basement door, which led into the kitchen. With the same result – it was firmly locked and she did not even possess the relevant key. Those locks too had been replaced, as had the iron grilles. She stepped back further on the sidewalk to examine the upstairs windows. Everything looked in impeccable repair but the house had the slightly neglected air of having been recently abandoned. Surprisingly, in this oppressive heat, not a single window was open even a crack. And then she saw it, on the second floor, the real estate agency's board. For a second she wondered if she had come to the wrong address, even checked the number to make quite sure. Then fished out her cellphone and dialled the agency's number on the board, only to get a recorded message saying that the office was closed for the night.

So then she sat on the steps and called Paige, her fingers almost too tremulous to make the connection.

'Anna?' said the alert, familiar voice, unleashing in her a torrent of emotion. She tried to explain but could not find the words. All she could do now was helplessly blub. And she had no idea what had happened to Sadie. The thought of her pet alone and abandoned practically broke her heart.

'Grab a cab,' ordered Paige with her customary efficiency, 'and get yourself over to my office right away.'

Paige sat serenely in her leather executive chair, the sunlight pale and ethereal on her hair. Even on a day like this, not a detail was out of place. Her neat linen dress displayed not a single wrinkle, her nails were shaped to a sensible oval and immaculately and expensively French polished. A secretary appeared with two glasses of iced water and Anna collapsed on the stylish cream sofa as though punctured by a pin. Which was, in effect, more or less what had happened. The air had been effectively knocked right out of her.

'Run it all through again slowly,' instructed Paige, handing her a box of tissues. 'When precisely was it that you first suspected anything was wrong?' Nothing had been mentioned in recent emails. There was no way Anna would not have turned to her first.

'Not really until the computer played up. Though I did find it odd that he seemed never to be there when he'd been so awfully keen to make the swap.'

'And you never got round to meeting him in person?'

Anna shook her head. 'It wasn't ever really feasible,' she explained. 'He was there and I was here. We were timed to pass in the air.' *Besides, he was a Yalie.* The words hung between them but remained unspoken. This was no time for 'I told you so's'. Anna was obviously much too shattered. And the situation did look bad. She was right to be so concerned.

'And what about the credit card fraud? Do you think that could have been part of the same scam?' It certainly looked so; too much of a coincidence. But again Anna shook her head.

'I really can't tell you. I seem to be losing my marbles. I no longer have any idea of what's going on.' And what about Sadie, what had become of her? A house, at the best of it, was bricks and mortar; an animal was supposedly for life. (*Get one from the animal shelter.* She remembered her father's advice. But she had spotted this kitten in a fancy Madison Avenue shop and fallen in love on the spot. *You get what you pay for,* she had tried to explain but she knew that, in some historic way, she had radically let him down. Though Sadie had become a great favourite of his, *the only grandchild he was ever likely to have.*) Now Anna brushed away her tears and tried to put a good face on it. A cat, however precious, was only a cat. Look what those people had gone through in September.

'So why didn't you email me about the credit card fraud?' Paige was only being professional but there was just the slightest hint of hurt in her eyes.

Anna, getting it immediately, was embarrassed. 'I talked to Larry,' she told her lamely. 'And he convinced me that everything was all right.'

There was no need for Paige to say anything at all; besides, she loved Anna far too much. She insisted that she come home with her and ushered her into a cab. Charles wouldn't mind, he was hugely fond of Anna, and they had a luxurious guest suite.

'Just waiting for you,' said Paige, pulling down the blinds and turning on the air-conditioning full force. She opened a row of empty closets, equipped with dozens of padded hangers trimmed with minuscule lavender bags. There was bluebell oil on the edge of the tub and chocolates next to the bed. Anna, who normally might have made fun, embraced Paige in a long and silent hug.

'Just for one night,' she agreed reluctantly, hating, as always, to impose, but Paige was adamant she stay for as long as it took; what else, after all, were best friends for? Or, indeed, lah-di-dah spare rooms. With luck, it would all turn out to be just some minion's colossal fuckup though, privately, her lawyer's brain was far from believing that so. For someone as smart and streetwise as Anna, this situation should never have come about. She remembered how down and depressed she had been; perhaps, for once, she had not been thinking quite straight. But now was no time for recriminations; the milk had been well and truly spilt. They had to get fast to the root of the problem and put in some speedy damage limitation before it got any further out of hand.

'What now?' asked Anna helplessly, after they had got her safely settled. Charles was home and mixing martinis; Paige had phoned for a Chinese takeaway. Anna's energy had been well and truly sapped. All she really wanted now was to sleep.

'First thing tomorrow, we're calling the real estate people and after that we will talk to Visa and the bank. In the meantime, try not to worry too much. There has to be some logical explanation.' Paige was always so gloriously upbeat. One of the many reasons that Anna loved her.

'Can't we do anything now?' asked Anna as she paced the Colliers' spacious living-room. 'Break a window? Force our way in? Call the firefighters to cut through the bars on the windows?'

'No,' said Paige practically, taking her hand. 'Anything like that would be a disaster. All you've got going for you, right now, are your rights. Break the law and you'll be in more serious trouble.'

'But it's my house.'

'I know, but it has to be proven. Just because somebody else broke the law does not automatically put you in the clear. These things, I'm afraid, have to be done in the right way. Trust me.' She laughed. 'I'm a lawyer.'

'Do you want to call your dad?' Paige asked later, once they had eaten and cleared away.

'No,' said Anna, quite positive about that. 'I really don't want to worry him at this stage.'

Paige nodded. She loved and revered the distinguished old man and saw him as often as she could. But she had noticed how, in recent months, he had started to look that much frailer. Anna had always been the pivot of his world and he was bound to feel he had somehow let her down. Best to leave him until things were properly sorted, when Anna's sudden return could be viewed as a treat.

First thing next morning, Paige rang the real estate office and got put through to the relevant person, a woman with a distinct attitude problem who seemed strangely and immediately on her guard. Yes, she agreed, the house was on the market, in fact she had already had an offer. She seemed uneasy to be talking to a lawyer and constantly on the verge of hanging up.

'Really?' said Paige, astonished. 'How can that be? Without the knowledge of the owner, Anna Kovac?'

The woman grew suddenly even more uptight. 'I'm afraid I don't know about that,' she said. 'All I can tell you is that we have the necessary authorisation.'

'May I ask who from?' Paige was at her silkiest and Anna could see she was right into her stride. Though a beautiful woman who cared much about life's luxuries, beneath the velvet glove was a fist of steel. She might equally have made it on the stage or, indeed, as a model. Instead the brilliant scholar had chosen the law. She flashed Anna an encouraging smile and slowly the burden of worry began to ebb. Paige would fix things; that was her special talent. Anna was grateful to have her taking charge.

'That is classified information,' said the woman, beginning to sound distinctly disconcerted. 'I am not empowered to tell you any more. Have you called to make an offer? I'm very busy.'

'Ask her about Sadie,' hissed Anna, before she could hang up, desperate to find out whatever she could.

'Can you tell me the whereabouts of the owner's cat?' said Paige. 'A pedigree lynx-point Siamese who was left in the care of the tenant.'

'I know nothing about a cat,' snapped the woman, who clearly could not have cared less. 'Now, if you'll excuse me, I have to go.' And rudely, without allowing Paige another word, she hung up.

'How could they sell my house without my knowledge?' Anna, after a proper night's sleep, was starting to bounce back.

'They can't. Don't worry. It will all come right in the end. But there's nothing to stop someone putting it on the market.'

'But how could they get away with it? Surely the agency should demand some proof of the vendor's identity.'

'Correctly, yes, but often they don't bother. Think about everything you have heard about real estate sharks. A bunch of shysters all competing in a very cutthroat market. What do they care about legal rights; they are in there solely to make a rapid killing.

Provided you have the keys and obvious possession, it is not the business of the agency to dig deeper or to demand any proof. Not until a deal is agreed; then it becomes more tricky.'

'What would happen in the event of a sale?' Anna was trying to remember. It was only months since she had been through the process herself but so many things had intervened, her recollection was hazy.

'They need the deeds, which should be in the owner's possession. That, they are bound to find, is the stumbling block. Without them, they cannot go ahead. What,' Paige added, 'as a matter of interest, did you do with yours?'

'At first they were with the bank, as security, but then, when the movie deal went through, they let me have them back. Now I keep them safely in my study, locked inside the safe.' At which she groaned. Along with everything else, that they would have removed.

'We will cross that bridge when we come to it.' Paige briskly brushed it aside. Though she tried not to show it, her heart was sinking. With every new piece of information, the situation was growing that much more complex.

Next Paige talked to the Visa office, explaining that she was Anna's lawyer. When she gave them the details of Anna's account they obligingly looked it all up. But the answer, depressingly, remained unchanged. She was way beyond her credit limit. There was nothing more at this stage they could do until she had paid it off.

'Right,' said Paige grimly, reaching for her purse. 'Now we are going to the police.'

The precinct was crowded and depressing. Paige and Anna had to wait their turn and were there for over an hour.

'Can't you pull rank?' muttered Anna frantically, still obsessing about the cat.

Paige shook her head. 'The very last person the cops respect is a lawyer.' Her smooth blonde hair was swept neatly into a coil. She looked as demure as a socialite at a charity lunch but inside that elegantly coiffed head existed a razor-sharp brain. She laid delicate fingers on Anna's wrist and exhorted her to stay calm. 'They have to go through the correct procedures. I am only sorry it is taking so much time.'

The duty sergeant, when it was finally their turn, looked weary and unkempt. He had obviously been working a very lengthy shift and was badly in need of a shave. When Paige started speaking, he produced a mountain of official forms which he laboriously started to fill in. The questions he asked seemed trivial in the extreme, with no apparent relevance to Anna's case. She shot Paige a glance of pure agony; this was obviously getting them nowhere and while they were stuck here, sorting out all this crap, anything could be happening to her cat. Paige conveyed to her silently that the man was simply doing his job, the questions purely routine. When they got to the details of the invasion of her computer, he raised cynical eyes and stared levelly at Anna.

'How come just anyone could access your files? Don't you use a password for security?' *Puh-lease.*

'Of course I do,' said Anna, stung. His assumption was making her mad, not to mention feel stupid. What sort of fool did he take her for? He seemed to be suggesting it was somehow her fault. This was the last thing she needed right now, some smart-ass cop poking fun at her. 'I use the name of my cat,' she said. Straightforward and easy to remember.

Theatrically, the cop covered his eyes. No doubt she listed

her PIN numbers too? At Anna's sheepish nod, he groaned and sadly shook his head. 'Lady,' he told her wearily, 'you women are all the same. Name of partner, name of pet. It's virtually routine.' He looked as though he were contemplating ripping up the forms until Paige rose suddenly to her feet and imperiously took command.

'Sergeant,' she told him, 'we have wasted enough time.' They needed some kind of investigation fast. She handed him her business card and watched as the penny slowly dropped.

'Come on,' she said crisply, steering Anna towards the door. 'We have far more important things to do.'

Back in Paige's office the two of them took stock. It now seemed fairly pointless to wait for the police to intervene. They were overburdened and slow-witted, plus far from sympathetic. Anna said she suspected that a man like that duty sergeant resented a woman like herself, independent, educated and obviously well-heeled.

'Or I was,' she wailed, recalling her vandalised account.

Paige made an appointment to talk to Anna's bank but the manager couldn't fit her in until the following week. 'We have to do something instantly,' she said. 'Let's start by proving that the house is legally yours before they go ahead and conclude a deal. The least it will do is save time.'

'But how?' said Anna, again in despair. 'My papers were all inside. Without access, why should anyone ever believe me?' She had lived there such a very short time, she had not even got to know her neighbours. With a plummeting heart, she thought of her fancy new filing cabinet; fireproof, rustproof, immaculately in order, finished in tasteful antique-looking wood to blend with the rest of the room. Only, alas, not locked; not that that would have made a difference. In any case, she assumed the house had been systematically swept clean. All her possessions would have been removed, including any relevant legal papers. If only poor Larry had not been killed. His death seemed suddenly sinister. She had tried calling Phoebe, who was still in no state to talk. All she knew was from that one brief conversation. He had apparently lost his footing and fallen. Nobody had witnessed it first-hand.

She told Paige about the woman who had been there, PA or girlfriend, Larry had not been sure. 'I am now beginning to wonder if it might have been his wife. That would make most sense, don't you agree?'

'I hadn't realised there was a wife. You never mentioned that before.' Paige had always had a shrewd suspicion that Anna rather hoped Sutherland might be single. She had been so delighted when the swap was arranged, had been perfectly willing to accept his credentials on trust. She remembered her cousin Wilbur's remark about Sutherland having no trouble with the ladies. It might be worth calling him again to find out what else he knew.

'I didn't think there was at first but now it seems to make sense. The villa is done in the most exquisite taste with all the fixtures and fittings exactly matching. Also, there are signs of children. Well, a daughter at least.' She told Paige about Hector's discovery in the nursery, out-of-date clothing that had probably been there for years.

'So you think his wife might be with him in New York? In which case, where is she now?'

'She presumably set up the sale and they've both headed for the hills.'

'So it's another case of *cherchez la femme*.' Paige became

instantly thoughtful. Though it really did not advance things in any way. They still had no idea what was going on nor where the elusive Sutherland might be.

'What about the previous owners? They must have a record of the sale. After all, you paid them a load of money. They must have hung on to the papers for the IRS.'

Miserably Anna shook her head. 'I bought it, remember, from a Japanese bank.' They had used it solely for corporate entertaining and sold in a hurry when they relocated. Anna, who had happened to be in the right place at the right time with sudden huge money in her account, had been lucky enough to buy it at a snip. Certainly they must have kept legal records, but she did not know where they had gone. Back to Tokyo was all they had said. She hadn't been interested at the time.

Paige remembered the occasion only too well. At the time of the purchase they had celebrated in style, rejoicing at Anna's propitious luck. She put a supportive hand on Anna's shoulder and implored her not to lose heart. It was early days yet, they had only just started. They would unravel these problems one by one and then take appropriate action.

'Why not call your dad,' she suggested, 'and go spend an evening with him.' He'd be thrilled to see his daughter back and she need not fill him in on too much detail.

'I might just do that,' said Anna slowly. At least it would help to take her mind off things.

14

Somewhat to Anna's surprise, her father appeared not to be there. She tried him at nine and again at eleven and then at one, when he would normally be having his lunch. She was mildly concerned. It was not like him to be out for so long, certainly not a whole morning. He taught his pupils in the front parlour at home and rarely walked further than the single block to the grocery store on the corner. It could be that he had a doctor's appointment or was out playing chess with a friend. She would try him again at a later hour, though remained cautious about alarming him. He did not, she reminded herself, even know that she was back and his life, after all, was his own. Like her, he was both independent and strong-willed. She had always been thankful for that.

Once Paige and Charles had departed for work, Anna's insecurities crowded in. She felt she ought not to impose on them too long, despite their generous insistence that she should stay.

She was far too fond of both of them to risk damaging the friendship, calling to mind the old adage about fish and house guests. Luckily she still had enough in her savings account to pay for a modest hotel. As soon as she got her old energy back, she would make appropriate arrangements to move on. Meanwhile, feeling the need of some loving kindness, she called her former neighbour, Colette O'Connor. They had been through a lot together, over the years, and Colette's door was always ajar, a fact well-known throughout her neighbourhood. She was an East Side social worker with a keen sense of community and one of the warmest hearts that Anna knew.

Not today, however. As soon as she registered that it was Anna on the line, Colette's voice became distinctly guarded. There was no effusive shout of delight at her friend being home prematurely. No invitation to come straight over and catch her up on the trip. Rather, Colette sounded positively evasive as she quickly muttered something about her workload.

'I'm afraid I can't talk to you now,' she said, as coolly polite as a stranger. 'All sorts of important things have come up. I have to go.'

Stunned, Anna stared at the abruptly silent phone, then slowly replaced the handset in its cradle. Could it be that her paranoia was really taking hold or had she just been well and truly snubbed? By someone she had considered a trusted friend and part of her innermost circle. She would have called Paige but hated to disturb her. Instead, she poured herself another cup of coffee and started ringing round the rest of her friends. All of them intimates who normally would have cared; none of whom seemed any more to give a damn.

'What's going on?' she asked Paige later. 'I'm beginning to feel

171

like Rip van Winkle, returned after twenty years, yet nobody cares.'

'You've been overstretching your brain,' said Paige, as always brisk and to the point, with little room in her soul for sentimentality. Considering how close they had always been, in character they were actually quite unalike. Anna, the dreamer; Paige, the pragmatist, yet the very best of friends since their student days. Paige had been working so hard herself, she had largely dropped out of the social scene. Though their circles of friends overlapped quite a lot, she had not been keeping up. Life for the past few months had been fraught, with little room in it for fun or entertainment.

'I am sure you are just imagining it.' Most New Yorkers, especially now, had their own preoccupations. Anna, for too long, had been living a dream. Normal people, Paige reminded her, had real jobs with regular hours. None of this lying around in the sun, awaiting inspiration from the muse.

Anna grinned. Paige always had had the knack of being able to cheer her up. On things like that were true friendships really grounded. She was doubtless being solipsistic again, writing was such a solitary occupation. Just because her own life had changed was no reason she should expect any special attention. She might have chosen to skive off for the summer but reminded herself that others had not. Soon they would start returning her calls, she was sure. They could not know what a crisis state she was in.

Anna told Paige of her plan for moving on. She could not, with any conscience, intrude any longer. Here, on the affluent Upper West Side, was wonderful for a while but she needed a space of her very own in which to get on with her writing. Just one modest room would be quite enough; she had to be alone for her concentration. Paige protested but Anna stood firm. There was a small, slightly drab hotel near where she lived that looked both innocuous and respectable. She had often passed it and been curious to see inside. Besides, it was on Madison, close to her house.

Paige, getting it immediately, withdrew her objections. 'You can always come back to us if you get depressed.' Tomorrow she had the meeting with the bank; with luck, very soon she could solve all Anna's problems and enable her at last to return to Tuscany.

Anna tried her father again but he continued not to answer. She thought about dropping in on him, then chided herself for being over-fussy. Nothing annoyed him more than being nannied and he had raised his daughter in exactly the same mode. She would wait a few days, until things were a little calmer, and then go round and surprise him. Cautiously, she phoned Phoebe instead and received permission to drop by.

The Atwoods lived in a new apartment complex that Larry's firm had helped to construct. Phoebe opened the door with red-rimmed eyes and stood with Anna for a long emotional moment, locked in a wordless hug. Eventually Phoebe pulled away and led her into the spacious open-plan room. She offered refreshment but Anna wasn't staying; really just wanted to check that she was all right.

'I still can't believe he's gone,' said Phoebe, nervously picking at the tissue in her hand. 'Whenever the phone rings, I expect it to be him, and still find myself setting the table for two.' In just a week she had lost ten pounds and her normally glossy hair was lank and greasy. Their children were grown and away at college; Phoebe faced a bleak future on her own. 'It's just not fair,' she said, crying again. 'Everything in our lives was going so well.'

Anna awkwardly patted Phoebe's hand and wondered if she really should have come. But the nagging question refused to go away; she had to find out exactly what had happened. 'Tell me about the accident,' she said. 'That is, if you can bear to.'

Phoebe had no objection. In a way it was a relief to be able to talk. 'I keep reliving it in my mind, though actually nobody saw it, not first-hand. The men had been taking the scaffolding down and were piling it on to their truck. Larry was up on the second floor, doing his mountain goat act.' Despite her grief, a pale smile lit her eyes. 'He always was a buffoon.'

'And then he fell?'

'Just like that, without warning. All anyone heard was his cry.' His dying cry was what she meant.

Anna digested this. 'Yet someone called the police, you said?'

Phoebe nodded. 'Though they still have no idea who it could have been.' A neighbour, maybe, though none had yet come forward. Or, alternatively, somebody in the house. It had happened so quickly, all had been confusion; he was dead on arrival at the hospital. Phoebe began visibly to fade again so Anna hugged her and quickly took her leave. There were questions still that needed urgent answers but she felt she had already exceeded her welcome.

'Take care,' she said gently, giving Phoebe another hug. 'And let me know if there's anything I can do.' She felt guilty; if it hadn't been for her house, Larry would still be alive. And that, even more than anything else that had happened, hardened her determination to fight on.

She moved her few belongings into the Caledonian Hotel, where she tried to revitalise her writing schedule. But sitting all day in a gloomy, shuttered room – especially in this terrific heat – proved not to be conducive to much work. She missed the freshness and shifting light of Tuscany as well as the constant freedom to wander at will. Most she missed the company of the other two, which surprised her even more than she would have guessed. Anna, from choice, had always been a loner, but she'd grown accustomed to their lively camaraderie and constant lighthearted banter. Even Hector, in retrospect, was just a bit of a goon; were she to bump into him right now, she might even give him a hug. All things were relative, after all, and he had provided some welcome light relief. She couldn't stop thinking about Larry's horrible death and whether it had been an accident after all.

Paige had her meeting with the bank, which turned out to be less than constructive. They had no idea how the account had been cleared and the manager was reluctant to discuss the matter. All he could confirm was that the money from Warner Brothers had been paid in, then withdrawn again in slightly under a week. The signatory had been A. L. Kovac; everything had appeared to be in order. Frustrated and furious, Paige called Anna and the two of them met for an after-work drink in the bar of the Plaza Athenee. It was mid-July and the city was stifling. Anna, now accustomed to pure country air, felt almost light-headed from the heat.

At first Paige made a feeble attempt to gloss over the gravity of the situation, then had to admit she felt seriously out of her depth. She still hadn't made any progress at all and now the bank, too, was being deeply disobliging. She ran a list of points past Anna to see what she might have overlooked.

'You checked your online balance, right?'

Anna nodded. 'Yes.'

'And the last time you did that, there was money in the account?'

Another nod. 'As it happens, quite a lot.' She had been surprised but then had never been very good at keeping up to date with her current earnings, particularly since nowadays most incoming money was paid straight into the bank.

'With another tranche due shortly from Warner Brothers?'

'Due at the start of the week.'

'And now it would seem to have disappeared, though the bank confirm it was temporarily in there. Long enough for them to have registered it. Someone succeeded in siphoning it off, using your family name and initials. What they can't explain, and neither can I, is how that could have been done without your PIN number. Or, indeed, your personal passcode calculator to which nobody else but you should ever have access.'

There was a shifty pause during which Anna looked uncomfortable. She knew all too well what was coming next.

'Oh no,' said Paige, reading the expression on her face. 'Please don't tell me what I think you are going to. I don't believe it. I can't cope.' Theatrically, she thrust her head into her hands.

So Anna had to confess. 'You know how bad I have always been with figures. I find it so much simpler to stick to just one.'

'Of which you keep a note on your computer . . .'

'So that I won't forget it.'

'But what about the passcode calculator?' asked Paige, once she had taken this in.

'I keep it safely in a drawer of my desk. Alongside my cheque-book and paying-in book. That way, I know where they are.'

'And you didn't bother to take them with you?' Or think of

locking the drawer? Not that, in the circumstances, that would have made a lot of difference.

'I couldn't see any point. I travel light.'

They drank in silence. What more was there to be said? Paige, for the moment, seemed to have run out of questions. Anna was feeling exceptionally dumb, but none of this had occurred to her before. As why, indeed, should it with a totally trustworthy tenant, whose credentials she had even bothered to check? With a member of Paige's family, no less, though that was something she wasn't about to mention. There was nowhere the blame could be laid except squarely with her.

'It has got to be Sutherland,' Anna said finally, 'without the slightest shadow of a doubt. A fool I may be but not to that extent. He set it up from the start, that is obvious now. But how are we ever going to pin him down? He appears to have got away with it and now apparently vanished.'

She had taken to wandering past the house, hoping for some sign of occupation. But the real estate board was still on display, though whenever she tried calling the agency, no-one was ever available to talk. Neither, unsurprisingly, were the police coming through. Paige felt she was banging her head against a wall. The trouble was that at this time of year, most of the people who mattered were out of town. She hoped it wouldn't drag on until Labour Day.

And then Anna was struck by a colossal realisation, the obvious trump card they had somehow overlooked. She had not been thinking clearly for days or else she could not have missed it. She stared at Paige with bulging eyes, then started to chuckle in a faintly manic way.

'What?' Paige was not in a mood for levity; she felt she had seriously let Anna down.

'Think. He may have pinched my house and drained my bank account but look what I have gained in return. He has not left me entirely empty-handed.'

'The villa.' Paige could have kicked herself but these were harrowing times. Like Anna, she had been scarcely sleeping for days.

'The second I get home, I am calling Montisi.' All Anna's energy came surging back. They could smash through those solid locked doors, if necessary, and likewise batter the truth out of Raffaele. Someone in that village had got to know something. They were all in it together, she'd be willing to bet.

'There's a guy at the bar who keeps on staring over here,' said Paige as Anna waved frantically for the bill. Anna distractedly followed her gaze to where a group of well-dressed men were standing. The one who had been showing interest was immaculately turned-out, with the dark and saturnine looks of a movie star. Aware of Anna's attention, he turned away and buried himself in conversation with his friends.

'Johnny Delano!' said Anna with joy, rising impulsively and making a beeline for him. 'Where have you been hiding?' she asked, giving him a hug, and Paige, from across the room, observed his sudden apparent unease. He returned Anna's hug, however, then introduced her to the group.

'Anna Kovac, famous novelist. One of my all-time favourite people.'

Anna brought him over to meet Paige. A former neighbour, she explained. Johnny was a TV director who had lived in her previous building, though she hadn't seen him since the move, almost eight months ago.

Paige, diplomatically, had to go. 'Catch you later,' she said, giving Anna a meaningful look.

'Can we talk?' asked Anna urgently. There were things, she realised now, that she felt Johnny might know. He obligingly fetched his drink and settled into the chair vacated by Paige.

'Am I glad to see you,' said Anna, from the heart. They had been good pals for a number of years. He was slightly younger but dead attractive and, like her, highly creative. Together they made an excellent team and also shared a zany sense of humour. She realised how much she had missed him.

'Who's the blonde bombshell?' He rarely missed a trick.

'Unbelievably, my lawyer. I can't believe that your paths haven't crossed before.'

'So what's the problem?' asked Johnny, relaxing, though his dark eyes still flickered uncomfortably.

Anna shrugged, at a loss to know where to begin, but Johnny fetched her another drink and she soon found herself pouring out her woes. It was a relief to be able to run things through and, at last, get them into perspective. She left out nothing and Johnny was transfixed; he listened until the end without interrupting.

'And you let this stranger into your house, just like that?'

Anna nodded, still feeling a fool. She no longer had anything to say in her own defence. She didn't even mention that he was at Yale.

'But what I need to find out from you,' she said, recalling the purpose of this drink, 'is what the hell is the matter with all my friends?' None of them seemed to want to know her any more, apart, of course, from Paige, who didn't count. She saw immediately she had scored a direct hit. Johnny shifted awkwardly and gazed silently into his glass. So she hadn't been paranoid at all; there really was something wrong. She patiently waited until he was ready to talk.

'Well, my darling,' he said at last, looking her straight in the

eye, 'I can't pretend that we weren't all a tiny bit shocked.' Anna
stared back blankly and allowed him to struggle on. She hadn't
the faintest idea what he was saying. 'I mean, a deal's a deal –
and well done you – but doing the dirty like that on your own
father? I'm afraid we all feel that you acted somewhat shabbily.
You have to admit such behaviour wasn't quite kosher.'

'What the hell are you talking about?' asked Anna, after a
stunned pause. This appeared to have nothing at all to do with
her current situation, though it was clear to see that Johnny was
upset and that there were tougher things to follow.

'So soon after 9/11,' he continued. 'It's hardly what might be
called patriotic.'

'Stop!' said Anna, frustratedly, on the point of giving him a
shake. 'Tell me what you are on about. I really don't have a
clue.' She sensed something even worse was coming and steeled
herself to withstand another blow.

This time Johnny heard her and filled her in. Shortly after
she had left for Italy, indecently soon in the opinion of her
friends, her father had been moved to a retirement home and
his house, the family home in which she'd been raised, immediately put up for sale.

'*What?*' screamed Anna, almost crazy with disbelief, but
Johnny doggedly ploughed on. An odd time, they had all agreed,
to be selling property in Tribeca, when prices had plummeted
to rock bottom and nobody had any money any more. Added
to which, and he was sure she would see their point, they all
felt that fine old man deserved far better. Failing he might be,
but not to that extent; he was still in pretty good nick for a
man of his age. He surely couldn't have many more years. Could
she not just have curbed her greed and waited for time to take
its natural course?

For a moment Anna thought she might throw up and clamped her hand to her mouth. The horror of Johnny's story overwhelmed her. There she had been, worrying about something as trivial as money, when all the while her father had been abducted. And she hadn't known because she hadn't called him. Selfish, as ever, to the last.

'Help me!' she said feverishly, clutching at Johnny's arm, and saw in his eyes, to her immense relief, that finally someone believed her.

15

'I have to find him. Fast,' said Anna, almost inarticulate with distress. They were sitting in Colette's cheerful kitchen, with its familiar pine table and bright enamelled mugs, and Colette was stroking her hand. Thanks to Johnny's persuasive charm, her former neighbour had at last accepted her story and was making up for her recent coldness with Irish coffee and sympathy and hugs. All of which Anna needed in abundance. She, more than anything, regretted that she had not been quicker off the mark. If only she had bothered to check up on her father the day she first failed to reach him on the phone, she might have discovered a whole lot sooner what had been going on. Not that they knew very much even now. Only what Johnny had already explained, that the house, apparently, had been placed on the market and George had disappeared.

'Where did you get the story about the home?' asked Anna, still finding it hard to take in.

'One of those street kids,' said Colette. 'I happened to drop by on a Sunday night with free-range eggs from my sister's farm and found the place deserted and boarded up.' The budding ball-players had filled in the rest. They had witnessed the old man being helped into a car and were told by his female escort that he was moving into a home for his own safety. Somewhere in upstate New York, they thought, but weren't too clear about the details.

'Shame,' one of them had said, with real regret. 'He was a great old guy and always looked out for us.'

'Naturally,' said Colette, 'I assumed that woman was you. Though now I realise I should not have jumped to any such conclusion. Especially since, at that time, you were travelling overseas. My fault, guess I just wasn't thinking too straight, it has been one hell of a year. Plus, I love you enough to confess, my judgement was clouded by anger.' George Kovac, a star in his own right, had always had his fan club. And had spent considerable time with his daughter's friends.

Tears clouded Anna's eyes again; she could still not quite believe what had happened. Who in the world could possibly wish a man like her father harm? Stealing her money and her house, she could see, was possibly fair game, part of the grabby society they now inhabited. But latching on to an unworldly old man? That was despicable beyond belief. Even forgetting his horrific past, all George had ever done was delight millions of music lovers until, when by his own perception his faculties had started to wane, he had passed on his gift to poor kids just for the love of it. George, in everyone's opinion, was a saint. Anna had always felt proud to be his daughter.

'So who was this woman?' asked Colette, splashing more Irish courage into their mugs. Someone who must have known Anna was out of the picture or else she surely would never have dared to attempt such an outrageous ploy.

'I really have no idea,' said Anna. 'Though the only person Larry reported ever seeing in my house was female. PA or girlfriend, he never found out, not as far as I know. All he said was that she was super-efficient and taking good care of the cat. That was all I needed to know. Until Sadie, too, disappeared.' The tears returned and Colette consoled her. The only good to have emerged from the whole wretched business was that Anna had regained the respect of her friends, now full of apologies, genuinely contrite, keen to do what they could to help make amends.

'Now,' said Anna, brushing away her tears, 'I am starting to think she was much more involved than that. It occurs to me that she might have been Sutherland's wife; his wife or whatever, and fellow conspirator. Doesn't that make better sense? It is obvious now I was set up from the start. And whoever did that also went after my father.'

'How would they know about your father if they didn't even know you?' It was a fair question; Colette had a point. But Anna reminded her of the rest.

'Once they had access to my home, they could find out whatever they liked.' All those neatly labelled files, the whole of her life laid bare. If only she hadn't always been so damned tidy; anally fixated again.

They sat in silence, absorbing all this. Put so bluntly, no-one could disagree.

'I doubt it was specifically aimed at your father,' said Johnny, after a while. 'More, I would think, just a predatory bid to gain possession of his house.' Effective, too; it had already been sold. They had established that fact though, once again, not the identity of the vendor. Somehow someone, while Anna was out of the country, had tricked George into signing his property rights away, then presumably kidnapped him as well. It was growing more sinister with everything they learned and Anna was seriously worried about her father's safety. Organised street crime, she had read about that, though never to this extent. The city supposedly had been cleaned up since the mayor had introduced zero tolerance, but clamping down on drug dealers was one thing, corrupt financiers quite another. These days the papers were full of cold-blooded swindles, much of it targeting the elderly and infirm. Luckily for Anna, she had good friends. Without them she did not know how she could have coped.

'First thing tomorrow, I promise you,' said Colette. 'I am going to pull rank with the social services and find out exactly what has happened to your dad.'

It took her precisely two days to locate him. During which period Anna collapsed in overwhelming anguish and remorse and spent long hours lamenting with Paige over what could have triggered this horrible sequence of events. She believed neither in God nor superstition, yet something in her stars was decidedly awry. She could work very hard and replace the stolen money, not that that even mattered in the scale of things, but in no way could she ever replace her father or her family home. In some way, its loss meant more than the loss of her own. It was the house in which she had spent her happy childhood, the backcloth to her parents' solid marriage, the secure environment that, she supposed, had made her who she was.

'I have been very selfish, I see that now,' she said. 'I should never have even considered being so long away. Had I stayed in the city and kept my eye on him, none of this would have ever happened. What sort of daughter must I be and what is he thinking now, wherever he is?' Assuming that he was still alive; they all steered clear of that one.

'A good one,' said Paige firmly, who knew her better than most. 'The daughter he raised to be clever and independent and succeed in a brilliant career. You know how proud he has always been of you. He wouldn't have you any other way.' No unsuitable marriages for Anna, nor messy divorces or children that hadn't been planned. And she had always been there to keep him company; less like father and daughter, more like real friends. George Kovac had much to be thankful for. And would not, for certain, be blaming her now. Whatever.

'But we don't have any idea where he is or whether he has come to any harm.' Anna frenetically paced the room and chewed at the corner of a cuticle. Usually she was immaculately groomed but the façade was lately wearing thin. Any more time and she might crack altogether and then whoever it was would have finally won.

'Try not to worry,' said Paige, who was worrying too. 'I am confident that Colette will find him.'

Charles was mixing them more martinis, not that that helped very much. The theft of the house as well as most of Anna's assets had seemed, at the time, the worst thing ever. But now the abduction of her father too had eclipsed even that. Whoever had been responsible for such a cruel and malevolent act had to be very dangerous indeed.

And the finger pointed at one person only, the mysterious and elusive D. A. Sutherland. Nobody else was even remotely in the frame, no matter what credentials he might have produced. Anna flinched now to recall her own naïveté, tossing aside any caution because they had both been at Yale. What a sucker she had been; he would have spotted that instantly when she eagerly responded to his ad. A sitting duck, a woman on her own, one no longer in the first flush of youth. With, furthermore, a recent financial windfall that had not gone unnoticed in the press. A natural target for a ruthless conman.

'Don't beat up on yourself,' said Paige. 'There is no way you could have known. Everyone these days is turning out corrupt. The worst thing lately, so Charles was just telling me, is that even Jack Welch, everyone's business hero, now admits he had his nose in the corporate trough. The world has changed a lot in the past year. We are none of us as innocent as we were.'

'I still should have known,' said Anna stubbornly. 'And not let this happen to my dad.'

As it was, she was relying on Colette's professional contacts to find him and help to bring him safely home. Paige's natural first instinct had been to involve the police but Colette had persuaded her, at least pro tem, to hold off until she had followed less official channels. After a lifetime in the social services, she knew what they were up against. And even though the process might be lengthy, she preferred initially to deal with the devil she knew.

'You won't achieve anything,' she finally convinced Paige, 'by rattling the cages of authority. I should know after all these years of constantly fighting red tape. I promise you, I won't waste time. I would just rather start by trying to fix things my way.'

Paige initially was set to argue, then saw the flickering hope in Anna's eyes. So, against all her lawyer's killer instincts, she grudgingly conceded to Colette. They had never been particularly close but both adored Anna and put her happiness first. That and, of course, her father's wellbeing. The old man was very dear to both of them.

At the end of two days Colette called in triumph to announce he had been located in White Plains. At the Park Residential Clinic for the Elderly, where he had been living for several weeks. Within minutes the three of them were on the road, heading towards the turnpike, Paige at the wheel, Colette with the map and Anna fretting silently in the back. She feared what her father must think of her for permitting this to have happened. After all the atrocities he had lived through in his life, now it must seem that he couldn't even trust his own daughter.

The street, when they found it, was dingy and run-down, the house colonial and shabby. A pair of old armchairs with sadly sagging springs lay abandoned on the porch, surrounded by a tribe of feral cats on the lookout for a meal.

'Now, leave it to me, girls,' instructed Colette, grabbing her briefcase determinedly and heading across the street. 'There is no point trying to frighten them with the long arm of the law. Someone, undoubtedly, was merely doing their job.' Which was always the answer with government departments; the buck was for passing on.

Paige, with admirable restraint, held back, though was set to put the frighteners on people should things not go according to plan. But Colette was accustomed to this sort of situation and greeted the buttoned-up woman who answered the door as though they had known each other for years. She briefly explained that they were here to visit Mr Kovac, and, when she had convinced her that Anna was really his daughter, the woman doubtfully made an internal call. After a brief discussion with whoever answered the phone, she indicated that they should follow her. It was obvious that Colette's air of calm authority, combined with the badge she flashed, had got them inside. This was a professional who knew what she was doing. Even Paige was impressed.

'Be careful what you say to him,' the woman warned as they trudged up the stairs. 'He is inclined at times to become confused and we don't want him getting upset.' She led them up a couple of flights that stank of urine and disinfectant, then punched out a code on an electronic door which opened to admit them. 'Security,' she explained to Anna, seeing the expression on her face. 'To stop them wandering off. At this stage in their lives, I'm afraid, we have to accept that they are little more than helpless children.' It was not an image that fitted Anna's father but now was not the time for any dissent. They had found him, that was the only thing that mattered, and soon, with luck, she would be taking him home.

The corridor was narrow and harshly lit. Identical doors bore cards with handwritten names; right at the end was one that read 'G. Kovac'. A nurse in a white overall ushered them in and stood, alertly attendant, at the door. And there he was, in a tiny cramped room, in a chair jammed between the washbasin and bed, wearing striped pyjamas that Anna had never seen and an institutional-looking navy blue robe.

'Dad,' cried Anna, rushing to hug him, appalled when he instinctively recoiled. His hair needed trimming and his fingernails were dirty. He looked like a refugee. He was obviously bewildered and not at all sure where he was. When Anna gently questioned him, all he knew was that some woman from social services had turned up on his doorstep one day. She had flashed some sort of identification, then insisted on being admitted and, after a cursory inspection, had declared the house structurally unsafe. Unless he vacated it instantly, she told him, she could not be held responsible for his safety. At any moment, the roof might well cave in; it was as crucial as that. She would make arrangements to move him, she had said, to temporary accommodation that was safe. Paige flashed Anna a complicit glance. It was becoming clear how the scam had been effected. Of course he had signed the papers on the spot – the woman had insisted – and since his only kin, his daughter, was currently travelling abroad, he had docilely gone along with what she wanted. Anything for a quiet life. Which, Anna had to admit, was George to a T. He had never had any interest in possessions.

Eventually things were sorted out and the matron agreed, reluctantly, to let him go. Whatever it was that had happened had not been her fault. There had been some sort of a misunderstanding; Anna was willing to leave it at that. Colette, who obviously knew her stuff, produced the necessary paperwork and soon they were able to pack his things and leave. While Anna was helping him into his clothes, Paige produced her business card and took the matron aside. How, she wanted to know, had this situation come about? Who, exactly, had brought him in and what had been her story? Seeing that Paige was not out for an instant conviction, the woman cast her mind back.

'She said she was a lawyer, acting for the family who were abroad. He was growing forgetful, they were worried about him. It was supposed to be just an interim stay until they could make a permanent arrangement.'

'And who was to be responsible for his bills?' demanded Paige. It could not be cheap to keep him here, no matter how down-at-heel it might appear.

'Standing order with the bank,' said the woman. 'It had all been set up by proxy. There was a family trust that would soon take over, or that's what this lawyer said.'

Paige and Anna exchanged a swift glance. Gradually the pieces were slotting in.

'I don't suppose she left her card?' The matron shook her

head. 'She said she'd be back in a couple of days. We never saw her again.'

'Can you remember what she looked like?' Paige was almost panting with excitement.

'Slim and dark and stylishly dressed. I remember thinking how young she was to have such a responsible job.'

'Let's get out of here,' said Anna, guiding her father to the stairs. She wished she had somewhere to take him back to other than her dismal hotel.

'Don't even give it a thought,' said Colette. 'He is coming home with me.' The least she could do for Anna, after such a treacherous breach of faith, was provide the poor man with a comfortable haven until they could sort something out. And, with luck, repossess his house. Paige was already on to that.

With her father now safe and being properly cared for, Anna at last got round to making that call. She found Genevieve and Candy on the verge of not getting on, bored and starting to be edgy with each other, suffering from incipient cabin fever. The barn of a house was all very well but unnerving now with just the two of them in it. Neither had ever quite adjusted to the night sounds of nature in the raw and it didn't help that their rooms were so far apart.

'Don't you sometimes miss Oxford Street?' Candy had asked Genevieve wistfully. Genevieve nodded. There were occasions when she could have killed for a burger or an afternoon at the sales. Even, perhaps, some bracing London rain, though she hardly dared admit it, it seemed so ungrateful.

'Hi!' said Candy, relieved to hear Anna's voice. It was after ten and they were thinking of turning in. Genevieve was still lingering on the terrace, sipping wine by starlight and watching the fireflies. The pungent aroma of genista hung heavily on the night air and there seemed to have been an invasion of crickets, sawing away in the trees.

They had at last succeeded in ridding themselves of Hector, who had flounced off to Florence in a huff. When Anna asked the reason for his departure, all Candy could do was giggle. She checked that Genevieve was safely out of earshot, then carried the phone into the kitchen and closed the door.

'He made a pass at me,' she hissed, 'and didn't like it at all when I batted him off.' Hector, who saw himself as a dashing Lothario, was unaccustomed to rejection. His standing as an opera critic gave him a puffed-up self-importance that didn't sit well with his squat, ugly body or his almost fifty years. He was used to women flattering him and listening with respect to his pronouncements. When Candy simply crumpled up with mirth, his pride, not to mention his ego, had been hurt. So, aware that Genevieve was no longer under his thumb, he had saved whatever face he had left and departed.

'Good riddance!' Candy had said, as his taxi drove away. 'Do you think you'll continue to see him back in London?' Despite her amusement, she had loyally not said a word. If Genevieve wanted to abase herself, it really wasn't any of Candy's business.

'I hardly think so,' Genevieve had replied, pulling a face. 'Somehow, I can't think why, he has lost his allure.' It was her turn to laugh now, at the thought of his pomposity, though that was not the main reason for her decision. Secretly, all she could think of these days was the handsome, hunky Raffaele whose smouldering eyes and curly black hair had the power to make her breathless. They were more or less sure now that he was unattached but having Hector in constant attendance certainly hadn't helped. She looked forward to being able to eat at the trattoria again.

Now she poked her nose round the door to find out what was going on.

'It's Anna,' said Candy, passing her the phone and automatically reaching for the grappa. These days, any excuse would do. It was certainly high time that Anna returned.

'What's up?' asked Genevieve, glad to hear Anna's voice. They needed her back to organise things and help keep them both on the level. Since she had been gone the days had seemed to drag and neither one was working as hard as they should. Even the absence of Hector had simply served to diminish their fun. Without his comical presence to deride, much of their childish humour just fell flat.

'Too much to tell you now,' said Anna, 'but I need you to do some urgent detective work.' It was vital, she told them, that they found out all they could about their mysterious and very much absent host. 'Dig up everything you can,' she said, 'no matter how trivial it might seem. Talk to Maria and Simonetta; someone has to know where the bodies are buried. I need to get all the dirt I can before he does any more damage. Bribe or batter, whatever it takes, just so long as you winkle out the truth. This man, I am certain, is a dangerous criminal whose activities have to be stopped and the only weapon we have, so far, is his house.' Which ought to be sufficient to barter but hers was worth a lot more. She asked them to force their way into his locked quarters and sift through his possessions. And, while they were at it, look out for his computer. She would fight him with his own weapons if she could.

'Surely he'll have it with him,' said Genevieve, who was rarely parted from hers.

'Maybe,' said Anna, 'but it's still worth a shot.' Anyone who could so effectively pillage her system had to be some sort of technological wizard. Her mind went back to Raffaele's friend, the arrogant stranger with the coolly mocking eyes, who had asked so many questions then walked away. She was now convinced they were all in it together, probably part of organised crime, even, maybe, an offshoot of the mafia. She had never entirely trusted Raffaele despite Genevieve's growing adoration. He was too effusive, too anxious to please; altogether too nice. Though she had noticed the steely glint in his eye, which was how her suspicions had been raised. Someone in New York, it seemed, had murdered Larry in cold blood. Although it was not yet proven, it did seem likely. And until the police came up with something definite, all of them had to watch their backs.

'One more thing,' she said, before finally ringing off. 'Find out all you can about Sutherland's wife.'

16

Paige and Charles Collier were sitting at dinner in a neighbourhood restaurant on the Upper West Side, around the
corner from their spacious eighth-floor apartment. Paige, these
days, seldom ever cooked; it was one of those mundane things
she had given up. Time spent together had lately become so
rare, they relished these evenings alone, just the two of them.
Charles, a banker, had been following Anna's plight with very
nearly as much interest as his wife.

'Tell me,' she asked him now as she picked at her salad, 'what
in particular would motivate anyone to act quite as ruthlessly
as that?'

'Greed,' replied Charles promptly, not even having to think
since he'd witnessed so much in the course of his business life.
'You wouldn't believe what people will do for money.' Especially
now with the stock market so insecure. Financial disasters were
thick in the news. Hardly a day went by without some new
corporate skulduggery being uncovered.

'But why would he take it all?' she said. 'The house, her assets, even the family home? It does seem rather excessive to leave her with nothing.' Beneath the steel veneer, Paige was softer than she liked to pretend and resolutely believed in fair play.

'Precisely because he could,' replied Charles. 'No point in leaving anything behind. This particular perpetrator knew exactly what he was up to. A professional conman, would be my guess, who has undoubtedly done it before.'

Paige ate in silence as she pondered this point, then wondered aloud how Anna had been selected. Could she have just been a random choice or was she specifically targeted?

'Think about it, it can only have been random. He couldn't have known she would even see the ad.'

'He must have had loads of other replies,' said Paige. 'It sounded unbelievably enticing. So why pick Anna out of all the rest? Simply her rotten luck, do you suppose?'

'Newly renovated townhouse in a highly desirable neighbourhood. Plus he will have found out that she lives alone.' They had, after all, exchanged emails about the swap. And Anna had foolishly trusted him because of Yale.

'And,' added Paige, 'she is now becoming quite famous. Is it possible he could have heard about the movie deal?'

Charles shrugged; in these areas anything was possible. 'Richer pickings is what you are suggesting. With a scam like this, nothing would surprise me.' The rogue was sounding more unscrupulous by the second; the measure of what poor Anna was up against. Wall Street was in turmoil, the Enron scandal on every front page. It was almost safer to keep money under the mattress than risk one's hard-earned savings in the markets. Anna had been well advised to put hers into property, though no-one could have imagined that this would happen.

Paige shuddered, unusually fastidious for her. 'He has to be stopped before he does any more harm. Where do you suppose he has stashed the money and how come he got away with it?' She was still frustrated that she hadn't tracked him down and that the bank was continuing to block her.

'Offshore account most probably,' said Charles. 'Somewhere safe where it can't be got at. As soon as he's bled her dry, he will disappear.' Which rather seemed to have happened already; to date there had not been a single sighting.

'We can't allow that,' said Paige with determination. If only the damned police would get up off their butts. 'But if he's disappeared,' she suddenly added, 'how is he going to handle the sale of the house? Putting it on the market is one thing; all he needed was proof of residence plus a great deal of gall.' And a shady realtor without too many scruples who could not be bothered to check on his true credentials. 'But what will happen if a deal goes through and money has to change hands?'

'That will be the crunch point,' said Charles. 'It will be interesting to see what happens then.'

'It does seem possible,' said Paige a little later, 'that he may never actually have been around at all. Nobody seems to have seen him or even heard his voice. What precisely do we know about him? Zilch. Except that he's a photographer, constantly on the move.' Which, now she came to think of it, could well be no more than a cover.

'Except that,' Charles reminded her, 'he's a former classmate of Cousin Wilbur. Who seemed to think the sun shone out of his ass.' It might be worth another word with Wilbur, in case he had anything to add.

'What would be his purpose, I wonder, in wanting a foothold in New York? It wouldn't appear to fit in with his way of life.'

'Money,' said Charles. 'Look at the real estate values. Apart from California, the highest in the country.' And, in these uncertain days of a totally bearish market, investors who had been heavily scorched were putting their savings elsewhere. Property was the investment of choice; not a lot could happen to bricks and mortar though even that, since 9/11, was not as safe a bet as had always been thought.

'So, assuming he was in it for what he could steal, how come he ran the risk of losing his own home? What's to stop Anna simply confiscating it? I can't see he'd have any comeback under the law.'

Paige paused while the waiter delivered their main courses, rare steak for Charles, a filleted plaice for her. She leaned across and filched one of his French fries; slim though she was, she remained a covert trencherman.

'Unless,' she said slowly, with a flash of sudden insight, 'the Tuscan villa isn't his at all.' Their eyes met as they absorbed this possibility. Slowly the disparate pieces were starting to fit. 'The only person that anyone has seen is the woman at Anna's house. Who Larry said had been looking after the cat.'

'And Anna now thinks might be Sutherland's wife.'

'Though that does seem a little too obvious.' If the police were less lethargic, they would be in there, rounding her up. Except that now she appeared to have vanished too. Whenever they passed, the house was bolted and barred, with never any sign of even a light.

If only poor Larry hadn't died. It was all so annoyingly frustrating. Paige longed to talk to Phoebe Atwood, though felt it still wasn't quite the time.

'What about Anna's cleaner?' she said suddenly. 'How come none of us thought of talking to her?'

*   *   *

Anna, of course, should have come up with that one herself. She had neither been sleeping nor keeping her eye on the ball. She cursed herself when she got Paige's phone call; Consuela had been with her eleven years and had come with her to the brownstone when she moved. Anna had paid her in advance for the full four months. She should be there, cleaning and keeping an eye on things, so where had she got to now? Finally galvanised into doing something constructive, Anna set off on the bus to East Harlem to track Consuela down. She located the house without any trouble, in a long narrow row with fire escapes at the front.

Consuela, when she opened the door and saw her, burst into tears of relief. 'Oh Miss Anna,' she cried, clutching her in her arms, 'I simply didn't know what I should do. The woman told me I was no longer required. I didn't know how to reach you.'

Anna hushed her and followed her inside where she was watching a TV gameshow with her grandchild. The little girl, with pink bows in her hair, placidly shifted to the far end of the sofa, leaving the women to talk.

'What can have happened to Sadie?' was Anna's first question, but Consuela just miserably shook her head. 'I don't know, Miss Anna, she seemed fine last time I saw her, stretched out nice and comfy on your bed.'

'And this woman, what was she like? Can you describe her?'

'Slim and dark. Polished manners and very good clothes. I think she was somebody's secretary, she had that air. Brisk and contemptuous, too grand for the likes of me. Could hardly be bothered to give me the time of day.'

'What was she doing in the house? Apart from feeding the cat? Did she appear to be living there? And keeping an eye on the builders?'

'I don't think so, Miss Anna, she didn't even take off her jacket. She was opening the mail and listening to messages, always in a hurry.'

'You don't think she could have been Sutherland's wife?' Now that Anna had got that idea, she was finding it hard to dislodge. It would help to account for all sorts of weird things, them working together as a pair.

Consuela considered. 'I really don't think so. Though I can't exactly say why. She didn't seem interested in the house, was merely doing her job. And she hardly took notice of the cat at all, which surprised me.' Sadie was one of the friendliest creatures. A person would need a heart of stone not to pet her.

'And you didn't get her name?'

Again Consuela shook her head. 'I found it very hard to understand her.'

'Look,' said Anna kindly, after some thought. 'I want you to know, the job is still yours. Whoever she was, she had no right to dismiss you. The problem is, I no longer have a house or anything else for you to clean. You should still have some money in hand. If not, I will let you have more.' She promised to stay closely in touch and let Consuela know as soon as the problem was fixed.

On the doorstep they hugged again and, when Anna was gone, Consuela privately called on Our Lady, beseeching her to find the missing cat.

Paige was interested to hear about Consuela, so far their one and only possible lead. She was still hesitant about intruding on Phoebe but at last legal inquisitiveness overcame her finer feelings. It was several weeks now since Larry's death and still the cops hadn't bothered to be in touch. Time to put a bomb up their backsides, starting with checking with the widow. Paige dropped by on the pretext of a sympathy call but Phoebe was unable to add to the little she had already told Anna. There had been an accident, he must somehow have lost his balance. The police appeared to have gone cold on the case.

On an impulse, Paige drove down to Baltimore to talk to Cousin Wilbur. He was gardening when she got there, late afternoon, portly and flushed, with a baseball cap on his head.

'Paige!' he said, embracing her heartily. 'What a wonderful surprise.' She had called from her cellphone to say she'd be passing through. Her legal brain was too cautious to let it seem urgent; until she knew what she was dealing with here, she was playing her cards very close. They walked, arms linked, across the immaculate lawn and he mixed them each a cocktail in the conservatory. Orchids and geraniums surrounded them in pots. The heady, earthy smell was quite exotic.

'Not too strong for me,' warned Paige. She did not want to risk getting booked; potentially disastrous for her career. She also needed to keep a clear head. Wilbur might be kin to her but she had not yet ascertained where his loyalties lay.

'So what brings you to this neck of the woods?' He lowered himself into a basket chair which creaked in protest at his weight. Gone was the one-time athletic jock; he was little more now than just a complacent attorney. Family money had provided this pile; all his children had been at private schools. Nancy, he explained, was off at a charity fundraiser. He seemed to be very content with his lot and none too curious about Paige. Which was just as well.

After a spot of idle chat, catching him up on the news, Paige steeled herself to cut to the chase without giving too much away. This could turn out to be the breakthrough she'd been seeking, but lawyerly caution held her back. Even within the family, she would not risk showing her cards, not to a one-time crony of Sutherland's without first discovering whether the two were still close.

'Tell me,' she said, after a suitable interval, aware that she should soon be taking her leave. The traffic at this time of night would be heavy. She didn't want to risk alarming Charles. 'Some time ago you mentioned Dan Sutherland. I think you knew him at Yale.'

'Sure,' said Wilbur, freshening his drink. 'A great guy, Dan. I've forgotten how you know him. It is years now since the two of us last met up.'

'Oh, he's just a friend of a friend,' said Paige vaguely. 'I was wondering if you knew where he might be now.'

'I do know he's almost always on the trot. Fellow always did have vagabond shoes. I admire that sort of inexhaustible energy, just thinking about it these days makes me feel tired. Very bright indeed, is Dan, with a sharp, original mind. Might have turned his hand to practically anything.'

'Instead of which he settled for taking snaps.' Paige could not keep the irony out of her voice. To her mind, photography wasn't a manly job but then, perhaps, she was thinking of Cecil Beaton.

'Only on a very superior level. He's won a lot of international prizes and has lately become something of a media star.' It could just be fraternity solidarity but Paige had rarely heard such praise from her ultra-conservative cousin. Interesting.

'And you've no idea where he might be now?' Her patience was starting to wear thin. What a silly old buffer he had become, with his amateur potting and over-noxious cocktails. And yet he was only a few years her senior, barely middle-aged.

Wilbur sat and scratched his head, oblivious of Paige's irritation. 'You could try *National Geographic*,' he suggested. 'Or some of the other big glossies. If they have him on assignment, which one or other of them is almost bound to, they ought to be able to tell you where he is.'

'One last thing,' said Paige, preparing to leave. 'Do you happen to know if he is married?'

Wilbur looked startled. 'Not that I'm aware of and it's the sort of thing that the alumni mag would certainly have picked up. Mind you,' he added, 'it's been years since I saw him. Who knows what the fellow's been up to in that time. I would just be very surprised if he'd got himself hitched. Dan always was pretty much of a loner. I doubt if anything's changed.'

Paige kissed him and muttered her thanks and apologies but said she really must be off. Sent her love to Nancy and the kids and hoped they could all meet up before too long. Wilbur walked her to her car and watched as she buckled up.

'My regards to Charles,' he said. 'Oh, and Dan Sutherland too, when you finally catch up with him.'

It took her less than a morning to track him down. Wilbur was right; he was with *Geographic*. Currently on assignment in Patagonia, where he'd been for more than a year.

'You mean he hasn't been working in New York?'

'No, ma'am,' said an obliging young woman. 'Not as far as I know.'

'And do you have a contact number?'

'Not one I can give out. When he needs us, he calls. It's as simple as that. Dan is very much his own boss.' Plus, of course, there was email but that often did not work, not when he was in transit through the rainforests. There were months on end when he was out of touch altogether, some of the areas he worked in were that remote.

'I can always take a message and pass it on.' The girl seemed genuinely keen to be of help.

Paige thought fast then told her it wasn't necessary. The truth was, she wouldn't know what to say to him even if she could. It seemed she was back at square one again except now she knew for certain he wasn't around. Nor, apparently, had he been all year, not since before the exchange of houses, which really didn't make sense. She wanted to bang her head on her desk. She felt as though she were trying to wade through mud.

17

'His wife!' echoed Candy, after Anna had rung off. 'Where did she get the idea that he's even got one? And how come she found that out in New York? I thought all the action was supposed to be happening here.'

'Dunno,' said Genevieve, equally in the dark. 'I suppose there's always a chance that she's tracked him down. In which case she's a meanie not to have let us know instead of just giving instructions for breaking and entering.'

'I think that right now she's got other things on her mind. She did sound awfully rattled.' Anna had filled them in quickly about her father but was in too much of a rush to talk very long. Things appeared to be hotting up on her side of the Atlantic. They would do whatever they could to help her out. Besides, since Hector left, they had time on their hands. First they had to interrogate Maria, who came in every Tuesday to supervise the housekeeping. It would not be easy since her English was so poor and, whenever they asked too many questions, a veil dropped over her eyes. But they would persist and try to charm her. And also chat up Simonetta, who seemed to know most of the village gossip and had once worked as an au pair in Enfield, of all places, the reason her English was so good.

When Anna called a couple of days later, she found both Candy and Genevieve in a state of giddy excitement. They had taken to amateur sleuthing like true pros, any slight tensions that might have built up having dissipated with the fun of this new game. Each clamoured to talk to Anna first; Candy, being quicker, grabbed the phone. Maria had dismally failed to come through, pleading the Fifth Amendment, *'non capito'*, but Candy had finally, after many patient hours, succeeded in picking the lock to Sutherland's rooms.

'Dressmaking scissors make an excellent burglar's aid,' she gleefully reported, 'though you do need a steady hand.' Luckily by now the grappa was finished and they were leading a slightly more sober life.

'So what did you find?' They had Anna on tenterhooks. This could be the crucial breakthrough she was after.

'We haven't dared go in there yet,' said Candy, lowering her voice. 'Didn't want Maria sussing what we were up to.' Maria was still in the kitchen, cleaning the stove, but soon, with luck, would be off to the market to shop.

'Be careful,' warned Anna, though she wasn't quite certain of what. Just longed to know what they'd find behind those locked doors. Progress at last and not before it was due; perhaps they would crack the mystery now in one throw.

'Don't worry,' said Candy. 'We'll ring you as soon as we can. Bye, Maria,' she called out loudly and stood with Genevieve, watching her walk away.

They left it a good five minutes, just in case, then cautiously twisted the heavy wrought-iron door handle.

'Bluebeard's cave,' hissed Candy, still in a whisper. 'Maybe we'll find what's left of his other victims.'

Another vast corporate scandal had broken, close on the heels of Enron. The news, as well as the financial pages, was covering it in minute detail. Two top executives of a telecommunications giant had surrendered voluntarily to the FBI and were photographed throughout the media being led away publicly in handcuffs. Later both were released on personal bonds, respectively of two and ten million dollars. The Bush administration was doing its stuff by trying, as publicly as it could, to stamp out corporate crime.

'What exactly is this all about?' asked Paige. Finance was Charles's department. Although she kept her eye on the headlines and knew just how shaky the stock market was, she was far too engrossed in her own massive overload to have followed it in any special detail. That, as she was fond of telling their friends, was her reason for marrying Charles.

Charles accepted another cup of coffee and glanced up from the newspaper he was reading. It was a quarter past seven and they were having breakfast. Both would be in their offices by eight-thirty.

'It is part of a series of law enforcements aimed at prosecuting corporate lawbreakers and protecting the savings and pensions of Joe Public.' Seeing the cynicism on Paige's face, he grinned. Neither one of them, by any stretch of the imagination, could be described as Republican.

'But what is it really about?' persisted Paige, suddenly tuning in. All these weeks she had been brooding on Anna's misfortunes and now it would appear to be happening to other people as well.

'It is nothing especially new,' explained Charles, 'but the chaos wrought by what happened in September hasn't exactly helped.' So many small businesses had been totally decimated, their records completely destroyed. It was a bit like London after the Blitz only this had all occurred in just fifteen minutes. Apart from the on-the-spot looting in the streets, it gave leeway for other, far more serious crimes. All sorts of charlatans had been taking reckless chances. The Security and Exchange Commission was working overtime.

'These guys,' said Charles, indicating the headlines, 'are not necessarily corrupt but victims of a tightening administration. It is more to do with politics than fraud. A sign of the current vulnerability of the White House.' A reflection, maybe, on the President.

What they had done, he tried to explain as concisely as he could with one eye on the clock, was create hundreds of 'special purpose entities' designed to raise debt through an outside company and keep it off the books, while also not losing control of the assets. They hired a bunch of so-called banking experts and gave them the chance of investing in these assets, fobbing it off as 'partnerships' to the big guys. That way they could conceal liabilities and, in some cases, create paper gains. And the banking experts were set to clean up, provided they had nerves of steel. That, in a nutshell was it, said Charles.

'Some of them are just kids,' he added. 'Late twenties to early thirties, often chancing their arm just for the hell of it. With impeccable pedigrees and expensive educations, cashing in on their fancy WASP connections. Investment advisors, they call themselves, and basically what they do is this. They build up a client base for whom they invest money – often, in order to appear more authentic, adding a percentage of their own. Then, after a suitable interval, they siphon off most of the funds to a personal account and stash it somewhere safe where it can't be touched. It is, pure and simple, white-collar crime and they richly deserve to get caught. Fastow, for instance, who allegedly screwed up Enron, faces up to a hundred and forty years in jail. Hence the current involvement of the SEC. Situations like this are popping up like mushrooms. Everyone seems to be in on it right now.'

'Well, I suppose it is preferable to bombing Iraq.' All these issues were very much in the news. Paige, not normally sentimental, silently blessed her stars for Charles as well as her rock-solid marriage. But, concurrently, her mind was embarking on an intriguing new avenue of possibility. It came to her like a nuclear blast and left her with a rapidly heightened pulse rate. Suppose there was something that you badly needed to hide, what better way could you possibly choose than simply to disappear? In the devastation of the terrorist attacks, thousands of innocent people had vaporised. It had made a huge tragedy still more insupportable for the relatives who felt that they could not yet grieve. It could be months, if not years, before things were finally sorted and even then a lot would be based on guesswork. The ideal cover, she suddenly perceived, for concealing all manner of crimes.

'Don't you know someone in the SEC?' she asked casually as she stacked the dishwasher.

'Yes, Dave Kelly. But what's that to do with this?'

'And what precisely does it do? The SEC, I mean.'

'In a nutshell?' He laughed; this looked like turning into a full-blown seminar. She was going to make him late if he wasn't careful. 'The Securities and Exchange Commission is an agency of the federal government, charged with keeping an eye on the securities business. It sets the rules for the brokerage firms and investigates any violations. Anything else you need to know now that won't keep until tonight?' He glanced up at her with narrowing eyes. 'What is your devious little mind up to now?' And saw from her bland smile that she wasn't telling.

'Just a hunch,' was all she would say. 'I promise I'll fill you in once I've figured it out.'

'You always were a Miss Marple manquée. You picked the wrong profession.'

The huge oak doors swung silently inwards and Candy and Genevieve stepped cautiously inside. Sutherland's quarters were dignified and sparse, with long shuttered windows leading out on to the terrace. The light filtering through the closed slats was dim but they dared not run the risk of opening them for fear of attracting attention from outside. No matter what Sutherland might have done, his private rooms were supposed to be off limits; Raffaele had made that abundantly clear and they did not want to risk his disapproval. The suite comprised a vast, high-ceilinged room, with two smaller ones leading off it. It was more spacious than an average townhouse, demonstrating how huge the villa actually was. Ancient frescoes in faded terracotta were still faintly visible in the plaster. One entire wall had been fitted with shelves, crammed to overflowing with learned-looking books. And opposite the windows hung an imposing portrait in oils, of a dark jowly man in uniform and medals, which dominated the room.

'Crikey,' said Candy, peering up at it in alarm. 'I wonder who this old geezer is? He looks like a general, Mussolini perhaps. I don't think I'd care to have him on my case. Certainly not watching me all the time.'

Genevieve, too, felt discomfited by the portrait's staring eyes, as if its subject knew they ought not to be there. She looked around for possible clues that might be of use to Anna, but couldn't see anything remotely intimate that could give them any sort of insight into the man. The suite looked as if it had been closed up for years, and was pervaded by a smell of ancient mustiness. In the corner, close to the terrace doors, was a vast mahogany desk, with a light box on it and stacks of shiny photo boxes. Next to it stood an antique plans chest which proved to hold negatives and prints; drawers and drawers of folders of them, all neatly labelled and dated. And above them, on the wall, a framed certificate – *Wildlife Photographer of the Year. D. A. Sutherland. 1998.* But no sign at all of anything private, nothing that Sutherland would not want a stranger to see. No trace, either, of any computer, nor even a telephone port. Even the old-fashioned telephone extension turned out not to be connected.

'That's really weird,' said Genevieve, 'considering this is his home. Not to have a computer modem nor anywhere obvious to plug one in. For someone who endlessly travels the world, it does seem oddly archaic.'

'Especially since his exchange with Anna was done entirely by email.'

Genevieve crossed to the bedroom doorway, where she saw filmy white mosquito netting looped above the bed. Again, that lingering aroma of decay, though everything had been meticulously dusted and polished. Maria had obviously done a stalwart job, keeping it all in immaculate order, though it must be a thankless task if the owner was so seldom here. Talk about loyal servitude: she was clearly one in a million. Which made it seem unlikely that she did not know more than she said. How to subvert that loyalty was the problem.

Genevieve opened the vast carved wardrobe, half-expecting a body to fall out. But all she found was a faded bathrobe that looked as though it hadn't been worn in years. Candy was rifling through the chest of drawers, which contained nothing more interesting than old sweaters and socks, with a gentle sprinkling of mouse droppings. No giveaway clues of any kind here, nothing to tell them more about the man. No framed photos nor personal knick-knacks; not a single thing to indicate that he was even coming back.

The bathroom was cavernous with a great claw-footed tub and black and white marbled tiles upon the floor. The old-fashioned lavatory tank dripped away relentlessly, causing a lengthy rust mark down the wall. There wasn't so much as a toothbrush on display, nor even a bar of soap.

'Surely he can't have taken everything to New York?' The less they found, the weirder it became.

'Unless, of course, he was planning not to return. A one-way ticket to the promised land to take up permanent residence in Anna's house.'

'And then sell it on?'

'At a mammoth profit before disappearing back to the jungle again.'

'But who would ever abandon a villa like this?'

'It's like the *Marie Celeste*,' said Candy, still whispering. 'Come on, let's get out of here. It's starting to give me the creeps.'

Anna was disappointed when they told her they had found virtually nothing. 'There must be something you overlooked. Everyone, surely, leaves some sort of a trail.' She seemed to be running around in circles, like a hamster in a wheel, while all the while that man remained dangerously at large, doing who knew what more damage without restraint. The world was falling fast into anarchy. She read it in the papers every day.

'You could try looking at his photographs,' she said, though what use that would be she didn't know. Any clue to the secrets in his life might give her the ammunition she required.

'You haven't seen how many there are. Stacks and stacks of boxes, going back years.'

'Full of rainforests and conservation areas.' At least, if what Paige's cousin had said was true.

'We still haven't spoken to Raffaele,' said Genevieve hopefully, willing Anna to give them the nod to proceed. Because of Hector, it was ages since they'd seen him and she was starting to suffer keen withdrawal pains. She yearned for his warm, admiring smile and the glint of libido in his eye. He was like a breath of Italian spring after an icy London winter. He, more than anyone, made her feel truly sexy, something she had been starved of for far too long. Anna hesitated then told her to go ahead. At this stage, she really had no other choice, yet still felt in her gut that they shouldn't trust him. But, face it, she had reached the bottom of the barrel. Almost anything now was worth a shot.

'Be careful,' she warned, 'and don't let him know too much.' They must not risk playing into the hands of the enemy.

'You'd not believe some of the stuff that is emerging,' said the SEC man, Dave Kelly. His shirt was wrinkled, his hair unkempt, he had not slept properly in weeks. In the aftermath of September 11th, the country's financial systems were all up the spout. The strain he was under was clearly visible and there was the glint of fanaticism in his eye. He was seeing her purely as a favour to Charles and Paige was suitably grateful. She had dressed with even more than her usual care, in a teal blue suit that had cost a small fortune, and her silver-blonde hair was drawn tightly back into a knot. The epitome of the no-nonsense lawyer, she was endeavouring to conceal her mounting excitement. After all these weeks spent chasing her tail, the gleam of a possible breakthrough was finally dawning. It was something that Charles had inadvertently said. About how to conceal illicit earnings.

'Things are coming to light that were hitherto unsuspected.' Dave Kelly ran his hands through his hair, the fever in his eyes as manic as hers. 'The general mayhem has provided cover for more than one case of quite unbelievable fraud. Even the FBI are now involved, though I beg you, please, not to breathe a word. Soon there may well be a major announcement. Heads in positions of power are likely to roll. The government is heavily implicated. You would not believe the half of it,' he said.

Paige's well-tuned antennae pricked up. 'You mean even bigger than Enron?' she said. 'Surely not.'

Dave Kelly looked at her and blinked and she knew she had got it in one. The whole world now knew the extent of the Enron collapse and that the SEC had filed a civil lawsuit against the Chief Finance Officer, seeking damages for defrauding Enron investors.

'Things,' she added carefully, intensifying the charm, 'unconnected with the terrorist attacks?'

Now he nodded, quite unsuspecting. Paige was the sort of lady he rarely encountered. Her beauty and razor-sharp intellect stunned him. He could not see what danger he was in.

'Criminal things that might have surfaced months ago, had not many of the records been destroyed. How we are going to sort it all out, I really cannot imagine. All we've uncovered so far is the tip of the iceberg. At least, that is how it appears as things stand now.' Again his hands went clawing through his hair and she noticed that his fingernails were chewed. This man was hurtling towards the end of his rope; it could surely only be a matter of time. She could not afford to let that happen, not before she had milked him for all he was worth. Paige thought fast and took a gamble, which was part of her stock in trade.

'Tell me something,' she asked him. 'If you had just succeeded in stealing huge amounts of cash, where do you suppose you would put it in order to be safe?'

He looked at her long and hard without replying. He might be fraught and on the edge of infatuation but he certainly wasn't a fool.

'I don't suppose,' she added carefully, 'that you'd let me look at your records.' Nothing ventured, nothing gained and, in the end, she invariably got what she was after.

He stared at her, profoundly shocked, snapped back to reality by her outrageous request. 'You know I can't do that,' he virtually spluttered. 'I'd be out on my ear in record time. Our work in this department is subject to Grade-A security. At the very least, I'd be facing criminal charges.'

Paige fluttered her lashes and switched on her little-girl charm; the things she would occasionally stoop to all in the name of duty. 'I can see you are busy,' she said sympathetically, 'so I'll be off. Thanks again. You really have been a great help.' You don't know how much.

'I wonder,' she added, as he walked her to the elevator, 'if we could meet again sometime, perhaps when you're not quite so pressured?' Her clear blue eyes were entirely without guile and he was suddenly acutely conscious of her perfume. One second was all it took and she had him hooked.

Even despite the accolades, they were unprepared for the quality of the pictures. The sky, for once, was overcast and it was still too early for supper, so they had crept back into Sutherland's rooms and obediently went to work on the plans chest.

Genevieve felt distinctly uncomfortable at Candy having forced the lock, even though it had been done with her total collusion. She was nervous that Maria might suddenly return and report their bad behaviour to Raffaele. 'No time like the present,' she said. Once they had completed their task, she knew she would find it easier to sleep.

They decided to leave the negatives alone, despite the convenient presence of the light box. This was photography of the very highest order; they must not risk doing any damage. Instead they each grabbed a handful of yellow folders and spread the glossy prints across the desk. And what prints they were; they were both astounded. No wonder he had won all those awards. Rare animals, exotic birds, waterfalls and mountains. A whole lost world captured in exquisite detail, a permanent record of things fast becoming extinct. The debate about photography not being art was in this case demonstrably groundless.

'What are we actually looking for?' asked Candy, after a while. She could have spent hours slowly sifting through the prints, so impressed was she by their excellence. This man, Sutherland, whatever his moral character, was possessed indisputably of a truly staggering talent. With work of this calibre, what reason could he have to steal? Still things failed to add up.

'Don't really know,' said Genevieve, equally affected, hating to have to tear herself away. 'Anything, I suppose, germane to the question of why he might have treated Anna in this way. Though I cannot see where conservation fits in, particularly since it means travelling most of the time.'

'He must be incredibly brave,' said Candy. 'It has to be dangerous work.' No lounging around in a cushy studio, posturing and chatting up models. He was out there in uncharted territory, possibly risking his life.

'Look at this crocodile!' Genevieve was appalled. With its scheming eyes and malevolent grin it looked close enough to the camera to swallow it whole. You could see every wrinkle of its leathery hide and the way its tail was thrashing about in the water.

'All he needed was one false step . . .' said Candy with ghoulish relish.

Genevieve shuddered. She was not an outdoors person. Though was mesmerised by the brilliance of it all.

They went on looking, but failed to unearth anything they could reasonably call a lead. It was getting late and Genevieve was hungry and wanted to tart herself up before going out.

'Time to stop,' she said, shifting the folders of slippery prints, succeeding only in knocking them all over the floor.

'Shit!' said Candy, on her hands and knees. 'Now he is going to know we've been in here snooping.' She tried to slide them back into their files and make some semblance of order. With luck, he wouldn't notice that they were no longer in strict date order, although he was clearly such a pro, that didn't seem very likely.

'Don't worry, by the time he finds out we three will be long gone.' Genevieve's eye was caught by the corner of an envelope jutting out from beneath the desk. It must have dropped from one of the folders. She bent to retrieve it and, as she picked it up, out dropped a handful of black and white prints, stylish and very atmospheric. Their subject was a striking young woman, glancing up from repotting geraniums as if caught unawares. It was a memorable face with bold dark eyes and heavily accented brows. Her thick, lustrous hair was artfully tangled and piled loosely on top of her head. It was difficult to tell, from the deliberately grainy texture, precisely when the pictures had been taken.

Genevieve caught her breath in triumph. 'She looks a bit like Elizabeth Taylor. I think we may have found her,' she said.

217

18

'Goodness,' said Simonetta when she saw the photographs. 'Where on earth did you get hold of these?' She carefully wiped her hands on her apron to take a closer look. Candy and Genevieve were instantly embarrassed, not wanting to reveal what they had been up to. They had dropped in on their way to the trattoria because Candy was out of tissues. It was seven-thirty, the shop would soon be closing, but the usual coven of garrulous old ladies was in there, chattering away. They passed the pictures from one to the other, clucking and sorrowfully shaking their heads. One, the oldest, dressed in black from head to foot, solemnly made the sign of the cross.

'Who is she?' Genevieve asked nervously. There was a distinct chill feeling of everyone closing ranks. She regretted ever having brought the subject up. They had certainly not expected this sort of reaction. All eyes turned to Simonetta, the only one among them who spoke English. She just shrugged. Clearly something was bothering her, it was not at all like her to be so unforthcoming. But the heavy-lidded eyes were guarded; she failed to meet Genevieve's gaze.

'Raffaele is the one to tell you, if he feels that you should know. It is something he rarely talks about any more.' She took Candy's money and rang it up on the till, then returned to the conversation she had been having. In fast Italian that they could not remotely follow. It was clear they were being deliberately shut out.

'Go easy on him,' said Simonetta as they left. 'It is something he may still not be able to handle.'

'Well,' said Genevieve, the moment they were outside, 'I wonder what in the world *that* was all about.'

'Raffaele's dark secret, from the look of things. Maybe it explains his apparent single state. Some private sorrow from the past that no-one will discuss, though, obviously, no secret in the village.' The woman in the photographs had clearly been something special. Not quite a traditional beauty, better than that. A sharp intelligence combined with a siren's smile. There was something about her brilliantly lucid eyes that positively sucked you in.

Genevieve experienced a powerful shaft of jealousy. She was mad to have even dreamed that he might be unencumbered, not a man as attractive as that and certainly not at his age. Every bloke she ever encountered came with a load of emotional baggage and Raffaele was the best she had come across yet. She wondered when the photographs were taken. From the stylised black and white grainy texture, it was not at all easy to tell. This year, last year; even, perhaps, decades ago? The way the woman was dressed certainly offered no clues. She was wearing a low-cut peasant blouse, revealing more boob than was strictly necessary. Genevieve instinctively hated her. She was already wrecking her dream.

'Maybe she was his mother,' suggested Candy, aware of Genevieve's sudden shift of mood.

'Maybe,' said Genevieve miserably. She could not bear to think that Raffaele's heart might be taken, yet it was pretty silly ever to have assumed that not to be the case.

'Are you going to ask him?'

'I don't know. Let's wait and just play it by ear.'

Raffaele, when he saw them walk in, looked almost as though he were relieved. It had been so long since he had last seen them that he'd worried he might have scared them off, which was not what he was intended to do. *Keep them under close surveillance.* The instructions had been more than clear. These foreign women who had invaded the villa had not found Montisi accidentally but were part of a convoluted plot. Or so his associate believed. But looking at them now, as they fluttered in the doorway, it was hard to believe that they were not as straightforward as they seemed. The taller one, Genevieve, looked particularly sensational and familiar regret flooded Raffaele's chest that he'd been ordered to keep well away. She was wearing a diaphanous delphinium blue dress, made for her by Candy in just two sessions. Her legs were long and slender and tanned, her toenails expertly buffed. She had shed more pounds which suited her well. Raffaele, at heart, was a true romantic but his purpose now was to find out as much as he could. He hurried across the restaurant to greet them.

'*Signore!*' he breathed with his faintly unctuous charm, then led them both to their regular corner table. As he pulled out Genevieve's chair and helped her to settle, Candy could not suppress an involuntary twinge of discontent at being so blatantly ignored. Genevieve certainly deserved brownie points for having finally had the guts to get shot of Hector but all this overt attention from a man as fanciable as Raffaele was secretly starting to stick in her craw. Genevieve did look good in her new creation but Candy was prettier as well as ten years younger. *Hello!*

On this particular evening the restaurant was relatively quiet so Raffaele fetched a bottle of wine and joined them, uninvited, at the table. It was a golden opportunity and one that he must not miss. Without their more forceful American friend, he hoped to be able to elicit more information.

'And where have you been since I saw you last? Enjoying yourselves, I hope.'

Genevieve, remembering their recent spot of burglary, flushed in sudden confusion and dropped her fork. As Raffaele stooped to pick it up, Candy frowned and rapidly shook her head. *Don't go giving things away*, was her meaning. *You could hardly look more guilty if you tried.*

'Just lounging around the pool,' she said. 'It's a shame to waste a second of this glorious weather.' Despite Anna's warnings about too much sun, Candy had almost perfected a beautiful tan. Raffaele smiled politely in agreement but his eyes kept returning to Genevieve. *Oh well*, thought Candy, *I suppose I can't complain.* Romantic involvement was the very last thing she was after at the moment. Her mind returned to Trevor again but she tried to suppress the thought. If he really was set on stealing her kid, there were no lengths to which she wouldn't go to stop him.

'What do you ladies do when the sun goes down? Those nights that you don't come here?' He could not believe they were simply on vacation, not for as long as four months. Surely no women on their own who were not extremely rich could find the time for so much idleness. Raffaele was a man who had worked hard all his life and disapproved of others not doing the same. He had been told to monitor their comings and goings and find out who they had really come here to see.

'I'm a writer,' said Genevieve, who had told him before, 'and so is our other friend, Anna. Candy here is a brilliant fashion designer, putting together her new collection for a very prestigious London department store.' She beamed proudly at Candy who looked a touch embarrassed. Surely this lusty Italian male would not be interested in that. 'It may not appear so, but all three of us are working really hard.'

'So how did you first find *Casavecchia?*' That recurring question again.

'Anna saw an ad in a New York magazine. From someone keen to go there for four months. Mr Sutherland, in fact, as you already know. Are you saying you haven't checked it out with him?' It all seemed most confusing; nothing added up. And something in Raffaele's tone sounded almost accusing.

'And will there be anyone else joining you here?'

Genevieve shook her head. 'There's bags of room but that's the whole point. We all needed peace and quiet in order to work.'

'Hector was an aberration,' put in Candy, 'but I'm pleased to say that now we've got shot of him.'

Raffaele's stern expression eased and he grinned. He had made no bones about disliking the arrogant Scot, though courtesy had prevented him speaking his mind. Not his business who they hung out with, but he had always been convinced that Genevieve could do better. But right now his mind was on more serious things. He needed some information to make his report.

'Signora Anna,' he said. 'Where is she tonight?'

'New York,' said Genevieve, suddenly radiant, turned on by his physical presence. She sensed he liked her though was too shy to show it. She wondered what she could do to egg him on.

But Raffaele was not in the mood to flirt. A guarded look had entered his eyes. 'New York?' he repeated, apparently startled. 'Why, if I may ask, did she cut short her stay?'

'Trouble,' said Candy cautiously, shooting Genevieve a glance, wondering just how much it was wise to divulge. But Anna had asked them to find out all they could and now seemed an ideal opportunity for some delving.

'And will she be coming back soon?' he asked.

'We certainly hope so,' said Candy. 'We miss her a lot and are finding it very hard to cope without her.'

Raffaele, preoccupied, put down his glass untouched and disappeared precipitately into the kitchen. Startled by his unexplained mood swing, Genevieve and Candy quickly conferred.

'What do you think?'

'I really don't know.'

'Should we, do you suppose, risk raising the subject?'

'What's there to lose?' Anna had requested it. 'The worst he can do, I imagine, is throw us out.'

When Raffaele, after a lengthy absence, finally returned, Candy slapped the photographs on the table and boldly asked him to tell them who it was. Predictably, Raffaele's face turned a paler shade and, when he picked them up, his hand was trembling.

'Where did you get these?' he asked her sharply, all trace of his former benevolence totally gone.

'We found them in the villa,' said Genevieve, not wanting to go into detail. 'And wondered if she might be Sutherland's wife.'

223

'Wife? What wife?' His voice was suddenly hostile. 'Daniel has no wife. And neither have I.' He passed one hand quickly across his eyes, then handed back the photographs. 'Put them back where you found them,' he said, 'and leave the matter alone.'

Anna had an uncomfortable awareness of possibly being stalked. It was not in her nature to feel so jumpy but the horrendous happenings of the past few months had managed to undermine her in many ways. She spent her days quietly at Colette's, writing and keeping her father company. Since the disruption of his life, his teaching had gone by the board. She had written a personal note to each of his pupils, explaining that he was temporarily indisposed, though in her heart she had a sinking feeling that for George this could well be the end of the line. He seemed older, frailer and still very much confused. All he could tell her about his abduction was that some unknown woman from social services had whisked him away. Who she was, he had no idea; he could not begin to describe her. His feisty independence had gone. Which, on top of everything else, was another bleak burden for Anna.

Usually they ate early, as soon as Colette got home, then Anna returned to her lonely hotel room to try to get on with her writing. Work on the novel was only limping along since, these days, she found it so hard to concentrate, but her pressing September deadline loomed large and now she had to rely more than ever on the delivery payment that would be due. No more winging it and trusting to the bank's benevolence should she fail to come in on time. No matter what else might be on her mind, she could not now afford to slack off. Colette, true to form, had come through with flying colours, with all the warmth and moral support she had unfailingly given in the past. The rest of the inner circle were rallying too. They were deeply contrite that they had ever thought badly of Anna, were doing all in their power to help make amends. Whatever else might be wrong in her life, she now knew for certain she could rely upon her friends.

Though not, so it appeared, on the police, who continued not to return her calls. All she had in the world was on the line, yet still she could not get them to take her problems seriously. Their inept indifference was making her crazy. Luckily Paige was very much on the case. She was pursuing a whole new avenue of her own which, for the moment, she was not divulging to Anna. Too many of her leads had proved false. She did not want to risk disappointing her again.

So life for Anna had become very restricted and she longed to be back in Tuscany with the girls. The happy memories of those glorious carefree days had now receded as if they had never been. Only the knowledge that they were still there, actively searching, brought any kind of solace to Anna's soul. The last she had heard, they were planning to tackle Raffaele. She hoped that, between the pair of them, they would get him to spill the beans. She still believed he was guilty as hell, despite all that beguiling Italian charm. Where men were concerned, Anna remained hard-headed. It took more than a sunset and a pair of empathetic brown eyes to get beneath her skin.

She made a point, on her way home from Colette's, always to detour via 74th Street to check if anything had changed. The feeling of being followed continued but never, when she turned, was there anyone there. It was still the height of summer and the air was humid and stifling. The streets of Manhattan were dry and parched and the traffic fumes suffocating. The terrible devastation that had destroyed life as it had been was gradually mellowing into recent history. The fires of Ground Zero had long been extinguished and the city was emerging from its mourning. People were slowly beginning to come to terms though not, of course, to forget.

The house, whenever she passed it, looked empty and forlorn. It broke her heart to see it like that after all her ambitious plans. One evening she noticed that the board was down, which meant, she assumed, that they must now have a firm offer. But when she called the real estate office, again they refused to talk and were positively rude when she attempted to force the issue. They would not even listen to her story, virtually accusing her of being some sort of impostor. She had no rights; they knew nothing about her. It was not her name on the title deeds though they also refused to divulge whose it actually was. She handed the whole thing over to Paige who was working on serving a writ. Everything legal dragged on for so long; Anna felt herself on the edge of despair.

On this particular evening she was standing, as she so often did, across the street behind a tree, as furtive as if she had no right to be there. Twilight was gradually creeping in and she was feeling more than usually despondent. What, she wondered, was the point of working so hard, only to have everything snatched away? The lights were off, the windows shuttered, no flicker of life there at all. She wondered again what had happened to Sadie and intense emotion surged through her. In some ways, the loss of her pet was the worst thing of all. Apart from missing Sadie's intelligent company, she felt she had seriously let her down. And the thought of that beautiful pedigree cat loose on the New York streets was driving her crazy.

From deep in the shadows, she experienced again the feeling of being watched. She swung round quickly but the street was deserted; even the traffic had thinned out. She waited another forlorn few minutes, then wearily trudged on to her dreary hotel.

'Get a grip,' she ordered herself severely. The last thing she needed now was to start feeling spooked.

He called two days later, sounding somewhat apprehensive. Women like Paige were way out of his league but he had been unable to dislodge her from his mind.

'I know it's short notice but is there any chance you could manage that lunch today? Only there's something in my office you might find of interest.' He knew he ought not to but, what the hell, he was smitten by her translucent porcelain beauty. Also she was a lawyer from a blue chip firm, married to a highly reputable banker. It was not beyond the bounds of possibility that she might even be able to help him in some way. That, at least, was how he kidded himself. After so many months of unendurable pressure, he was reduced to clutching at straws.

'Great!' said Paige, though with a sinking heart. She had not expected him to come through quite so quickly. Fortunately she was adept at coping and a little light flirtation could do no harm. She agreed to meet him in a restaurant in his building, after which it was up to him how things panned out. The thought of Anna's anguish spurred her on. They were more, far more, than just lawyer and client.

Genevieve sounded unusually subdued when she called. Normally, because of the time difference, they left it for Anna to make contact first but today she had something she needed to get off her chest. In the past few days, since the departure of Hector, Genevieve's voice had sparkled with happiness so that Anna, disregarding her own miserable situation, had been pleased when it dawned that her friend might be falling in love. Well, good for her, she deserved some sort of break. In the several years since they had first met she had been having a rotten deal. First the husband and then that dreadful man. It was time something magical finally worked out for her despite what Anna might privately think about Raffaele. But, crooked or not, he was certainly appealing and a million times preferable to Hector. She would keep her mouth shut and her fingers firmly crossed that all would eventually work out.

Genevieve, however, was solidly in the dumps and feared her budding relationship might be over. She described how they had discovered the photographs and also the reaction of the women in the shop.

'They acted as if she were the Antichrist,' she said. 'One even made the sign of the cross. Whoever she was, they were not about to discuss it. Even Simonetta wouldn't talk.'

'So what did you do?'

'We took them to Raffaele. And that was our biggest mistake.'

Anna could hear the quaver in Genevieve's voice and sensed she was getting close to tears.

'He was positively rude when we asked him who she was, virtually told us to mind our own damned business. Said we should put them back where we found them and leave the matter alone. And then he went into the kitchen and that was that. He only came out when we paid the bill and even then was barely civil. Whatever it is we have stumbled into, we clearly should not have been messing with Sutherland's photographs. There's a lot going on that we simply don't understand.

'Oh, by the way,' she added, 'Sutherland isn't married, so there goes your theory about him being there with his wife. Raffaele isn't married either but it was more than clear that the woman in the pictures means a great deal to him. Means or meant; I am certain she is dead. Which is pretty macabre, when you think about it. It seems that I'm playing second fiddle to a fucking ghost.'

'You can't know that for sure,' said Anna, though it certainly did look that way. Clearly there was some mystery surrounding the woman which no-one in the village was ready to share. 'I'd just hang in there and see what happens. But better not go back into Sutherland's rooms.'

It had been worth the try but again they had drawn a blank. Why did that no longer surprise her? Anna confessed her own fears about being followed but also conceded it was probably just in her head.

'Take care,' she said. 'I will call you as soon as there's news. Paige is on another new trail but refuses to let me know what it is. I think she feels I have been through enough. And, you know something, she's dead right. And please don't worry about upsetting Raffaele. Behave as normal and I'm sure he will soon come around.' Genevieve was so gentle and sweet. There was no way he could stay mad at her for long.

'Take a look at that,' said Dave Kelly, his barely suppressed excitement making him sweat. His hand was shaking like a hardened junkie's, he looked like a man in urgent need of a fix. He moved aside to allow Paige to study his screen. She read the list and was instantly skewered by a sharp adrenalin jolt that felt like hope.

She raised an enquiring eyebrow at him. 'What exactly is this?'

'A list of the companies that had offices in the twin towers. Not just the big ones, like Cantor Fitzgerald, but everyone in the financial world who lost staff.'

'Why are you showing me this?'

'I am not exactly sure. You will see that, apart from the tax department, almost everyone else was a bond trader.'

Her theory again; how smart of him to have deduced it. Maybe he wasn't such a klutz after all. She glanced around for the water-cooler, checking to make sure it was nowhere in sight.

'I wonder,' she said at her most feminine and appealing, 'if I might possibly have a glass of water.'

'Sure,' he said, delighted to do her bidding, and disappeared obediently down the corridor.

Swift as a cobra, Paige struck and, within seconds of his leaving her alone, was rapidly working his printer. By the time he returned with a paper cup in his hand, the printout was safely in her purse. What he did not know he need never fret over, though she had a shrewd instinct he knew more than he let on. Unethical, maybe, but she was a lawyer who had been fumbling in the dark for far too long.

They chatted for a further few minutes, then Paige made her pretty excuses and said she really must go. She thanked him profusely for giving her lunch and promised that next time it would be on her. *Fat chance,* she thought as she hailed a cab. The one good thing about gullible men was that they were so easy to manipulate.

19

It was early morning and the streets of Montisi were deserted. Simonetta, in a flowered pinafore, was sluicing the pavement directly in front of her shop. Candy, for once in her life up with the lark, had bravely volunteered for breakfast duty and was down in the village, stocking up with supplies, while Genevieve lazed on in bed. Simonetta, putting aside her pail, greeted her with her usual radiant smile.

'*Buon giorno!* You're up early,' she said. 'It looks like being another glorious day.'

Candy followed her inside, inhaling the powerful aroma of freshly ground coffee. 'I'll take some of that,' she said, 'and also a chunk of the pancetta.' She picked out some figs and a box of fresh farm eggs and lined them up on the counter. When she did make the effort, she enjoyed this time of day, with the sky a limpid pinkish blue and the cuckoo spit still on the grass. She took a gamble on Simonetta's mood. 'I guess we boobed where the photos were concerned. I hope we didn't offend you.'

'Not at all,' said Simonetta, slicing the pancetta, 'it was just a bit of a shock.'

Candy thought quickly and wondered if she dared. 'I am also afraid that we might have upset Raffaele.'

'Don't worry about it,' said Simonetta rather too fast, revealing that she obviously already knew. 'It's just something he's going to have to learn to cope with. All of us, in fact.'

'I assume that means she is dead?'

Simonetta nodded. 'It hit the whole village very badly.'

'Especially Raffaele?'

She nodded again. At which point, to Candy's intense irritation, one of the gnarled old harpies came hobbling in. No point now in even trying to continue. She would simply have to wait for another chance. She paid, picked up her groceries and left. On the short drive home she thought hard about what she should do and decided not to say anything to Genevieve, who was depressed enough as it was, poor thing. No point in making her feel worse.

Time passed and still Paige sat on at her desk, engrossed in the purloined list. In addition to the big names Dave Kelly had mentioned, there were fourteen single-spaced pages of them. Mainly bond traders, some of them one-man shows, whose offices had been in the World Trade Centre. If her latest theory held any substance at all, one of these names might be a cover for something considerably more sinister. The Enron chief had used characters from *Star Wars* in order to cover his tracks.

She remembered what Charles had explained to her at breakfast; the concept of off-balance-sheet partnerships. If a company structured a special borrowing arrangement, in which the obligation to repay failed to appear on its statements, then it could reduce the liabilities shown on the balance sheet. The investors would never see the transaction; only the phoney brokerage statements. And by the time they discovered the truth, much of their money would be gone, magicked away by the crooked trader and stashed in a secret account. Most of this was gobbledegook to Paige yet she was starting to get the gist.

A faint draught fluttered the air behind her where the door to the stairwell stood ajar and, looking up at the clock, she realised just how long she had been there. It was Friday night and growing late; everyone else would be gone now. Soon she too would have to be off; in thirty minutes' time she was meeting Charles. She ran her eye down the list again, on the lookout for something unspecified. The name she had expected to find was Sutherland; instinct told her that he had to be somehow involved. The little about him that they did know all seemed to fit; his silence, his evasiveness, the fact that he worked mainly abroad. Yet now it seemed that he might have been stalking Anna; Paige was still at a loss to understand how. There were still a lot of missing pieces but a picture was slowly emerging, if incomplete.

The facts remained indisputable. Anna had innocently answered an advertisement, suggesting a home swap from April to July. She had checked out the references and done it in good faith, exchanging her own extremely valuable property with a stranger who had hailed from the same alma mater. It had all seemed perfectly cut and dried at the time, regardless of Paige's initial misgivings. But Anna, in some ways, was that much more trusting; Paige admired her for that. Next she had had trouble with her credit card which someone had run well above its limit and, after that, all the money from her bank account had mysteriously vanished without trace. Then she had found that the house was on the market and her father had been temporarily abducted while his own house was peremptorily sold. The money from that had never been recovered. This had to be organised crime. Paige, after all her weeks of fruitless research, was now convinced that the secret lay in this list. If she could only establish that one missing link, she would be able to turn it over to the FBI.

That draught again and the feeling that someone was out there. She glanced around but the light was no longer on. Just a couple more minutes and then she'd be off. She stapled the pages together. She wondered if Charles would be awfully cross if she worked through the weekend.

Simonetta lived above the shop, with a balcony crowded with flowering plants and a cheerful, melodious canary in a wicker cage. She was busily watering as Candy passed beneath and found herself suddenly drenched.

'Oi!' she shouted. 'Are you trying to drown me?' Luckily she was wearing her versatile hat. Simonetta peered through her phalanx of brilliant foliage and laughed when she saw what she had done.

'*Vieni!*' she said, beckoning, beaming with delight. 'Please come up here and have a glass of wine. I am sorry if I have made you wet.' It was almost lunchtime and business, for once, was slow. Candy, returning from the market, needed no second invitation. Genevieve, for a change, was actually working; it would do her good to be left in peace for a while. They had shaken down to a new routine, more relaxed than Anna's but nonetheless effective. Besides, there were things Candy was keen to find out and now seemed the perfect opportunity. She wanted to ask more about the woman in the photographs but sensed she would have to work round to it. So she began with something relatively safe.

'Have you always lived in the village?' she began as Simonetta bustled around, pouring wine into tiny fluted glasses and arranging the sweet, dry biscuits on a plate.

'Since I was three years old,' she said. 'My grandparents were from Siena.' Presumably the boundaries of her universe until she grew up and mysteriously landed in Enfield.

'And how on earth did Enfield come about?' asked Candy, impressed by women who radically changed their lives.

Simonetta shrugged expansively. 'God moves in mysterious ways,' was all she would say.

'But you ended up back here?'

'I had no choice. My father died and my mother needed help in the shop. Besides, by then I had seen the world and was ready to settle down.' Simonetta's wide grin was irreverent and infectious. It did not appear that she had suffered too much.

'Yet you never married?' Candy was curious, despite her own rebellion in that department. Simonetta, though not a beauty, was fun with lively intelligent eyes.

'No-one asked me,' she said with a chuckle. 'And here, in Montisi, there isn't a lot of choice.'

Which brought them neatly to Candy's main agenda. 'Tell me about Daniel Sutherland,' she said.

'Daniel, ah, what a lovely man. One of the most generous I have ever known. He'd do anything for anyone, especially if they're in trouble. Would give away the shirt off his back if need be.' A faraway look came into Simonetta's eyes and her expression perceptibly softened. 'I have known him most of my life, you know. We grew up together in this village.'

'Here?' said Candy, taken aback. 'We sort of thought he must have married into Montisi.'

'Daniel, alas, is not the marrying kind.' She made no attempt to conceal the regret in her voice.

'But with a name like Sutherland and educated at Yale . . .'

'His mother was the Contessa di Valdombrone. She married the Count when Daniel was just a child and he raised him here as his step-son and presumed heir. Daniel and Raffaele have always been close; they are, after all, step-cousins.' Then, observing Candy's growing confusion: 'Raffaele is the nephew of the Count.'

It was a lot to digest but explained a good few things. She would have to go away and think it all through.

'You should have seen them as young men,' said Simonetta fondly, 'forever up to mischief of some kind. Once they even competed in the Palio, sporting the family colours, carrying the flag. They were both so handsome, all the women were crazy about them. And yet, in all those years, unbelievably, they managed never to fall out.' It was clear, from the sudden slight quaver in her voice, that neither had she been entirely immune.

'So *Casavecchia* was part of his inheritance?' They had assumed it was something he had bought.

'*Si, si*, it is part of the Tolomei estate.' Simonetta obviously thought Candy knew more than she did.

And now she was definitely out of her depth. Her look of total bafflement made Simonetta laugh. 'The Contessa's husband and also Raffaele's uncle was the Count Ildebrando Tolomei di Valdombrone.'

It was not entirely the dry biscuit that made Candy choke; she needed to get away as fast as she could. It was siesta time for Simonetta and Genevieve would be waiting for her lunch.

'I've got to go,' said Candy, draining her glass. 'Please may we do this again some other time?'

Charles Collier had been waiting a full twenty minutes; the concert was scheduled to start in fewer than ten. He looked repeatedly at his watch as he paced the concrete plaza. It was not like his wife to cut things quite so fine. Lately, he knew, she had been hugely preoccupied, trying to sort things out for the wretched Anna. Five more minutes and he'd leave her ticket at the box office. He did not want to risk missing the opening Dvořák. His mobile rang and he answered it impatiently. He had had a taxing day himself and was anxious to unwind.

'Sorry, honey,' said Paige, 'I am on my way. I'm just at Columbus Circle, crossing the street. Be with you soon.' She sounded hugely excited. '*Wait* till you hear what I think I have stumbled upon—'

She was interrupted by a sickening screech of tyres and a violent scream before the phone went dead. Charles shook it in bewilderment, for a second not comprehending, then threw himself into the heavy traffic, in reckless disregard for his own life.

Emboldened by all she had learned from Simonetta, Candy persuaded Genevieve to return with her to the trattoria that night. They had kept away since the incident of the photographs, scared of once more inciting Raffaele's wrath. They still didn't have the full picture, only that he had suffered a bereavement with which he was trying hard to come to terms. A look of relief crossed his face when he saw them; he hurried across and took both of Genevieve's hands.

'*Signora,*' he breathed, 'I had started to worry. I'm afraid I spoke to you harshly last time we met.'

237

She squeezed his hand. 'It doesn't matter. We were interfering where we had no right to be.'

Raffaele, relieved, gave her an affable smile. 'Soon I will tell you everything,' he promised.

While he was getting their order, they conferred. Should they press their advantage while the going was good? Candy thought definitely though Genevieve was cautious. She feared to invoke that coldness again in his eyes. But Anna, in New York, continued to suffer. Their first priority must surely be to do what she had asked.

So once the food was on the table and Raffaele, still beaming, hovering, Genevieve plucked up the courage to ask him about his relationship with Sutherland. Simonetta had been talking, she explained. They were both intrigued to know more about their mysterious absentee landlord. Raffaele hesitated, his eyes inscrutable, clearly struggling with powerful inner conflicts. But Candy was gazing at him with spellbound attention while the candlelight threw a halo round Genevieve's head. He could not resist these two lovely English ladies and felt in his heart he probably could trust them. So he eased himself comfortably into a chair, loosened his tie and embarked upon his story.

Daniel's mother, Alicia, was a society beauty from San Diego who had married Daniel's father while still in her teens.

'It was – how you say it? – a true love match. One look and for them that was it.' He kissed his fingers expressively, the embodiment of the sentimental Italian. A frisson of excitement flickered down Genevieve's spine. The plain-speaking earthiness of this man, especially after Hector, made her giddy.

The couple settled in Colorado where he worked as a mining engineer. They were blissfully happy until, when Daniel was five, his father was killed in an aircrash in the Rockies and the feckless Alicia, unable to cope alone, soon after remarried a much older man. Raffaele's uncle, Count Tolomei, owner of most of the land in these parts. Genevieve's eyes met Candy's. It must have been his portrait they had seen, though they dared not let Raffaele suspect they'd been in there snooping.

The Count raised Daniel as his son and heir but died when Daniel was fifteen, leaving the bulk of the estate to Alicia and *Casavecchia* to Daniel.

'Plus an expensive education in the States. I tell you, he looked upon him as his son. Daniel is as close to me as a brother. We grew up together as children in this village. There is nothing in the world I wouldn't do for him. Or, indeed, he for me.'

One by one the pieces were slotting in; slowly it was starting to make sense. It explained the strong bond between the two men and the fact that, in Raffaele's eyes at least, Sutherland was something of a saint.

'So where is he now? That's what we need to know.' Enough of all the sentimentality; the urgency was sharp in Genevieve's voice. She sat up straighter and her cheeks were becomingly flushed. If he doesn't crack now, thought Candy, amused, then he's tougher than he would appear.

'You tell me. You said New York,' said Raffaele, instantly back on his guard. 'His work means he moves around all the time. Often we have no contact for months though he knows I am always here, should he ever need me.'

'How much time does he spend here altogether?' asked Candy.

'Very little,' said Raffaele, 'which is sad. Only when it fits his busy schedule.'

'But he was here in November,' Candy persisted. Which was when the ad appeared and it all began.

Raffaele calculated then shook his head. 'I would say it's at least a couple of years since Daniel last set foot in *Casavecchia*. His occasional visits are always very rushed and even then he only comes if there's something that urgently needs fixing. He has been in Patagonia for months, before that in Nepal. It's the life he chose though it's sometimes hard on those of us who love him.'

Silently they absorbed this information, then Genevieve made a bold decision. She hesitated to incur Raffaele's wrath, yet felt the time had come to spill the beans. Nothing would be gained by prevarication; the situation was far too serious for that. She leaned across and gingerly touched his hand.

'There's something you ought to know about,' she said.

Briefly, choosing her words with care, Genevieve filled him in. She told him everything that had happened so far, beginning with Anna seeing the ad, right up to the callous abduction of her father. The credit card fraud, the missing text; most of all, the cold-blooded theft of Anna's house.

'I am afraid your saintly Daniel is a crook who has ruthlessly preyed on our friend.'

Raffaele's eyes were suddenly icy. 'How do you figure that?' he said.

'Because,' said Candy, leaping in, 'he's the only person with legal access. No-one else has the keys to Anna's house. Not now the architect is dead.'

Raffaele stared blankly, as if not comprehending, so Genevieve started to run it all through again. But Raffaele silenced her with a curt gesture. His charm had vanished along with his good humour.

'The architect is dead?' he repeated.

'Yes, I was certain you would know that. He had a fall.'

Candy was starting to grow impatient but Raffaele looked as though he had seen a ghost.

'*Scusi,*' he muttered and bolted from the room. They heard him in the kitchen, frantically phoning.

By the time Charles got there a crowd had gathered and all he could see through their legs was a flash of teal blue. They told him an ambulance was on its way but, from the expressions of the nearest spectators, he grimly surmised it was probably already too late. He pushed his way through them to where she was lying, on her back with her hair all unpinned. He wanted to cradle her in his arms but knew he had to wait for the paramedics. Instead he picked up her bloodstained purse and silently cursed the relentless ambition that had snatched his darling from him so abruptly and far too soon. Since college he had only ever had eyes for Paige; she had been the whole focus of his life.

'Hit and run,' said a sympathetic bystander. 'Guess the poor lady never really stood a chance.' But Charles, in his heart, remained unconvinced. He knew from their discussions of the securities frauds that something underhand had been going on. And his beautiful, headstrong, impetuous Paige had done her usual thing and leapt straight in. For once, however, and it broke his heart, she had unknowingly been batting way out of her league.

20

Right around the corner from where Anna was staying was a basement café in which she occasionally ate. Today being Saturday, she dropped in there for brunch. For once she had left her father alone with Colette. There were times when she felt that she badly needed space. Too much was presently weighing on her mind for her to be any sort of company. She had brought the newspaper and intended to read it but found herself with zero concentration. At six that morning she had been awoken by the phone – Candy and Genevieve, bursting with news, eager to fill her in. They did their customary double act, passing the receiver back and forth while they told her all about their evening with Raffaele. Culminating in his unexpected exit without so much as a word of explanation.

'It was all most odd,' said Genevieve plaintively. 'Suddenly his attitude totally changed.'

'It was when we let slip about Larry,' chimed in Candy. 'He disappeared to make an urgent phone call.'

'And never came back.' Which had really upset Genevieve. More had been hanging on that one contrived meeting than she cared to admit.

Now Anna sat and contemplated all the underlying implications. She had asked the girls to continue their good work while, at the same time, exhorting them to be careful. The more convoluted it all became, the more potentially dangerous. No-one knew for sure what it was they were embroiled in but it was wise to remember that Larry had ended up dead. And, despite their belief that he was a good guy, she feared they might have played straight into Raffaele's hands. Words like mafia flitted through her brain; something positively shady was going on. It all boiled down to two basic facts: someone had been responsible for the crimes and still none of them had yet encountered Sutherland.

She was mopping up her eggs Benedict and looking around for more coffee when a man descended the stairs from the street and halted in front of her table. Since he was effectively blocking the light – the restaurant was gloomy and the stairway unlit – all Anna could make out was that he was tall.

'Mind if I sit here?' he asked casually, even though the place was far from full. Then, without even waiting for a reply, he plonked himself down on the opposite chair and asked a passing waiter for coffee and toast. Because the street door was temporarily open, all Anna could make out was his silhouette.

'Well,' he said calmly, removing his mirrored shades. 'Finally I have succeeded in tracking you down.'

The eyes, which she had never seen before, were as tawny and probing as an eagle's, but the teeth were familiar the moment he smiled and reached across the table to offer his hand.

'Dan Sutherland,' was all he said, as the waiter brought his coffee, then he relaxed and waited for Anna to react.

For a full sixty seconds she was frozen with disbelief, then the anger boiling inside her began to erupt. He had the gall to sit there, invading her space, as though it were the most natural thing in the world. This man, who had methodically sucked her dry, appeared now to be offering the hand of friendship.

'You've got some damned nerve,' she spluttered, once she had regained the power of speech, seriously wondering whether to call the police. But, since the chances of them ever showing up were minimal, she might as well take the time to hear him out. It was, after all, their first real encounter, aside from that single brief brush in Tuscany. Then his manner had been supercilious when he had coldly and rudely grilled her about the house. She also remembered, with a dart of sudden alarm, the gun in the back of his Land Rover. He had not even deigned then to tell her who he was; now it seemed he was offering some sort of a truce.

She bit back her rage; there was little point in fighting. She could always change her mind and summon help. Besides, she was curious to hear what he had to say. Whatever his story might be, it had better be good.

'How did you find me, in any case?' No-one outside her tight circle knew where she was staying.

'I have my ways.' He tested his coffee and then his toast arrived. He took his time before answering her question. 'Sooner or later you were bound to show up. So I hung around your house and simply waited. And, speaking of nerve,' and now his voice grew colder, 'what the fuck were you doing in my house?'

Anna was too surprised to answer. How dare he try to grab the moral ground. 'Why didn't you tell us who you were?' she came up with feebly. 'What was it with all the cloak-and-dagger stuff?'

Another long pause while he considered her thoughtfully. 'There were reasons,' he eventually said.

'What kind of reasons? You knew who we were. It had all been covered by email. Your secretary even called Raffaele from Patagonia to tell him we were on our way.'

'I have no secretary,' he said.

Silence again and, again, deadlock. They seemed to be going round in circles.

'I had to be certain.' He stirred his coffee. 'When Raffaele called, I came straightaway to find out what the hell was going on.' He looked at her with those clear perceptive eyes and suddenly, for no reason she understood, Anna started to feel slightly less embattled. Despite the fact that his story didn't add up, she believed that he wasn't lying.

'You thought we were trespassers?' she suggested.

He nodded. 'And why not? You had no right to be there. The villa is private and has been shut up for years. The only people who ever go there are personal guests of my own.' The smile had gone and now his eyes were flinty. His face was stern with a strong and resolute jaw. Like cats preparing for a fight, they sat rigid and sized each other up.

Until, unnervingly, he started to chuckle. 'You must admit, it does have its farcical side. Don't worry,' he added, in a gentler tone. 'Raffaele has brought me up to date. It seems we have both been the victims of a trickster. Let's call a truce, at least for the time being, and exchange what information we both have. You, so I'm told, have lost everything whereas I am hot on an entirely different trail.'

245

He picked up both bills and paid the cashier, then courteously escorted her into the street. It was clear, from the easy way he took control, that he knew exactly where she would be heading. His stalking must have been more thorough than she had known; no wonder lately she had started feeling spooked.

'Look,' he said outside her hotel. 'There are things I have to do that can't be postponed. Could we, perhaps, meet up later for a drink? It is vital that we put all our cards on the table.'

Gradually Anna felt her anger abating. His suggestion was, at the very least, constructive. She had been through so much in the past few weeks, she no longer had the heart to keep on fighting. All she wanted was some sort of resolution. And something about him made her feel she could trust him. Despite all the evidence to the contrary, in person he came over as absolutely straight. Why, if he weren't, would he have bothered to track her down? The very least she could do, she supposed, was give him the benefit of the doubt.

'Come here at seven,' she said, mollified, and watched while he scrawled down her number. She was drawn by his unnervingly steady gaze that seemed to see into her soul. He was lean and fit and, yes, attractive, with the sort of permanent tan that came from an outdoor life. A feeling of cautious hope swept through her. Maybe, after all, it would be all right.

Until she entered the lobby and saw Colette, white and shaking, clearly waiting for her.

'Anna,' she faltered, coming forward with arms outstretched, and Anna was overwhelmed with sudden terror.

'Dad?' she whispered, not sure she could face the answer. She didn't believe she could handle anything more.

Colette shook her head. 'It's Paige,' she said.

And Anna knew, without having to ask, what had happened.

So now New York's finest were belatedly on the job, keen to discover the identity of Paige's killer. For murder it had been, of that there could be little doubt. Eyewitness accounts simply did not tally with a straightforward traffic accident. The driver had swerved up on to the sidewalk and sent her flying as she waited to cross the street, then vanished into the rush-hour traffic while a crowd of horrified bystanders looked helplessly on. Who, the police were keen to know from Charles, might conceivably have wanted to kill his wife? The only answer he could logically come up with was that she was, by profession, a criminal lawyer. Until he looked in her purse and found the papers.

For the moment, he decided not to tell the police; he wanted to think things through before he did. Shock meant he wasn't entirely rational; he turned to Anna instead. They clung to each other in their inconsolable grief, unable to believe that such a thing could have happened. They'd been friends for as long as he had known Paige, since their second year at Yale, in fact, though Charles had been at Princeton and two years older. After all these years, they felt as close as family. It wasn't a lot of comfort but it helped.

'Whatever I do,' swore Charles, fists tightened, 'I will get the bastard responsible for this.'

He showed her the slightly bloodstained pages, now also spattered with his tears. 'These are top-security SEC documents which Paige should never have been allowed to see.' Let alone carry away in her purse; there were so many questions without answers. What she had been up to, he still didn't know; bitterly regretted that she hadn't told him. 'She said she thought she had a hot new lead and got me to introduce her to Dave Kelly. My friend at the SEC,' he explained. 'They met up a couple of times.' Many men, blessed with a wife as glorious as Paige, might have felt the occasional twinge of insecurity. Not Charles Collier; nor had he ever. One of the many reasons that Anna had always envied their marriage.

He wondered if he should talk to Dave, though hated to implicate Paige. On the other hand, now that she was dead what could it possibly matter? Lawyers were hardly known for keeping their noses clean and Paige had always been one of the best – probing, insightful and thorough.

'So she didn't discuss it with you in any particular detail?'

'Only ever peripherally, though I knew it had something to do with your case. She told me she'd fill me in when she'd worked things out.' That was his feisty, unstoppable wife, always prepared to go that extra mile. Tears came flooding back and he started to weep. The two of them had only ever had eyes for each other. What on earth was he going to do with the rest of his life?

Anna hugged him and waited until he was calmer. Her mind was fixed on the SEC and Dave Kelly.

'You think he might have given her some sort of tip-off?'

Charles shrugged. 'I really can't say.'

'So go and talk to him instantly. Find out everything he knows. If you want, I'll come with you.' She held out her hand. For the first time in all the years she had known him, Charles looked on the brink of cracking up.

Dave Kelly, as Charles had rather feared, could not tell them very much more. He was shattered, of course, by the news of

Paige's death, but also completely at a loss to imagine what conceivably might have triggered it. When Charles produced the stapled pages, he explained it was something he had wanted her to see.

'Strictly against the rules, of course, but I had a gut feeling she might be able to help me.' He had been hugely impressed by her agile brain and obviously formidable intelligence. He ran through her theory, which coincided with his own, that someone was using the September devastation in order tactically to disappear. 'The first time we talked, I thought she was being over-fanciful but then I received details of everyone who was missing, along with the companies they ran. Some large, like Cantor Fitzgerald, some small; one-man shows that had only recently been set up. Among the jumble of them on that list, there's a chance one's a cover for a shady operation.' Which was why the SEC had become involved.

'Sorry,' said Anna, 'you have lost me completely.' Maths had always been her very worst subject at school. Her own particular talents lay in a different area of her brain, one of the reasons she had never learned to drive.

Charles explained briefly about special purpose entities and the gangs of small brokers linked to corporate fraud. It all went back to Enron, he said, whose recent demise had dramatically blown the cover on all types of corporate skulduggery, previously unguessed at. 'Paige believed that the person who swiped your money might have ploughed it back into a bogus account and used it as bait to attract bona fide investors.'

'So what's with the list?' She still didn't quite understand. What had been Paige's fascination with those names?

'I had been through it so many times,' admitted Dave, 'and it still didn't make any sense. But because she appeared to have reached similar conclusions, I gambled on allowing her to see it.' He caught Charles's eye and gave him a guilty grin. 'Well, you knew Paige,' was all he said.

She had acted so swiftly, he had been impressed and had never let on that he knew. Another thing Charles understood completely; the only way to control her had been always to let her have her head.

'The last time we spoke, she sounded excited.' Charles well recalled the jubilation in her voice when she called to tell him that she might have found a new lead. And then the screeching of brakes and she was dead. He furtively wiped his eyes to stop the flow.

'So what exactly had she discovered?' asked Dave. 'I confess that I am still in the dark.' He suppressed his dream of that longed-for third meeting when she would have explained it succinctly over lunch.

Charles sniffed and shrugged. He didn't know either. A penalty of loving a maverick woman.

'Here, let me,' said Anna, grabbing the list. What they were saying made no sense to her; perhaps a fresh eye might throw some new light on the matter.

It took her three minutes of intensive skimming before it simply leapt off the page. Tucked away near the end of page fourteen, a bond company listed simply as 'Ptolemy'.

The blood started hammering wildly in her ears. 'Got it, that's him!' she almost shouted. 'That's Dan Sutherland, I know I am not wrong.' There was no other person it possibly could be.

21

'Why don't we simply turn him in?' Charles was visibly panting for a fight. 'I will slice off his balls and stuff them down his throat if ever I get my hands on the fucking bastard.' Nothing he could devise would be bad enough for the man who had cold-bloodedly run down his wife and for no reason that Charles could understand, which was infinitely worse.

Anna felt much the same but more controlled. She put her arms gently around his neck and rested her cheek against his chest. He was hurting so much it was painful to observe but she was suffering too. Emotionally she agreed with him but first they must think things through. Larry and Paige had already died; this was not a children's game they'd become involved in. Dan Sutherland, for all his apparent honesty, now looked like being the dangerous killer they had initially taken him to be.

A man who could look her squarely in the eye only hours

after murdering her best friend had to be deeply unscrupulous and also very probably deranged. They must not run the risk this time of allowing him to slither off the hook. If they turned him over to the cops right now, the chances were he would slip through their demonstrably incompetent fingers. Before they could shop him, they needed hard evidence which could only be achieved from another meeting. That was how Anna reasoned, at least; reluctantly Charles agreed.

The original appointment had been cancelled because of Paige but Anna had rearranged it for two days' time. She knew that might appear to be a bit on the callous side but Paige would have been the first to urge her on. She had done so much and now she was dead. They owed it to her not to bungle things now. Anna explained to Charles, as gently as she could, exactly what it was she intended to do. He thought about it, then nodded agreement. Any sort of action was better than none.

'Mind if I tag along?' he asked. 'I feel so pathetically useless.' Until the autopsy was out of the way, time hung heavily on his hands. He could not face the bank nor being at home on his own. Paige had been the sum total of his life; they had not even bothered to have a family. He was feeling murderous since their meeting with Dave but rational enough to acknowledge that Anna was right. Despite all the pointers that appeared to incriminate Sutherland, they must tread very warily to ensure that he didn't get away. Softly, softly, catchee monkey. That was the only way to play it.

'Do come,' said Anna, 'I could certainly use some backup.' It would give him something to focus on and her the reassurance of having him there. A man as dangerous as Sutherland was not the kind of opponent to face alone. Anna was slightly scared but also intrigued. She could not equate the man she had met with the monster that lay beneath.

She had fixed to meet him for drinks at The Mark so Charles came by and they strolled up Madison together.

'I can't guarantee my behaviour,' he warned her. This was, after all, the man who had ruined his life.

Gently Anna took his hand. 'Let's hear him out first and then make up our minds. We can always call in the cops if we decide to. But first we really need to hear what he has to say.'

It was hard to imagine what story he could come up with. She worried about its effect on Charles, who at Princeton had been a pretty nifty wrestler.

He was taller even than Anna remembered when he rose from a corner banquette to greet them. He was wearing jeans and a battered leather jacket and, without the shades, looked much more human. A camera case was on the bench beside him; even in circumstances like these, he was obviously always on the job. She made the introductions without explaining who Charles was, nor his reasons for having come along. No point in making him suspicious at this stage; a friend, was all she said, and left it at that. Despite the recent ravages of grief, Charles Collier was still a fine-looking man. She was proud to have him there at her side.

'So now, where were we?' asked Sutherland briskly, once the waiter had taken their orders and gone. 'Talking about this fic-titious house swap.' He pulled out a palmtop computer and flicked to his notes.

'And the way you have ruined my life,' flashed back Anna, instantly on the offensive. Something about the very maleness of the man always succeeded in getting her hackles up. Last time they'd met he had ended up charming her but that was before what had happened to Paige. Now she hated him unequivocally. It was he who, by placing that fateful ad, had started off this whole horrible sequence of events.

Charles, beneath the table, kicked her foot. Trading insults was not constructive and so far, to his huge surprise, he was favourably impressed. This gaunt-faced stranger with the world-weary eyes had the air of a man of some distinction. Despite the agony in his heart, Charles's pent-up belligerence subsided. Let them hear him out and then decide what the verdict should be. The drinks arrived, creating a minor diversion, then Sutherland resumed his interrogation. Charles could see, from the glint in his eye, that he was taking Anna more seriously than she might think.

'Tell me,' said Sutherland, sipping his bourbon. 'Why do you suppose I would ever have considered allowing total strangers into my home?' Money's no object was implicit but unsaid. This man could afford the finest hotels.

'Because you needed four months in New York.' That's what the ad had said.

'For Chrissakes, I am a *wildlife* photographer. Hardly my natural territory, wouldn't you say?'

'But I didn't know that,' said Anna, flustered, still spoiling for a fight. 'It just seemed the ideal arrangement at the time. Me to Italy, to finish my book, you to Manhattan, presumably on a job.' She remembered vividly how depressed she had been, wanting only to quit the city of sorrows and hide herself away in some rural retreat.

'And it never occurred to you to check?' He might as well have had the shades back on, his eyes had become so inscrutable.

'I did that,' she said, 'with Paige's cousin.' Charles supplied the name. 'Who thought you were an A1 guy. Told us to tell you hello.'

The corners of Sutherland's mouth quirked slightly. He was laughing at her again. After all she had been through, the misery he had caused, she couldn't believe that he still wasn't taking this seriously. Because of him she had lost two dear friends, her house, all her money as well as the family home. She was destitute with nowhere to go and he still didn't even know about the cat. This was no moment for levity; she was on the verge of losing it altogether. Charles again touched her foot beneath the table, silently begging her not to give way now. Far too much was riding upon it and this man was beginning to intrigue him.

'You are claiming that you never placed that ad?' She tried to get a grip on her emotions.

'Damn right,' he said forcefully. 'Finally you get it. And now you seem to suggest I have stolen your house. I spend most of my time on the far side of the world and have only come here now because of Raffaele.'

'Raffaele? He called you?' Anna was startled. So the two of them had been in contact all the time. Another deception, her instincts had been right. They never should have trusted that fawning Italian.

'You bet. He keeps an eye on my affairs and has my best interests at heart. And, therefore, instantly alerted me when you ladies first blew into town.'

'But he told us he never knows where you are,' said Anna, suddenly feeling rather foolish.

'He lied.' The eyes were clear and now disconcertingly amused. For the first time she noticed the scar across his cheek, something that had been much more than just a scratch. 'Look,' he said in a gentler tone, seeing how upset she had become,

'I'm as keen as you are to get this whole thing sorted. It seems someone must have been taking my name in vain and that I cannot allow. Yet no-one apparently has ever encountered that person. Doesn't that strike you as odd?'

'Just your secretary.'

'I told you, I don't have one.'

'Nor a wife?'

He shook his head.

'So who is this woman?' Who had fired Consuela, checked the mail and been boldly in and out. Who might have been there when Larry died and possibly called the police. Who was solely responsible for losing the cat, of that Anna had little doubt. And taken her father, on false pretences, to a run-down retirement home in White Plains before disposing of his house? If she wasn't in some way connected to the scam, then who in the world could she be? The woman from the real estate agency? They had only ever talked to her on the phone. Or any of the countless others who had acted to stop Anna sorting things out and left her practically destitute and alone. She lowered her eyes, on the brink of tears. It was much too painful to go on.

'That,' said Sutherland calmly, ordering another round, 'is exactly what we are here to try to figure out.'

Charles, now totally absorbed in it all, was fast coming round to respecting him. He had come here today in a mood to break someone's head but instead had been unexpectedly won over. This man, with his calm demeanour and rock-solid confidence, impressed him more by the second. All the signs were that he was innocent, or why else would he be here at all instead of on a flight back to Patagonia?

'It is even worse than you think,' he said, after careful deliberation. He owed it to Paige to show his hand in order to catch the hare that she had started. 'There have already been two unnecessary deaths. We must not run the risk of any more.'

'Two?' said Sutherland, obviously taken aback. 'I had only been told about the one.' He seemed genuinely startled and concerned; Charles was certain now that he couldn't be faking.

'My wife,' said Charles, 'was killed yesterday. Apparently on the brink of a major breakthrough.'

'Your wife? The lawyer?'

Charles nodded.

'I am so sorry,' said Sutherland, reaching across and briefly touching his arm.

Anna watched all this with fascination. He appeared to be totally sincere. If not, then he must be a brilliant actor. In order to save Charles the ordeal of giving details, she now stepped in and told him about Larry and then Paige. Two senseless accidents in the space of just a few weeks. The odds against it happening to close friends had to be infinitesimal.

'So you think they were murdered?'

'I am positive,' said Anna. 'Although, so far, we have no actual proof. The only reason, by the way, that we haven't yet called in the cops.'

Sutherland listened attentively. A small nerve started ticking at his jawline and it looked as though his blood was draining away. When he spoke again, his voice had dropped much lower. He seemed to be talking primarily to himself. 'I thought we were dealing with just theft and deception. I honestly didn't know things had gone quite this far.'

Anna, alert to his sudden mood change, was shocked to realise she found him disturbingly attractive. At any other time . . . but that was not why they were here. She was still working up to lobbing her hidden grenade.

257

'Tell us what you know about Ptolemy,' she said, watching closely for his reaction.

His gaze remained level, without so much as a flicker. 'I have not the slightest idea what you're talking about.'

'Ptolemy, as in the Pharaohs,' persisted Anna. 'Cleopatra and all that stuff.'

There was a sudden brief flash of recognition which was just as instantly snuffed out. Anna would swear before a court of law that he knew precisely what she meant. There followed a long pause, while he swirled the remains of his bourbon, putting his thoughts together before he replied. She had got him; she felt her adrenalin rising. Actor or not, she knew that she now had him nailed.

Eventually he looked up at her and his eyes were as clear and unwavering as before. Amber, she realised, was their actual colour; they seemed to change with the nuances of light.

'I think what you are referring to,' he said, 'is the fanciful local legend in Siena that the Tolomei family dates back to Ancient Egypt. Not true, of course, although they have been around for some time. Their forebears were bankers and that is what they are now. Bankers and landowners and pillars of the community. The rest, alas, is just a lot of baloney. I would love to believe that my relatives had been kings.'

He grinned and suddenly looked boyish and much younger. The shadow had faded from his eyes. 'But you still haven't told me what all this is about?' His bewilderment, she would have sworn, was genuine.

So, encouraged by a nod from Charles, she plunged in and told him the rest. About Paige's incursion into SEC records and her search for a phoney corporate name, one that might lead to the perpetrator of all that had happened to Anna. Ptolemy had seemed to ring instant bells but Sutherland was shaking his head. 'Nothing whatever to do with me, though I'd love to hear more some other time.' Here he looked pointedly at his watch. 'Pretty soon I am going to have to go. So may we, please, now cut to the chase?'

His sudden brisk mood change startled Anna but Charles took over the narrative. He explained about Paige's investment theory and where she believed Anna's money had gone. Sutherland listened with rapt concentration, asking a few perceptive questions and entering notes into his palm pilot. He then brusquely snapped it shut and rose to his feet.

'You have both been a lot of help,' he said, 'but now I have to go. There is something I need to do that cannot wait.'

'Hang on,' said Anna, struck by a sudden thought. Something about this man still didn't quite add up. 'If you're not actually working in New York, how come you are here at all?' *Geographic* had seemed unaware that he had left Patagonia.

He slung his camera bag over his shoulder then paused. For a moment he stared at her with those clear inscrutable eyes as if wondering how much he could trust her.

'I am looking for someone,' he said.

22

The sea was flat and almost white in the hazy afternoon heat. Genevieve, paddling at the edge of the surf, was glad she had remembered to bring her hat. Raffaele, in shirtsleeves with his pants rolled up to his calves, laughed as he waded beside her. They were like two kids on a Sunday-school outing, willing it never to end. His muscular arm was tight around her shoulders; she was keenly aware of his body's urgent heat and the musky aroma of masculine sweat heightened her own visceral excitement. She knew exactly what he had in mind, it was what she yearned for too, but this was neither the place nor, indeed, the time. The Hector memories must first be cauterised and that was not going to happen overnight. Added to which, anticipation is very often the greater part of seduction. For the first time ever, with her new-found confidence, she was prepared to string it out for as long as it took.

They were at Castiglione della Pescaia, thirty minutes' drive away. Raffaele had, after weeks of procrastination, eventually summoned the courage to ask her out.

'Bellissima,' he had pronounced with approval when he'd turned up at the villa to collect her. After several months in the open air, she had truly blossomed and was looking quite stunning. Candy, in her generous way, had run up yet another of her effortless creations, this time in heavy embroidered cream cotton which did wonderful things for Genevieve's tan. Beneath the demure straw hat, her hair was heavily sun-streaked and healthy eating had made her even more svelte. Raffaele took one look and visibly melted; it was clear he wanted to ravish her on the spot. Since his cousin, Daniel, had been on the phone he had come to the welcome conclusion that he could trust her. And now wanted only to make up for lost time. Not for nothing had Raffaele been born Italian.

'Now, behave yourselves, children,' Candy had said, mock-stern. 'Don't do anything that I wouldn't do.' She felt a shade wistful as she waved them off, then climbed the steep stairs to her studio and her drawings. The fashion portfolio was very nearly done and she knew in her gut that it was good. Inspired, in fact; the others had raved and assured her that Harvey Nichols were bound to snap it up. Soon she would have to face going home to sort out the stark realities of life. Trevor was still looking after the child. There had been no more news of his wedding plans and she was privately hoping that they might yet fall through. A man in his forties with a commitment phobia could scarcely be considered a good marriage bet, not for a woman several years older, anxious to settle down.

She still had occasional nightmares when she considered all the implications. No other woman must ever be allowed to meddle with the upbringing of her son. Yet love appeared to be suddenly all around her, or so it certainly seemed from where she sat. The light of desire in Raffaele's eye could scarcely be misconstrued and she had never seen Genevieve looking more incandescent. She felt a pang, which was loneliness, and wished that Anna would come back. The role of third wheel was not one she was cut out for, though the last thing she would ever do was begrudge a friend genuine happiness. Especially after the horrors of Hector, it was the very least that Genevieve deserved.

It was interesting, Candy thought, as she sat by the window and sketched, the amount of emotional rubbish even intelligent women would put up with. Forceful women with lives of their own could turn into putty in the hands of a domineering male. Although she had had to raise Hugo on her own, she had never experienced a moment of regret. Yes, it was tough and she had often been scared but would not have wanted it any other way. Anna and Genevieve were opposite poles but Candy fitted somewhere in between. She could not have borne to be without her son, yet hated the concept of needing to rely on a man. Anna had made a huge issue of staying single, boasting that she had never experienced a maternal urge in her life. Genevieve, on the other hand, was an entirely different animal. She essentially needed male approbation to boost her confidence and make her sparkle, to oil the wheels of her everyday life.

She resembled a Japanese paper flower; her petals only unfurled when they were watered. Seeing her now with the clearly besotted Raffaele was seeing her at her very best. How she had ever put up with Hector, Candy would never understand. But until Raffaele slashed his way through the thicket, the odds had been that the relationship would have dragged on. Genevieve just wasn't strong enough not to jump at Hector's whim the next time his diary had a sudden vacant slot and he needed a stopgap date. She shuddered to remember his puerile pass; he was the absolute worst type of British male. The notion of even being touched by him continued to make her skin crawl.

She thought about Anna, marooned in New York when all she wanted was to be back here with them. The terrible events that were happening in her life were way beyond all logical comprehension. Whatever it was she was up against was taking a frighteningly darker turn. With two fatal accidents so close together, the situation had become exceedingly alarming. Candy hoped Anna was being careful and not doing anything too rash. Anna, in turn, had warned her to stay on her guard and keep an especially beady eye on Raffaele. For all that romantic Italian charm, she still could not quite bring herself to trust him. Anna probed deeper than superficial sex appeal and something about him made her slightly uneasy. He was almost too friendly and anxious to oblige, yet look what had been happening since the house swap. Total disaster; the decimation of all she had owned. She still could not believe he was not involved.

'Something most definitely doesn't add up,' she had said when she called the previous night. Genevieve was in the kitchen fixing supper, and didn't even hear the telephone ring. 'Please don't alarm her. Just keep your wits about you.' She described her two meetings with Sutherland, omitting the fact that he had disturbing eyes. Nor did she bother adding that she found him unnervingly attractive. Candy had seen him for herself and she was nobody's fool.

Before they paddled, he had treated her to lunch, a four-hour idyll on a sun-drenched terrace overlooking the sea. The innkeeper, part of a tight fraternity, had welcomed them both with elation. The food, none of which appeared on the printed menu, was the best that Genevieve had ever tasted, each dish personally and lovingly selected by the landlord, especially for them. From a basket covered by a fresh linen cloth, he produced his pièce de résistance, a knobby excrescence, covered in black warts, looking like an ancient and gnarled potato. Raffaele applauded and reverently sniffed it while Genevieve watched him curiously.

'*Tartufo!*' he exclaimed delightedly, passing it over for her to sniff too, then handed it back to its owner. One of the rarest of treats, a summer truffle, to be thinly shaved over a bowl of fine angel hair pasta. 'The food of the gods,' Raffaele declared, omitting to mention its famed aphrodisiac powers. After that, lobster fresh from the ocean, rushed from the barnacled pot to the restaurant's stove. Served with a crisp green salad and tiny potatoes and a generous dollop of garlic mayonnaise.

'Only perfection for such a beautiful lady,' said Raffaele, kissing her hand, and Genevieve experienced a small shiver of excitement as she saw the unabashed longing in his eyes. But that, she reminded herself, would simply have to wait. First there were far more urgent things that had to be sorted out.

'Go on with your story,' she said, gently withdrawing her hand.

Raffaele, duly rebuffed, did as bid and continued his narrative.

On the death of her second husband the Contessa had panicked, unable, or so she believed, to manage without a husband. First time round she had married straight out of the schoolroom and barely had any single life at all. She had walked down the aisle with Ildebrando within months of becoming a widow and had grown accustomed to being indulged like the pretty, headstrong girl she essentially still was. Daniel was off in the States by that time and only ever came home for the long vacations. There was ample money but very little to do, with far too much empty time on her hands. She found the forbidding palazzo in Siena cavernous, chilly and austere. Also stuffed with priceless antiques that continuously made her nervous. This was no life for a woman of her age, not yet into her forties. Alicia was unwilling to dress in black and resign herself to a permanent back seat along with the other Italian widows who clustered like crows on a chimneypot. She had loved her husbands, both of them, but still had a lot left to give. To hell with propriety, all she really wanted was to get back out there and dance.

And dance she did, more than she ever could have dreamed, when, in less than a year, she married again. She hoped the Tolomei family would forgive her but she was not yet of an age to commit social suttee. This time the pendulum swung right back and she opted for somebody younger. Julio was handsome, in a swarthy Mexican way, and twenty-seven years to her thirty-nine. An unusual choice after her first two husbands, he was, by profession, a dance instructor on a cruise ship. Alicia met him in a bar in New York where she had gone for a spot of remedial shopping. Later she declared it was love at first sight.

'To begin with they were happy,' said Raffaele. 'He made her laugh and she really liked to dance.' Because of the money the Count had left her, pursuing pleasure presented no restrictions. She closed up the palazzo and moved to Rome, to a vast apartment close to the Spanish Steps where they entertained as lavishly as royalty. Her friends in Siena viewed Julio with mistrust, recognising the charlatan he eventually turned out to be. He was sleek, he was charming, with oily slicked-back curls and a smile as meltingly seductive as a fallen angel's.

'Alicia was infatuated,' said Raffaele, looking back. 'My uncle had left her secure and well off but now she was crazily in love.' His brown eyes softened as he recalled how she had been, a giddy girl in a spin of excitement, thrilled at last to have found her handsome prince.

'And Daniel? Where did he fit in? What did he think of him?' It could not have been easy for a boy that age to acquire such a youthful step-father. Genevieve thought of her own two sons. At least she had never done anything like that to them.

'Daniel was sixteen and inclined to be judgemental. Luckily, though, he was still away at school.' Raffaele, for the moment, was being unusually discreet. The fact of the matter was that Daniel had loathed Julio. He had scarcely known his own father, who had died when he was just five, but had learned to revere and trust the man who had made him his surrogate son. To lose him too, at such an impressionable age, had helped mould the loner he was now.

'And then this bounder appears on the scene. I think you can imagine how he felt.'

Genevieve, looking back to her own failed marriage, empathised with someone she had once thought a crook. All they had gleaned about the elusive Mr Sutherland had added up to a totally ruthless man. Yet now this warm Italian, whom she trusted more and more, was throwing a whole new light on the situation. Despite what lingering reservations she still had, she was more than willing to put her trust in Raffaele.

'He suffered,' explained Raffaele gravely, 'yet was powerless to intervene. Imagine, a sensitive youth of that age having to watch his mother's descent into hell. Right in front of his eyes when he was there. They danced, they squandered, they threw expensive parties and Daniel saw his heritage being eaten away.

266

Not that he cared particularly, money has never impressed him, but Alicia, always so fearless and independent, was suddenly in thrall to a petty tyrant. The dancing master, with his foppish, elegant ways, was bit by bit revealing his monstrous side. Not unexpected to Roman society but devastating to her only son.' Daniel took after his father, he explained, basically serious though worldly-wise and a bit of a puritan at heart.

The innkeeper, beaming broadly, was back at the table, anxious to find out how they were liking the meal.

'*Magnifico,*' declared Raffaele in a way she had learned to expect.

'*Bene, bene,*' said their delighted host, satisfied that his honour was not at stake, and brought them a basket of summer fruits and a plate of chocolates.

'As the years went by, the money began to run out. Daniel, having graduated well, elected to stay in the States. He felt he no longer had a proper home here apart, of course, from *Casavecchia,* but his chosen career involved him in a vast amount of overseas travel and there wasn't very much scope for him here in Italy. I kept an eye on the house for him and occasionally some of us used it. He has always been very generous in that way but what else would an unmarried man be doing with a villa of that size?

'And then one day, out of the blue, Alicia returned, having been dumped by Julio. He had gone through her fortune, found himself a younger woman and disappeared as mysteriously as he arrived. Sadder, wiser and considerably more cynical, she rented out the palazzo to make ends meet and took up refuge in *Casavecchia.*'

'Rented out the ancestral home?' Genevieve's heart went out to her. She understood all too well how she must have felt. No wonder

Casavecchia was so exquisite and had such a feminine touch.

'All she had left to lean on was Daniel. Plus, of course, her daughter.'

'Her daughter?' Genevieve was doubly surprised. The story was growing more complex with each new revelation. 'So Daniel has a sister?' she said. Odd that had never been mentioned before. All sorts of facts about Daniel's family were now beginning to emerge.

Raffaele's face clouded; for a moment he went silent. 'A half-sister, Mercedes,' he explained. 'Child of the villainous Julio who disappeared.' Mercedes, he told her, was seventeen years younger than Daniel, with her mother's looks and wayward streak but also a strong dose of her father's instability.

At this point, he looked curiously contrite; it was not, indeed, his nature to speak ill of anyone.

'She was inclined to be wild and headstrong at times,' he said, 'but Daniel always adored her. Me too,' he admitted, a touch self-consciously, 'though she rarely even gave me the time of day. To her all I was was a slightly besotted older cousin, there to give her treats and keep her amused but not to be taken seriously.'

'What did she do?' asked Genevieve curiously. There was clearly a lot that he was still holding back.

'Investment broker. Incredibly bright. She moved to New York the moment she graduated from Stanford.'

That sudden silence again which was not at all like him. Genevieve looked at him with suddenly dawning concern. 'What's the matter?' she asked, struck by his expression, all her maternal feelings out there in force.

'That we don't know where she is right now. Daniel hasn't heard from her since September. Naturally he has had to assume the worst.'

Genevieve got it instantly. 'The woman in the photographs?'

He nodded miserably. 'I'm afraid I made a bit of a fool of myself. Though that was all over a long time ago.' He thought for a while and a tender smile crossed his face. 'You should have known her in her heyday,' he said. 'She was, as they say, a regular piece of work.'

What a truly terrible situation. Genevieve was at a loss to know what to say. 'And her mother?' she asked, after a moment's pause.

'Dead these past two years,' he said. 'She married a fourth time and retired to Palm Springs. She remained a great beauty right to the end, well into her late sixties.'

'So at least she won't be worrying about her daughter.'

'That,' said Raffaele sombrely, 'is the only blessing,'

23

Anna was finding it increasingly hard to sleep. The hum from the archaic air-conditioner in her hotel room gave the illusion of being in an engine room but the alternative was worse: she had tried that too. In temperatures of almost a hundred, New York was not a comfortable place to be. In Tuscany she had grown used to sleeping with the covers off and the windows wide open, though only when the mosquito screens were in place. Here, if she opened the window even slightly, the dull roar of Madison Avenue traffic permeated her dreams. She tossed and turned and tried hard to drop off but her brain remained stubbornly acute. She was thinking obsessively about Dan these days and whether or not he could be trusted. Although, logically, all the evidence weighed against him, both she and Charles were inclined to believe that he was, almost certainly, telling the truth. He seemed like a man who would not stoop to lie; if arrogance could be considered a virtue, in his case it worked in his favour. Charles, who had every reason to mistrust him, had, against all the odds, been completely won over.

'The guy's sincere. I'd put money on that. He seemed to be genuinely shocked when he heard about Paige.'

'Not just faking it?'

'Absolutely not.' The confrontation seemed to have stimulated Charles; the hopeless, lacklustre look had gone from his eyes. Once more he was back at his fighting best, committed to bringing Paige's killer to justice. Which, since they now agreed it wasn't Dan, meant they were back where they had started, depressingly at square one. 'So where do you suppose he was racing off to?'

'I haven't a clue,' said Anna. He had left within minutes of the Ptolemy revelation, while claiming absolute ignorance of the matter. Regardless of which, she strongly suspected that there were things he was deliberately suppressing. She and Charles had stayed on at The Mark and eaten supper, while trying to analyse everything that had been said. Neither had taken notes, which she now regretted. She remembered Dan's small, efficient palm-held computer into which he had punched out his notes.

'You think he was telling the truth about the house swap?' That story, even despite their change of heart, still sounded somewhat contrived. Who else but Dan could have placed the ad, with the certain knowledge that the house would be empty and that Raffaele was the holder of the keys? And what had stopped Raffaele simply standing his ground and summoning the local *polizia*? Instead of which, he had conferred with Dan who had graciously permitted them to stay. All Dan had done was drop by to check them out, then left without even telling them who he was. Odd behaviour, to put it at its mildest, in view of all the things he was now claiming. He could, just as easily, have evicted them on the spot. He wasn't what one might call a welcoming man.

'In theory, practically anyone in the village could have set it up,' said Anna. In a small, tight-knit community like that, everyone always knew each other's business. Except that almost none of them spoke English and, even then, just a few uncertain words. 'And why,' she added, 'should any of them want to? Swap Dan's sumptuous villa there in order to live in New York?'

'Greed,' said Charles promptly, his standard reply. People would do almost anything for money. A smart opportunist, with a knowledge of what was what, might easily have done it simply to make a killing.

'But how would they know about the Yale connection? Or, indeed, the alumni magazine?'

Charles thought carefully but failed to come up with an answer, the more so because he didn't know Montisi. He knew equally little about Dan Sutherland, only that he now trusted him which, with Charles, went a long way. He hadn't rocketed to the top of a banking career without an understanding of human nature. They sat on in silence, pondering this equation, both uneasily suspecting that the answer might be staring them in the face. If only they could figure it out without having to wait for Dan.

'They are not all peasants,' said Anna, considering, calling to mind the ebullient Simonetta. Her English was pretty fluent; for a time she had lived abroad. She made no secret, so Candy reported, of her ongoing passion for Dan. The sole strike against her had to be her high profile. If she ever happened not to be in the shop, the whole of the village would know. Unless, of course, she had some sort of accomplice. Which brought them neatly back full circle to where they had first come in.

'Guess all we can reasonably do now is wait,' said Charles. 'I am sure he will let us know as soon as there's news.'

So here Anna lay, in her stuffy hotel room, unable to blank her mind to those probing eyes, tawny as a jungle cat's. Intelligent and insightful, Dan had a way of looking at you as though seeing more than you cared to let him know. He was tall and lean and obviously fit, with a physical presence, she was well aware, that rarely failed to turn heads. She was faced with an unpalatable truth, one that shook her to the core. Against all her more rational instincts she was falling under his spell. It was years since she'd felt this way about a man or, indeed, anything at all. One moment she was resenting him for his acid superiority, the next fervently praying, like a besotted adolescent, for the telephone to ring. She liked the bone-crunching firmness of his handshake and the way he fired straight from the hip. She also liked the disconcerting way he looked at her which made her feel jittery inside. There was nothing too complex about Dan Sutherland; what you saw was precisely what you got.

'A real man' was what they would have said in the old days. Someone straight and dependable who would always be there for you. A dream, maybe, from a Fifties movie but, nonetheless, still seductive. If she didn't allow her intellect to take charge . . . but Anna Kovac was an extremely bright woman who had always preferred to be in control. Unlike Paige, but that was a different matter. Despite the fact they had roomed together and been best friends from the start, Anna had always been cautious about commitment whereas Paige had known her own mind and gone right for it.

They buried Paige on the hottest day of the year. Anna recalled now the stultifying heat and the limp bunch of freesias, Paige's favourite flower, that she had somewhat ineffectually dropped on the coffin. She'd been driven out there in a stretch limousine, provided and insisted upon by Charles, to the small upstate village on the edge of the Hudson River where Paige had spent her childhood years. Anna had always been happy here, loving her roommate's mother as much as her own. Paige's father had mainly been absentee, stuck in meetings in the city or jetting around the world making loads of money. Before the ceremony she walked the perimeters and Paige's dogs, remembering her well, had slunk up beside her and licked her hand for comfort. Why had it had to happen to Paige, so beautiful, so clever and so nice? She stood on the edge of the river and finally cried. Paige, who was perfect; Paige, her best friend. Paige who had only died in the course of duty. If it hadn't been for this horrible mess, Paige would still be alive and thriving today.

Anna turned, and the dogs did too, to retrace her tracks back to Paige's mother's house. The funeral crowd was already gathering; even from this distance she could pick out a host of familiar faces.

'Anna,' they said, coming forward to greet her, kissing her and smothering her with hugs. Anna, the valiant; Anna, the best friend. Anna who was becoming slightly famous, and but for whose existence Paige might still be alive.

Charles found her sobbing against the boathouse wall. Having seen she was missing, he had also absented himself. 'What?' he asked, as he gathered her into his arms and, in the same spirit, she had finally broken down.

'Is it my fault?' she asked him, soaking his shirt with her tears. 'If it hadn't been for my problems, would Paige still be alive?'

'Hush,' he said, the valiant Charles, stroking her hair to calm her. 'If you hadn't been around all these years, who knows what might have happened to Paige.'

On that note he had left her, striding away, head held resolutely high, to shoulder the coffin and face the future alone, a strong man who had lost his reason to live. Anna stood and watched him go and wondered, as she occasionally did, whether she had, after all, seen all of the picture.

'Anna darling,' said Paige's mother, leaning a lavendered cheek against her own. 'You know there was no-one she loved more than you. I am only grateful that you were there at the end.'

But I wasn't, thought Anna, *I was somewhere else entirely. Worrying about my own petty problems, uncaring of the safety of my friend.*

Meanwhile there was the book still to finish and her father's affairs to sort out. In the weeks since his rescue he had perceptibly rallied and some of the old fighting spirit had filtered back. There was no room in Colette's cramped apartment for him to be able to resume his teaching, apart from which, she didn't possess a piano. It was time he made plans to move on but, where to? Both he and his daughter remained destitute and homeless; nothing seemed to have changed for a number of weeks. Anna made numerous trips to Tribeca to try to establish the situation with his house. As Colette had reported, it was heavily boarded up, with a property developer's sign on prominent display. Instant action was obviously called for. It was vital that the demolition programme be stopped before they brought in the bulldozers. Paige had been trying to impose an injunction; Anna had no idea how far she had got.

She chanced dropping in on Phoebe for advice, praying she wasn't being too intrusive. Phoebe, through Larry, knew most of the building trade and was glad to have something to take her mind off her grief. She was adamant that, in principle, there was no legal way they could just go ahead and demolish the house without formal authorisation, though few of these cowboys paid much attention to the letter of the law. Phoebe, pleased to be useful again, made a few calls that endorsed all Anna's fears. This so-called developer's reputation was, put at its mildest, fairly shady.

'No honest contractor would buy property in such circumstances. An old man coerced under heavy duress into signing bogus documents.' Phoebe's old spunk was back there in a flash; she had washed her hair and was even wearing makeup. 'I'd love to help you,' she volunteered, 'I could certainly do with the diversion.' Too many empty hours alone in the state-of-the-art duplex were threatening to drive her slightly batty. The problem, once the children had left home, was the much-talked-about empty nest syndrome. Sure, they would visit but it was not the same as having an ongoing solid, caring marriage. Sometime in the future, maybe, Phoebe and Charles should get to know each other better. For two decades, since they had all been at college, they had merely been peripheral friends. But not until after a decent interval, they still had their grieving to go through. Anna filed a mental aide memoire to get them both together over dinner. But only when, she reminded herself with a jolt, she had a home of her own in which to do it.

With Phoebe behind her, she confronted the developer and warned him, in no uncertain terms, that an injunction was imminent. She then went to see Paige's law practice partners who reassured her that this was indeed the case. For the present the property could not be touched. It was up to Anna, as its owner's daughter, to take the next legal step.

*   *   *

All this took time, which came as a relief, since it helped to stop her thinking too much about Dan. In any case, realistically, she knew him to be a lost cause. He lived his life thousands of miles away and would doubtless go back there as soon as he was finished with whatever it was he had come here for in the first place. Anna had managed to remain single all these years by always being the first to walk away. There had been endless admirers, she was blessed with many friends and almost never felt the lack of male company. But as soon as any relationship showed signs of even slightly changing gear, Anna was off in a cloud of dust. Despite the advice she doled out to her girlfriends, she was never capable of heeding it herself. She swore by the joys of the single state, mainly because she lacked the courage to change it.

But over the years she had watched the Collier marriage with openly envious eyes. What Paige had achieved was what Anna would have liked; more than a lover, a soulmate too, someone to share her secrets and her hopes. Paige and Charles had been the ideal couple, always an inspiration to spend time with. Their dinner parties were legendary in New York; once Paige decided to quit the kitchen, she had fallen back instead on stylish caterers. Leaving her free to talk to her guests and ensure that everything went smoothly. Anna, accustomed to being on her own and out of the habit of entertaining, now had to face a crucial truth. Regardless of her growing success, beyond the superficial, she was lonely.

She kept in almost daily contact with Genevieve and Candy, updating them with what was going on. Which, at the moment, was precisely nothing. There had not been another word from Dan; for all she knew, he might even have left New York. There was no real reason why he should have said goodbye. If, as they now believed, he had done no wrong then, equally, he owed her nothing. She had lost her home, her money and her cat and Charles had lost his wife, but what was any of that to do with him? He, on the other hand, was letting her friends stay on in his villa and, as of now, had not asked them to leave.

Genevieve sounded on top of the world, deliriously excited about Raffaele. They still hadn't done it but it was only a matter of time.

'To travel is often better than to arrive,' said Anna cynically. There she went with her homilies. What did she know, anyhow, about the mechanics of love?

Candy's portfolio was virtually complete and Hugo was due back from his fishing trip. Soon she would have to return to the real world. Their summer idyll was almost at its end.

'But not before I get there,' pleaded Anna. She hated the thought of their threesome breaking up.

'I will stay here as long as I can,' promised Candy. 'Provided you hurry up and sort things out.'

So she worked on her book and worried and dreamed about someday being with Dan. She reflected on his chosen lifestyle, saw him as a latter-day Thoreau. A man of money and education who had opted instead for simplicity. She envied him his driving sense of purpose. All she had ever achieved was a handful of novels.

'I think you may be in love,' said her father shrewdly. 'When you feel the time is right, I hope you will permit me to meet this man.' His daughter was the most precious thing he had; all he cared about now was that she be happy. She had done so well in her writing career but it was time she found something more. Living and working alone was not good; she needed to widen her perspectives. She was a good-looking woman with a bright intelligence and a talent far greater than she thought. She needed to get out into the world a bit more and live a properly fulfilled life.

'I'm too old,' said Anna, though secretly, in her heart, she felt like a foolish kid. If Genevieve could find happiness with Raffaele, then she wanted some of it too. Though how to achieve it, she no longer knew. She had never been any good at making the running. And Dan remained a complete enigma. She knew almost nothing about his life except what he'd volunteered.

She sat in her stuffy hotel room and fretted. None of the bad things had yet been resolved. She felt life was passing her by.

24

A nd then, just as she was on the brink of losing all hope, he called.

'Meet me tomorrow at your house,' he said. 'Four o'clock. Be there on time.'

'Why?' she asked.

'You'll see,' he said.

'Can Charles come?'

'That's up to you.'

Anna flew into a fervour of excitement and checked the wardrobe to see what she had to wear. Since she had only brought with her that single bag, she had very limited choice and now no money with which to indulge herself further. The weather was still uncomfortably hot so that, in the end, it had to be the linen safari suit he'd already seen. She would have to make do with sponging and pressing it; she could not risk the hotel messing it up. She pined for the Sienese sandals she hadn't bought, settling instead for a pedicure. It made little difference in any case; he was hardly likely to notice how she looked.

'What do you suppose he is up to?' asked Charles.

'I really have no idea.'

As Dan had requested, they arrived there on the dot and this time found the house abuzz with people. The blinds were up and the windows open while the door had been left on the latch. For the first time in weeks Anna mounted the front steps and cautiously crossed her own threshold. Dan appeared to be acting host. He came forward to greet her and welcomed her into the main parlour. She glanced with approval at the expertly restored plasterwork, although it still wrenched her heart to see that all her possessions were gone. Empty, the room looked far larger than before, with its walls of palest apricot and highly polished wood floors, though without the sofas and the Botticelli rug it seemed to have lost its personality.

Rather to Anna's surprise, Dan placed a slightly proprietorial hand on her shoulder and steered her round to meet the other people. The frumpy woman with thick pebble lenses turned out to be Esther Feldman, the real estate agent, while two of the suited men were lawyers, there at Dan's request. A black man, tall with distinguished grizzled hair, was simply introduced as Mr Roberts. He remained in the background watching the proceedings. Someone from Larry's building firm, Anna guessed.

'I wanted you here,' said Dan to Anna, 'to witness the closing of the sale.'

She stared at him in blank astonishment but all he did was smile. It fell to Esther Feldman to explain. 'Mr Sutherland is the purchaser of the house.' Her eyes, behind the thick lenses, were uneasy. It was clear she knew now exactly who Anna was and remembered her own brusque rudeness on the phone.

Anna noticed, with quiet satisfaction, the smear of fuchsia lipstick on her teeth. One thing now, though, was instantly clear: this was not the mystery woman who'd been seen in the house.

'May I please know what the hell is going on?' Charles was suddenly growing truculent. He did not like the look of this at all, more fishy business to sort out. Dan, however, held up one hand in a mollifying gesture, begging him to be patient.

'All we need now,' he said to Esther Feldman, 'are your formal instructions as to where the money should be paid. I'll deposit cash in the vendor's account as soon as you give us full details.'

Charles, with a sharp inhalation of breath, gripped Anna's elbow in sudden comprehension. He was there way ahead of her, saw what Dan was up to. His admiration for him grew even more. Esther Feldman, flustered and out of her depth, scrabbled in her briefcase for her notes. Everyone stood and quietly looked on until she produced the appropriate piece of paper.

'Here,' she said, proffering it to Dan. 'The details of the off-shore account and the trading company's name.'

Dan held out his hand for it but Mr Roberts was in there first.

'I'll take that, thank you,' he said to her courteously, flashing his FBI badge.

Everything else was a blur of confusion which Anna, later, found hard to recall. Hands had been shaken and documents signed and then Dan had handed her the keys.

'Yours,' he said, with the same quirky smile. 'I can only apologise for taking so much time.'

'So now you have to tell me everything,' said Anna. 'Leaving out nothing, please.' They were dining at Jean-Georges to celebrate and Anna had rashly splurged her remaining dollars on something chic and nifty from Armani. Charles had been invited too but pleaded diplomatic fatigue. Anna still ached for him, the way he was grieving, and knew he was in no mood to socialise. Still, he was pleased for her, on more than one front. He had always seen something not apparent to her, the light of admiration in Dan's eye.

Dan went pensive as he crumbled his bread. 'It is very, very complicated,' he said.

'No hurry. Take your time.' She was cautiously happy to be here with him, even though she still wasn't sure that she could trust him. There was a lot he hadn't yet clarified; she hoped he would do that now. For the occasion he was wearing a conservative dark suit with a blue shirt that accentuated his tan. Cleaned up, he was a remarkably handsome man. Anna still couldn't quite believe her luck. Or the fact that he genuinely seemed to like her; the world-weary cynicism was gone.

He savoured the excellent wine he had chosen and gave it his full consideration. 'I'll tell you something about the rain-forests,' he said. 'They don't do a lot for one's palate.'

Bit by bit, throughout the excellent meal, he filled her in on what had happened. The FBI, he could now reveal, had been on the case all along. And even had an informed idea of who might have murdered Paige and Larry, though that they had only come to recently, in the light of new information. There was still a lot of checking they needed to do.

'Wait,' was all he would say at this stage. Anna must learn to be patient. Despite his good humour at the joyfulness of the occasion, trouble still lurked in his eyes. Eventually, when the plates had been cleared, he gave her his absolute attention. 'You certainly deserve to hear the whole story, though it isn't going to be easy. I am sorry I couldn't be more honest with you from the start.'

He was working in Patagonia, where he had been for several months, when the events of September 11th had occurred. He had watched the devastation, along with the rest of the world, then placed an urgent call to his sister, who lived in Brooklyn Heights.

'Her apartment is right on the promenade, facing the foot of Manhattan. Since her office was in the World Trade Centre, all she had to do was cross the bridge.'

He called as soon as he heard the news but there hadn't been any answer. It was almost nine-thirty; she'd already have left for work. But when he then tried her direct office line, all he got was static. So he hopped on a plane to New York right away and went straight to her apartment. 'I pulled a few strings with *Geographic*,' he explained. 'The airlines were all snarled up.'

Anna stared at him, aghast with horror. This was worse than anything she could have imagined. 'You found nothing?' she asked, with her hands to her mouth.

Dan simply shook his head. 'Worse than that. I found her passport, in her desk alongside her chequebook. Unwashed dishes in the sink, the newspaper still on the mat. And apparently none of her personal things missing. I checked as far as I could. No-one from her building who survived remembered having seen her. I could only surmise she was there when the terrorists struck.'

'I am so sorry,' said Anna in a whisper, unable to imagine what he must have been going through. Losing her house and her money had been bad but this was a million times worse.

Dan stared into the middle distance and a warmth she had never seen before came slowly into his eyes. 'Mercedes,' he said in a far gentler voice, 'always was something of a rebel. She was seventeen years younger than me so I really helped to raise her. My mother found her a bit of a handful; she was always running wild. From the day she was born, I looked upon her as my special charge.' The baby sister he had always longed for arrived just a little too late.

'By then I was off at school in the States but I saw her whenever I came home. She loved *Casavecchia*, considered it partly hers, though my step-father actually died some years before she was born.'

'The Count?' questioned Anna.

He nodded. 'Ildebrando. He was like a real father to me. If he hadn't died suddenly when I was fifteen, things would have turned out quite differently. I, I suppose, would be managing the estate. And Mercedes would never have been born.'

He paid and they left and went back to her dreary hotel. Now that the house was hers again, she would shortly be able to move in. First, however, there was the question of furniture. The FBI were still hot on its trail though Anna strongly doubted that it hadn't been immediately dispersed. Still, now that they had frozen the offshore account, soon she should have her money back and be able to replace it. She could hardly believe it, it had happened so fast, and she owed everything to Dan.

'Go on,' she said as he poured them both a nightcap and they settled on the cramped sofa which smelled of stale ash. 'What happened next?' His story was enthralling though she hated to see the pain in his eyes as he told it. This was his little sister he was describing, whom he had spent the best part of a year believing dead.

'What happened next was the FBI. They called without warning while I was staying in her apartment, still frantically trying to locate her.' It was one of the biggest heists in history, millions coolly filched from her clients' accounts. She was always exceedingly bright, he explained, with the beauty and panache to carry it off. Plus the expensive American education, paid for by Ildebrando's legacy. 'My mother sent her to Andover, then on to Stanford Business School when it became obvious how good she was with figures.'

'And before that to boarding school in England?' asked Anna, suddenly getting it.

'St Mary's, Sherborne. But how could you possibly know that?'

Anna flushed with embarrassment. She remembered Hector's exuberant triumph as he'd burst in on her, while she was trying to work, brandishing the school boater. 'One of our house-guests discovered her trunk. He really had no business to look inside.'

Dan smiled, quite unconcerned, his mind back in the past, immersed in a sea of memories that had suddenly come rushing back. 'That was my mother all over,' he said. 'Hoarding things in case of a rainy day. Though Ildebrando left her so well off, she need never have had another financial worry. Not until she married Mercedes' father.'

Back to the present. Anna was still curious. The past they could resurrect some other time. From the things he had hinted at and the way he was looking, it seemed there might be other occasions for that.

'So you think she may yet be out there somewhere?' Why else would the FBI still be on the case? They had found the money and were extraditing it. They could surely have called it a day.

'Now I do, after all that's been happening to you. Only Mercedes knows enough to have engineered such a sting.

Including the fact that I am almost always travelling and often incommunicado for months at a time. Without a passport, it's unlikely she's left the States but since the whole scam was set up by email, that won't have presented much of a problem.'

'Why do you think she did it?'

'Very simple. My guess is that, once she saw her office building collapse, she recognised a perfect chance to disappear entirely. The Feds had been on to her for months and were rapidly closing in. It could only have been a matter of weeks at the most. In some ways, she was very lucky. She always was an opportunist. Got that from her father, I suppose.'

'So why the house swap?' It still wasn't clear.

'Think,' said Dan, as though he had known her for years.

Anna, usually so bright, was puzzled. She had never pretended that maths was her strongest suit. Any discussion of finance left her reeling; even Charles had given her a headache when he tried to explain the workings of the SEC. 'All I know about money,' she explained, 'is when it is there to spend.' Which reminded her of the credit card theft, presumably also Mercedes.

'If she's disappeared, presumed to be dead, she no longer has an identity. Right?' No passport, no checking account, not even a home. The Brooklyn apartment had now been sealed by the FBI.

Light dawned and Anna began to nod. Of course, how obtuse could she be. 'So she needed to steal one from somebody else? Preferably youngish and female and single.'

'With a fancy address in Manhattan. Right. When you answered the ad, she must have felt like a pig in clover.'

Anna sat silently and thought it all through. What a brilliantly devious plan. 'She must be exceedingly clever,' she said.

He grinned. 'It runs in the family.'

'So why immediately sell the house?'

'It could only ever be a stepping stone. In four months' time you were going to come back and then the shit would have really hit the fan. She needed the house to sell it on and establish a new identity in the States. And she would have succeeded if it hadn't been for Raffaele, who alerted me just in time. By the way,' he added, 'to answer your earlier question, that's what I've been doing in New York.'

'And in Italy?' He had turned up unexpectedly. Anna still remembered the frost in his eyes.

'To suss you out. Raffaele called and I came right away. Both of us hoped you might lead us to Mercedes.'

'So you thought that she and I were in league?'

'It made sense. So we had to check. Remember, at that time, we still thought she was dead. Your arrival was the first spark of hope we had had.'

'And Raffaele was in love with her?'

'Briefly, a long time ago. He always did have too big a heart. I guess he's probably over it by now.'

I hope so, thought Anna, thinking of Genevieve. She seemed finally to have run out of questions.

'I'm so very sorry,' she said and gripped his hand. 'It seems that both of you must have been through hell.'

25

The sunset was spectacular with a pinkish-golden light that irradiated the darkening hills with its glow. The main thrust of summer was gradually petering out. From now on it would be woodsmoke and chillier evenings.

'This is Tuscany at its most impressive,' said Dan, his arm resting lightly on Anna's shoulders. 'Now you can see precisely where the Renaissance painters got their inspiration.' The colours at this time of year were luscious; deep, reverberant and vital. Like the crude poster paints she remembered from school; the exuberance of Titian and Caravaggio.

Many things had happened in the intervening weeks, not the least of which was that Anna had finished her book. It was safely in her publisher's hands which meant an abrupt change of pace. No more leaping out of bed at the crack of dawn for that first shot of energising coffee. These mornings she lingered on beneath the duvet; now she had more important things on her mind. For she and Dan were fast becoming an item, to the extent that he'd put off his return to Patagonia. They had started dating and he'd then invited the whole lot of them back over here.

They were out on the terrace for the cocktail hour, this time formally as Dan's guests. Candy with Hugo; Genevieve with her boys. Even George Kovac had been persuaded to come. Maria was preparing a gala dinner to celebrate their reunion while Dan and Raffaele danced gracious attendance as hosts. For the first time in years, the villa was full and, from the satisfied smile on Maria's face as she bustled about in the kitchen, creating magic, it was clear she felt that at last it was filling its proper potential. It had stood neglected for far too long. That must not be allowed to happen again.

'Any changes you care to make, feel free,' Dan had said indulgently. 'It could do with a female touch.'

'Nonsense,' said Anna. It was far too soon. Besides, she couldn't see that it could be improved. The Contessa, Dan's mother, had had excellent taste and Maria had worked miracles all these years, keeping it up to scratch. Provided they came here as often as they could and also threw it open to their friends, *Casavecchia* should have a new lease of life with all the cobwebs of memory blown away for a far more positive present. Whoever could have guessed, when she had recklessly answered that ad, that Anna would ever end up here with an open invitation.

They'd had many discussions, in the past few weeks, about how their separate careers might interact. *Have laptop, can travel* had long been her boast. Now she was going to try putting it to the test. There were projects on which a photographer and writer could successfully and profitably liaise. It would be a challenge she would gladly welcome. She had worked far too long on her own.

'You could always try an adventure novel,' said Candy, the pulp fiction queen. 'Perhaps become a female Wilbur Smith.'

'Or,' cut in Dan crisply, 'write an *Oscar and Lucinda* and win the Booker Prize.'

Anything seemed possible now. Life was opening up. As long as I am with him, thought Anna, nothing else really matters. She would follow Dan wherever he went, do what he wanted to do. She looked at him, slouched elegantly against the terrace wall, head bent, listening intently to her father, and felt that her heart might implode with happiness. It was all due to Dan that George was here at all, though he had come with the minimum amount of protest. George had made remarkable strides since the snatch and was almost fully restored to health and fitness. He liked this man with the taste to be courting his daughter, admired his vision and stalwart old-fashioned values. He saw, from the way Dan's eyes followed her around, that this latest suggestion that they try working on joint projects was not altogether altruistic. Both had succeeded brilliantly on their own and both were pretty set in their ways. There had to be more to it, he hoped that was so; it would be nice for Anna to have someone to care for her as well as he had done himself. Not that Anna needed looking after any more; she had been her own woman half her life.

George's own future had also been arranged. He was going to move into Anna's house, under the surveillance of Consuela. This was a perfect solution for Anna, since in future she'd be travelling so much. The house, restored to its state of perfection, cried out for a permanent tenant. And the music lessons could now be resumed for those children whose parents would allow them to come uptown. Colette was putting out feelers for more; the house fell within her catchment area. Dan had donated a Steinway baby grand which took pride of place in Anna's study.

'I hope it won't get in the way of your work,' worried George, hating the idea of imposing.

'No problem,' said Anna, who had grown to prefer the laptop. She could write wherever she liked in the house, which sometimes improved inspiration. '*Mea casa, sua casa.* That's what families are about.' She liked the idea of her father living there, of having him to come home to whenever she could. She had spent so much money and time doing it up and wanted him to share its harmony. At heart she remained the intense little girl who had always sat on her daddy's knee. Now she had two men to spoil her but that was okay. It would not be too hard, she felt, to get used to that.

Dan also took it upon himself to sort out the business of George's house. It turned out the developer had bought it in good faith so that, now that the FBI had frozen the offshore account and George would be getting the purchase price back, they might as well let him keep the house. Anything else would involve lengthy litigation and Dan was against George being harassed in that way. His twilight years should be happy and serene, with his music, his pupils and his family around him.

'They are going to knock it down,' lamented George. 'Almost forty years of my life.' It had been his first foothold on American soil after he had left everything else behind him. Here he had brought his beloved bride; here he had raised his daughter. He would miss the immigrant community a lot, though could always pop back downtown for his regular chessgames.

'But where you are going is so much nicer,' coaxed Anna. Safer, too. With Colette and Johnny on hand should he ever need help. No more threats of a retirement home. Anna and Dan would ensure he was taken care of for the remainder of his life.

And then something truly miraculous had occurred. Consuela had turned up on the doorstep of East 74th Street one day holding Sadie in her arms. The real Sadie, cautiously purring, not just a lookalike. Consuela had, through the cleaning ladies' grapevine, succeeding in locating her at last. She had been found, wandering collarless, by a neighbour on the block who had taken her in and asked around but failed to come up with any leads. Anna was relatively new in the area; few people knew that she even had a cat. Sadie was sleek and looked well-fed and entirely at her ease. She had regarded Anna with her customary hauteur before stalking around the house, tail held high, and imperiously demanding food.

'She looks fit as a fiddle,' said Anna, overcome, though she took her in for a checkup, just to make sure. The neighbour was telephoned and profusely thanked, then granted perpetual visiting rights for life. 'I think she will probably get a kitten of her own,' Anna told Consuela. 'The vet has a list of the top few breeders and she has clearly now become addicted to Sadie.'

'Nice of her, then, to let her go,' said Dan. 'And good to know there are still some decent people in this city.'

'Everything's working out so well,' whispered Anna, hoping the future might be similarly bright for her friends.

George and Hugo instantly bonded and spent hours together in earnest conversation. The child, just turned nine, was an unexpected delight, with his mother's unstoppable energy and infectious grin. His latest enthusiasm, encouraged by his father, was collecting and preserving rare bugs. Rural Tuscany proved to be an exciting new hunting ground. Often they would be seen wandering off together, the tall, stooping man with a shock of iron grey hair, escorted by the lively child with his newly bought butterfly net. They would put what they caught into sterile screw-top jars and Hugo would industriously label them.

'That boy's considerably brighter than people give him credit for,' George told Anna when Candy was not around. 'Which is often the case with children with special needs. I've a shrewd suspicion he might turn out to be musical. I'd certainly love to have the chance to find out.'

Which was not, as it might have seemed, so very far-fetched. When George told Candy she whooped with delight and confided her next daring plan. The completed portfolio had been an instant success. The buyer from Harvey Nichols loved it and offered her a contract on the spot. Macaskill Modes would actually just be called 'Candy' and aimed mainly at the late-teen shoppers swarming in every high street. Anna, remembering the buyer from Barneys who sat on the breast cancer committee, offered to introduce them some time if Candy were ever in New York.

'Bring Hugo over in the holidays,' she said. 'You can always stay in my house. I know Dad would really enjoy having him around. Look how well they get on.'

It would also put distance between Hugo and his own father, not entirely a bad thing. A wedding was still scheduled but no date had yet been set. Hugo told Candy that they were constantly rowing.

Genevieve's two lanky sons were tossing a frisbee on the lawn.

They were almost men, with their hairless, concave chests and brightly coloured bead necklaces round their throats. One was sporting a David Beckham haircut and a tiny tufted beard that he'd soon shave off. Their manners were acceptable though their laughter often loutish. Their mother had made a passable success of trying to bring them up. At night they would usually go off to the village, where they had found the centre of Montisi's social whirl. Not exactly bright lights, big city but a certain improvement on staying at home with their ma.

Ma, in any case, had little time for them now. Her full attention was focused these days on Raffaele. She was thinner, prettier, more vivacious than in years and, they both agreed, looked ten years younger. Not that they'd ever let her know but secretly they were proud. Their father's new wife was a bit of a nag; it was a great release to come over here and slob about uncontrolled.

Raffaele was organising a lunchtime barbecue, having closed the trattoria for the day. 'Unheard of,' said Dan, with his endearing quirky smile, rapidly cuddling Anna in the kitchen.

'Do you think he loves her?' Anna was still concerned. Genevieve was such a fragile plant, she could not bear to see her let down again.

'Undoubtedly,' said Dan, 'as never before.'

'But Mercedes . . .'

'. . . is in the past,' he said, stopping any more questions with a kiss.

Maria had spread the long garden table with an immaculate white linen cloth and chosen matching ceramic platters that set off the food to perfection. Raffaele was cooking while Dan did the carving. They made an unbeatable team.

'You can see they grew up together,' said Anna. 'As co-ordinated as skaters.'

'It is like a wedding reception,' said Candy, not without an element of wistfulness.

'Your turn will come,' said Anna and Genevieve in unison. Candy had much to achieve before she settled down. Besides, she was ten years younger.

The feast was consumed and the speeches made. And Raffaele had another surprise up his sleeve. Maria, it now turned out, was his mother. Sister to Ildebrando and the lynchpin of the family. Between them they ran the estate for Dan, which was why she kept such a careful eye on the house. And explained the loving tending of the garden. She had always hoped he would come back.

In a perfect world, thought Candy whimsically, Maria should really marry George. Then, at last, they would all be part of the same family.

Which reminded her: 'Whatever happened to Hector?' And was unanimously ordered to shut up.

It was evening now and the sky was sprinkled with stars. Everyone, having had their siestas, was out on the terrace again. Dan discreetly led Anna away to take her on his favourite cocktail walk. Each of them carrying a glass of wine, they followed the path that bordered the firefly meadow, a fairyland of shimmering light, enhanced by fragrant *genista*.

'All right?' he asked her, his arm around her shoulders, and Anna silently nodded. She had never, in her lifetime, felt more fulfilled; her heart was bursting with hope. The future, she felt, held the answer to all her dreams, dreams that till now she had never allowed to surface. She had convinced herself she was best off on her own. Now, at last, she admitted she might have been wrong. Perhaps her theory about the poppies was truer than she had believed. Certainly something was making her feel giddy, though her glass was still almost full.

Above them, in the brilliant sky, a shooting star streaked across the heavens and they watched it together, in companionable silence, her head resting gently against his chest.

'Are you thinking about Mercedes?' she asked.

He nodded and she felt how tense he was. 'There is something I haven't told you yet, that I wanted to keep till the others were not around. Early this morning I had a call from Bob Roberts. They think there's been a sighting of her in New Mexico. Nothing definite but they are still on her trail. He has promised to keep me informed.'

'New Mexico?' said Anna, puzzled.

'Her father, Julio, is Mexican,' Dan reminded her. 'When he left my mother he headed home. He had spent most of her money by then and went rapidly to ground.'

'So you think she is trying to cross the border. Without a passport?' said Anna.

'There are ways and means. And one thing about my sister, she has never lacked initiative.'

'One final thing that's been puzzling me.' She hated to upset him more but it was something that had been bugging her for days. 'Why Ptolemy if the Count wasn't even her father?'

Dan laughed. 'Mercedes was always a vain little thing and fancied herself as looking like Cleopatra.'

Anna hugged him and he responded but she saw that his eyes were sad. And so she silently clung to him and they went on watching the night sky. This woman she had never met had nearly wrecked her life and her father's and murdered two of

297

her closest and dearest friends. And yet, without Mercedes, Anna would not have met Dan. It was a hard one to figure out; she would leave it till later.

'I am sorry you never knew her,' he said, obviously reading her thoughts. 'Though now, of course, I am hoping you never will.'

And, hand in hand, they retraced their steps to join the riotous gathering on the terrace.